KISSING MY KILLER

by Helena Newbury

Second Edition

© Copyright Helena Newbury 2015

The right of Helena Newbury to be identified as the author of this work has been asserted by her in accordance with the Copyright, Design and Patents Act 1988

This book is entirely a work of fiction. All characters, companies, organizations, products and events in this book, other than those clearly in the public domain, are fictitious or are used fictitiously and any resemblance to any real persons, living or dead, events, companies, organizations or products is purely coincidental.

Cover photo: Alexei - Konradbak / Depositphotos
City - Appalachian View / Depositphotos

ISBN: 1519144539

ISBN-13: 978-1519144539

ACKNOWLEDGMENTS

Thank you to Liz, who deserves pizza.

And thank you to my readers, who allow me to do what I love.

Helena Newbury

ONE

Alexei

I MET HER ON MY WAY TO KILL SOMEONE. I was heading up to the tenth floor of the building, to check out the target's apartment. But there was a coffee shop on the ground floor and I figured I should get some coffee as a prop. The first rule of a job like this is: *wear a suit,* because no one stops a guy in a suit. But a guy in a suit carrying a cup of coffee from the coffee shop downstairs? People will actually hold the door open for you.

The place had big plate glass windows that were running with October rain, turning the street outside into a rippled gray blur. Inside, it was all warm golden light and polished beech wood. I shook off my coat and stood there for a second, soaking up the music and the heady tang of coffee.

I bought a black Americano, pure and uncomplicated, the way things should be. And I was just burning my lips on it when I turned around and almost ran into her.

I didn't know it then, but nothing would ever be the same again.

TWO

Gabriella

I DIDN'T REALLY WANT to take a break but I'd been at my screen for ten hours and the other two—Lilywhite and Yolanda—were starting to chant in the chat window: *TAKE A BREAK, TAKE A BREAK* and refusing to talk to me until I did. So I grudgingly went downstairs to get a coffee.

The coffee shop had become an extension of home, so I didn't bother to change. I knew it would be warm down there so I just put on some sneakers and went down in the leggings and tank top I had on. Hell, I debated whether to bother with the sneakers. I knew I probably looked a mess, but no one was going to see me and, if they did, they weren't going to notice me.

I headed towards the counter. A big guy in a raincoat was ahead of me in the line, so I twisted and looked out of the windows while I waited. A gray world—even the yellow New York cabs looked muted and cold. Who in their right mind would want to go out in *that*? Besides, I was crazy busy and it would be dark soon—

My stomach lurched at the realization. Another day gone. It was now forty-two days since I'd left the building.

I was getting worse.

It's fair to say I was distracted. I heard the big guy move, in front of me, and just assumed that he'd move to the left, towards the little rack of milk and sugar and wooden stirrers. It was only when I took a step forward that I found he'd just turned around, and now we were practically touching.

I looked up.

And up.

My first impression was one of hardness. Everything about him was brutal, but not brutal and ugly. Brutal and beautiful. His suit was so black and its creases so sharp that it looked as if it would hurt, if you ran your hand down it. His gray raincoat glistened like a wet sword blade. The sheer size of him—a head taller than me and heavily muscled—made me think of some military machine, all power and strength. He looked as if he could go through a brick wall.

His shirt may have been white and pure, but it only worked to contrast the danger underneath. A powerful chest swelled under the soft fabric, pushing it out, drawing my eyes to follow the hard lines of him all the way to his shoulders. The collar almost hid his tattoos—I could see the very edge of them, a hair-width line of blue-black on his tan skin. There was no way to know what they were. But the very fact they were designed to be hidden meant they must be some sort of code, only to be revealed to the right people. I wanted to be one of those people.

He was gorgeous...but in a way I'd never seen

before. His face was utterly uncompromising, as if a sculptor had carved it from ice-cold granite, filing away rock to form the high cheekbones, chiseling out that solid jaw. The fact he was still wet from the rain only added to the effect. It was like watching raindrops slide down a rugged cliff face, chasing each other over the valley of his upper lip, sliding down over the swell of his full lower lip—the one part of him that looked soft—and breaking up as they hit his darkly-stubbled jaw. He was thunderstorm-beautiful.

I heard coffee hit the ground and realized he'd spilled it towards himself, rather than spill it down my front. I looked down at his shoes, now steaming and wet. Then I looked back up and—

This time our eyes met and I felt a *wrench*. Like something had caught hold of my soul as it flitted along in life and brought it to an immediate, shuddering stop.

His eyes were steel-gray, shockingly light. I've never seen eyes like them, bright and clear but completely without warmth. Eyes that decided your fate in a millisecond. They had such an utter sense of purpose that they made everyone else look as if they were sleepwalking. Being under his gaze was scary as all hell. If I could have remembered how to move, I would have taken a step back. They were eyes that made you run.

Except....

As I stared into them, I thought I saw them change. I thought I saw the faintest hint of blue, like clouds breaking apart to reveal the sky. And that *wrench* happened again, pulling me towards him instead of away. I rocked on my heels, my brain screaming at me to go one way, the rest of me drawn forward.

And then I didn't have a choice anymore, because he grabbed my wrist.

THREE

Alexei

THE FIRST THING I noticed was her scent. I caught it in the air before I'd even fully turned around: *zhimolost*—what the Americans call honeysuckle. My grandmother used to grow it in her garden. And some strawberry-scented soap and, beneath it all, the smell of a woman: warm and sexual and calming on a level beyond all the other senses. I wasn't used to smelling that. All the women I'd been with, in the last few years, had doused themselves in too much perfume and hairspray. But this woman...I could have just inhaled her scent for hours.

I looked at her and she was...*soft*. Perfectly soft, in the way only a woman can be. She was so close, as I turned, that some of her hair brushed against my chest. It was the color of walnuts and its ringlets made it seem even softer and more sensuous. It fell past her shoulders, brushing the pale skin left bare by her tank top. I wanted to bury my fingers knuckle deep in it and feel the silk of it against my skin.

Her face was all flowing lines and sweeping curves, from the arched brows and big, hazel eyes to the elegant nose and broad, full lips. I wanted to sweep my palms over the soft skin of her cheeks, my thumbs sliding over the satiny skin, and lean down and explore those lips.

It wasn't an attraction. It was something far more than that.

I knew, in that second, that I'd glimpsed the perfect face. I could see ten thousand more and I'd never see one like hers again. I wanted her in a way I'd never wanted a woman before. I wanted to kiss her and lose myself completely in her softness.

And then I realized my coffee cup had tipped forward when we almost collided and that I was about to spill scalding coffee all down her front. I tilted it back, instead, dumping a good portion of it onto my shoes. We both looked down.

But she was shorter than me. That meant I was looking down at her body, at the twin swells of her pale breasts as they pushed out the front of her tank top. They were the most gorgeous breasts I'd ever seen, full and yet pert, bouncing just a little as she moved. Her whole outfit was black, throwing her pale skin into sharp relief and making her body into one perfect, smooth silhouette. Her waist was slender but her hips and ass flared in a way that made me want to growl aloud. Her legs were long and the lines of them drew my eyes all the way down her thighs to her shapely calves and then back up. The mood in my head shifted in an instant. I'd been getting all fucking poetic about her beauty and softness. Now, I wanted to scoop up that gloriously soft body and do very bad things to it.

I wanted to fill my hands with her breasts and squeeze them together into one sweet valley and lick my way up it. I wanted to press her down over one of the tables and jerk her leggings down over her creamy-white ass, rip away her panties and—

She looked up, right at the second I looked up, and we locked eyes. Everyone I meet, in my line of work, has the same eyes: tired and suspicious, bitterly cold. Hers were so innocent, so untouched by all the horrors of the world. It was like finding one perfect flower in the rubble of a building. I almost felt guilty at what I'd been imagining. Almost. On another level, her innocence just made me want to do it more.

She started to move back and my reaction was instinctual. I grabbed her wrist because I couldn't let something so incredible get away.

FOUR

Gabriella

I LOOKED DOWN at his hand on my wrist. Warm and soft and yet iron-hard in its grip, no give there at all, and his hand was so *big*. The heat of him throbbed into me, sending prickles up my arm. I opened my mouth to speak but nothing came out. God, he was so gorgeous...and he was looking down at me with an intensity that blasted straight through to the very center of me, making me catch my breath. It rolled down through me, changing to heat that soaked downwards....

I lifted my arm and his grip didn't falter, his arm lifting too. He didn't exactly resist my movement—he didn't have to. He was so big that just trying to lift the muscled mass of his arm was an effort. If he actually wanted to hold me in place, I realized, he'd have no trouble at all. He could probably hold me against the wall, or down on the floor, with just one of those big hands—

Another, unexpected wave of heat, starting

somewhere deep inside and twisting between my thighs.

I glanced around. People were starting to look at us and I wasn't used to that. No one ever looks at me. It's not just that I'm unremarkable, it's that I'm not normally around people. I was suddenly very aware of what a complete mess I must look—leggings and tank top, sneakers...I'd just run into the hottest guy I'd ever seen in my life and I looked like—

Well, like a girl who never goes out.

I swallowed. "Um." The first thing I'd managed to say to him and it wasn't even a word. I waggled my wrist.

He looked at his hand as if seeing it for the first time and slowly, reluctantly, released me. My wrist immediately felt cold: I missed his touch. I started to say something but he cut me off.

"Who are you?" His accent sounded like icebergs crashing together in the blackest night. The *who* was a bitterly chill wind and the *r* was like the grind of ice on ice. He snapped it out, a demand, but it somehow didn't sound rude. It sounded more like he just *had to know*, right now, and there wasn't time for pleasantries.

I tried to answer but the first thing on my tongue, the honest answer, was: *no one* and I was sure that wasn't what he wanted. And his accent was doing something to me, vibrating through my body and making my chest go light and fluttery, my toes dancing inside my sneakers. I hadn't heard anything like it before. I'd known a guy who was Polish, once, but his accent had been like a faded photocopy of this one. I tried to gauge his age. Twenty-seven, twenty-eight? About five years older than me.

He seemed to realize that he'd been abrupt because he frowned and said, "Sorry. What is your name?" The *is* sounded like *izzz*.

I started to say *Gabriella* but, at that second, the person behind me in the line got tired of waiting and asked me, "Are you going to order?"

And suddenly the whole reality of it came back to me. Echoes and brightness and polished floors and stifling, air-conditioned air. I was in the coffee shop, which is just borderline manageable for me on a good day, and I was surrounded by people and I didn't remember the room being this big or the doors being that far away and I didn't have his hand on my wrist anymore so I felt like there was nothing solid, nothing to hang onto and and—

I bolted. I threaded between the tables, hauled open the door to the lobby and sprinted into the elevator, thumped the button for my floor and panic-breathed all the way up to apartment 1006. I slammed the door behind me and locked it. Then I sat and panted with my back against the door.

As I calmed down, the shame took over, hot and all-consuming. I'd met someone and it had felt important—something that might never happen again. And I'd fucked it up because I was a pathetic, panicking freak.

He's probably still there. Go back down there.

I almost laughed at that thought. Now that I was panicking, the corridor outside my apartment might as well have been black, airless vacuum, completely impassable. I'd never see him again.

The part of my mind that made me panic, the part that kept me shut up in the apartment, whispered that my mistake had been going downstairs in the first place. I would have been okay if I'd just stayed put. I wouldn't go to the coffee shop again.

FIVE

Alexei

I STOOD THERE for a moment, trying to process what had just happened. She'd been *there* and then she was *gone*. It had happened so fast I could still smell the scent of her.

I'd seen something in her eyes just before she ran, a sort of realization. She'd woken up to something and been deathly afraid of it. I would have understood if she'd been afraid of me, but she hadn't known what I was. Something else, then. Something that lived inside her.

It hit me that I had no way to find her again. I didn't know if she even lived in this apartment building.

The guy who'd been behind her in line was shaking his head as if to say, *some people.* He stepped forward to take her place.

I'd never see her again. And it was his fault.

I put my hand on his chest and pushed. The guy staggered backward and knocked over a table, winding up in a heap on the floor. A couple of people screamed.

In the silence that followed, I realized I was panting. I was angry, and I never get angry.

I stalked out into the lobby, got in the elevator and hit the button for the tenth floor. What the hell had I been thinking? Hitting that guy would attract attention. I'd never even contemplate doing that normally, even if he'd been up in my face. And he hadn't been. He'd just scared her away.

Her. Those hazel eyes and that pale skin. She'd made me completely lose reason.

And she'd made me forget who I was...*what* I was. I'd seen an angel but I'd forgotten that angels are out of reach of mortal men...let alone devils.

For a second there, I'd seen a different world—a world of warmth and comfort and laughter. That wasn't my world and it never would be. Doing what I do means living outside that world, in a place that's cold and unforgiving. The harshness of it is what makes me keep my edge. If I lose that edge, I'm nothing.

I'd lost it just then, just for a second, when I'd hit that guy. No, before that—when I'd asked who she was. I should have just walked away.

I shouldn't have been interested in her in the first place. Oh, sure, I love to fuck. I'll take a blonde from a bar home for the night. Some of those women have a thing for gangsters—they soak their panties, right there in the bar, because it's so *dangerous* and *wrong* to fuck us. I take those women home and show them exactly what it's like to be pounded by a bad boy. I give them every sweaty, gasping orgasm they can manage and more and it feels good, for a few hours.

But in the morning it's over. I never see them again and I don't care.

Her, though...I'd barely met her and yet the idea of not seeing her again made me crazy.

Get yourself together!

I straightened my tie and stepped out onto the tenth floor. All I wanted to do was to get the layout of the place. I walked down the hallway, counting rooms and figuring out which window it would be. One, two, three, four, five, six.

I stopped outside 1006. That's all Nikolai had given me—Apartment 1006. I didn't even have the name of the guy.

It was almost tempting to knock on the door right now and get it done. But I've survived this job so long because I do things carefully, step by step. The guy could have five men in there with him, or a girlfriend or even a kid. I'd check it out first through the window.

Then I'd kill him.

SIX

Gabriella

WHEN MY BREATHING had slowed, I walked through to my office and sat down at my desk. Working would make me feel better...and stop me thinking about what had just happened downstairs. Lilywhite and Yolanda were waiting for me in the little chat window we keep running in the corner of our screens.

diamondjack> Back

I've been *diamondjack* forever. A male name makes things about a thousand million times easier, in the hacking world.

lilywhite> Good break? :)

diamondjack> Yup, great. Let's get back to it.

There are three of us, all women. We talk on the

phone sometimes, so I know the others are women as well, but we've never actually met. I don't even know what they look like or where they are in the world. Lilywhite says she used to live in Texas, but I don't know where she is now. She didn't sound like a Texan on the phone—in fact, she sounded like she was from New York. Yolanda I have no idea about—complete mystery. Yolanda's the best hacker but we all have useful skills. Lilywhite has back doors into all sorts of international databases, Yolanda writes malware to open up machines and I'm good with firewalls. All of us break into things in one way or another. Together, we're unstoppable.

We call ourselves The Sisters of Invidia.

yolanda> Are you into his email yet?

diamondjack> Working on it.

We'd first broken into Nikolai Orlov's computer a few days ago. Since then we'd gone in a few times, searching for a way into his email account, which in turn would help us get into his bank account.

We weren't looking to rob him. We're hackers, but we're not criminals. Well, *technically* we're criminals but that's not the point. We do what we do for a good reason. The men we hack deserve to be hacked. Nikolai Orlov, for example, had—

Ah, *there* it was. I finally found the chink in his email account's armor and breezed on through.

diamondjack> I'm in. Grabbing now.

I started downloading his full email archive. Most

of it would be in Russian but we could search for keywords. I sat back from my keyboard, watching the progress bar. There must be years of emails, because it was going to take a half hour to download them. Half an hour with nothing to do. I could try to work—I do freelance coding gigs for websites to pay the bills—but I knew I was too burned out from the day's hacking.

I glanced around the office. It had been laughably described as a bedroom by the rental agency but it was less than eight feet on a side. It held my desk and chair and pretty much nothing else. There was one window, looking out at the buildings across the street. Given how much time I spent in my office, I'd got tired of the view pretty fast. So I taped posters of far-off locations over the glass instead, giving the illusion that it was Tahiti or Monaco outside. Places I'd never visit.

The rest of the apartment was more normal. With just me living there—no partner, no kids, no pets—it stayed pretty neat and it wasn't as if I had a lot of stuff. Buying new clothes seemed stupid when you knew no one was going to see them. And I wasn't trying to impress anyone with fancy furniture or art. In theory, I could have had visitors—I was fine with people, as long as they were in a space I controlled. But to have visitors, you have to get out and meet people first. The only people who'd knocked on my door, in the last forty-two days, had been delivery guys. I knew them better than anyone else on their delivery routes, but I was pretty sure I wasn't allowed to count them as friends.

I checked the progress bar again. Twenty-nine minutes. I could sit there and mope...

Or I could go and wash the day off me. I was still jumpy from freaking out downstairs. Maybe a shower would help me relax. I could forget about the bad parts of the coffee shop and focus on the good. Like the part that came wrapped in a black suit and white shirt, pants stretched over his muscled thighs and ass. The part that had freezing gray eyes that pinned you right where you were and didn't so much as undress you as sear the clothes right off of you.

I thought about telling the other two about him. I shared everything with Lilywhite and Yolanda—they were the closest thing I had to best friends. Maybe it was because they'd be so enthusiastic and happy for me, even though I'd only managed to say "um." It seemed a long way from Lilywhite's red-hot anecdotes about outdoor sex with her cowboy boyfriend and I was betting that Yolanda had a colorful sex life and a string of men, too. She didn't talk much about herself but I couldn't see any way she could be as lonely as me.

I couldn't see *anyone* being as lonely as me.

diamondjack> I'm outta here. Talk tomorrow.

lilywhite> later

yolanda> sleep tight

I started to get undressed.

SEVEN

Alexei

WHEN I GOT BACK TO THE CAR, Lev didn't even give me time to close my door. "Is it done?" His mouth was full of sandwich and there was a coffee in the cup holder—he must have strolled down the street to the deli, even though he was meant to have stayed put. He had his smart phone in his hand, too, browsing porn sites when he should have been keeping a look out for cops.

I sighed. "You need to learn some patience," I told him in Russian. "That was just to scout the building. Now I want to check out his apartment. *Then* it'll be time."

Lev rolled his eyes and muttered something, but he made sure to do it under his breath. He was meant to be learning from me—that's why Nikolai had paired us up.

It isn't that Lev's never killed. He's killed plenty of times—on the spur of the moment, in alleys and abandoned warehouses. But that's a world away from what I do, where the aim is to sneak in and out unnoticed. If the police are able to trace a killing back to the Bratva—or, even worse, specifically to the Malakov family—I've failed.

There's another difference between us, too. I've been with Lev when he's killed and I saw the gleam in his eye, the way he pulled his shoulders back and put his chin up. Killing made him feel powerful. That's dangerous. Killing's what we do—it's *necessary*. But I don't enjoy it. People who enjoy it...they're the ones who wind up doing it more and more.

I grabbed some stuff from my bag—my rifle, a crowbar, wirecutters. "I'll be back when it's done," I told him as I got out. "A half hour or less. Watch the building I go into—call me if anyone follows me in."

Lev nodded, bored, glaring at the door I still held open. I knew he wouldn't have my back—I'd have to look out for myself. "Hurry," he said. "There's nothing to do out here."

I stood there staring at him, my hand still on the door. I wanted to say that it was a half hour in a warm car with a cup of coffee and a sandwich and fucking internet porn on his fucking phone. That he should try lying in a muddy ditch in Kazakhstan for eight hours, while icy water seeped into your uniform and eventually refroze in tiny, jagged ice crystals next to your skin.

But Lev hadn't come to the Bratva that way, shifting from the brotherhood of the army to the brotherhood of crime. He'd come up from the street gangs, where violence was about making a statement, not getting the job done. Beating and killing was how he'd maintained his position. And I suspected he'd developed a taste for it.

"Stay out of trouble," I grunted, and slammed the door.

***

There was a vacant office building opposite the apartment block. Breaking the chain on the fire escape, cutting the alarm and slipping in was easy. There were no security guards because there was nothing to steal. Just an echoing, gloomy space and a few broken office chairs.

I crept up to the tenth floor and sat down next to the window, invisible in the shadows. Then I took the sniper scope off my rifle and focused it on the apartment building across the street. Six apartments in from the west end. Three, four, five—

There.

1006 had three windows. The outer two had their blinds open; the one in the center was closed. No, wait...not a blind. Someone had taped something over the glass.

I needed to know if the guy was home and if he had company. Once I'd confirmed he was alone, I could go over there and get it done. Shooting him from the office building would have been easier, of course, but if a man's shot with a sniper rifle in the middle of New York, the police, FBI and media go into meltdown. It gets labeled as an assassination. But a knife or a gun, up close? That's just a *robbery gone wrong*.

I've done a lot of *robberies gone wrong*. They're even better than *tragic accidents* because accidents get investigated and there's hell to pay if you don't make everything look exactly right.

A light came on in the apartment. I sat up straight,

adjusting my focus on the window....

And then I cursed out loud.

It was her. It couldn't be her, but it was her. She was stretching and lazily yawning, arching her back like a cat, shaking out that long, walnut-colored hair.

I'd made a mistake. It must be a different apartment. I counted again. I even checked I had the right floor, in case I'd got eleven or nine by mistake. But I was definitely looking at apartment 1006.

The girl I'd met in the coffee shop was living with the hacker Nikolai had sent me to kill. His girlfriend, probably. I was going to have to go in there and kill the guy, right in front of her.

I lowered the sniper scope and just stared at the apartment building. Part of me was asking how fate could be this cruel. Another part was laughing its ass off at the first part. *Of course she's his girlfriend. What did you think? That you'd kill him and then come back here, another day, and track her down again and go on a date with her? Cotton candy and Ferris wheels and winning her a fucking teddy bear?*

Like an idiot, I'd forgotten who I was. Maybe it had been building for a while, under the surface, each killing gnawing away at me. I'd seen her in the coffee shop and I'd fantasized, for just a moment, that I could be somebody else. And now fate had slapped me in the face to wake me up.

I put the sniper scope back up to my eye. *No more dreaming.* I had to figure out if the hacker was home.

The girl was still in the room on the right-hand side, stretching and pacing around as if she was thinking. There was a TV in there and I could see kitchen units in the background. Then there was the room with the covered window. The lights were off in the final room so I couldn't see shit. But it looked like she was alone. I'd have to wait for him to come home.

I swung back to focus on the girl, just to check what she was doing. God, she was beautiful. I zoomed in more, holding my breath so that my hand steadied. I could see her expression and she looked...troubled.

She moved suddenly and I lost her. When I found her again, she'd walked through to the room on the left and turned the lights on. A bedroom. And, through the open door, I could see a bathroom across the hallway. I was making a mental map of the place in my head. Living area, bathroom, bedroom...that just left the mystery room with the covered window. Maybe the hacker was in there. I wanted to be sure, though. If I showed up at the apartment and he wasn't there, I'd blow the element of surprise. And what I was *really* hoping for was that the girl would go out for the night and leave the hacker alone, so I could do it while she wasn't there.

I'd wait. I'd watch the place and wait until she—

...

She pulled her tank top over her head. I sat there stunned, staring at the perfect pale globes of her breasts in their black bra. God, the skin looked so soft, so flawless. The sniper scope made it feel as if I was six feet from her.

She reached behind her, feeling for the clasp of her bra.

I took the scope away from my eye and she became a fuzzy pale blob on the other side of the street. *This is wrong* went through my head. Which was almost laughable, given what I was going over there to do. It was unprofessional, though. I should be remaining detached and indifferent and I was anything but.

I was losing myself in this girl. I needed to back the fuck away and get some space, so that this could go back to being just another job.

It took me all of three seconds to decide.

I got the scope back up to my eye just as she unfastened her bra. I caught my breath as her breasts swayed free. Her nipples were so pale, so delicate. And her breasts were larger than I'd pictured them: full and heavy. I could almost feel them under my hands, warm and soft, the nipples rising to attention as I pushed her back on the bed....

My cock was rising and swelling against my thigh. I didn't move. I barely dared to breathe. There was no way she could see me, but it felt like I was right there in the room with her, and any noise might startle her away.

She bent a little and I had to suppress a groan at the way her breasts bobbed and swayed. She hooked her thumbs into the waistband of her leggings and started to push them down her legs. God, she was going to strip off completely, right in front of the window. And why wouldn't she? She was ten floors up, well out of view of the street, and the only thing across the street was an abandoned building.

Again, that little pang of guilt. And again I crushed it down.

The black leggings rolled slowly down her legs, which were just as pale and finely shaped as her breasts. I could imagine my hands following the fabric: down over the curve of her ass, tracing the shape of her thighs, all the way down to her calves. And then back up, this time on the inside....

When the leggings were a thick black figure eight of fabric around her ankles, she kicked them off. Then she bent again, stripping off her panties—

I leaned forward.

I got just a glimpse of dark brown hair and then she was turning and walking away, her heart-shaped ass towards me. She went into the bathroom and closed the door behind her.

I lowered the sniper scope. My cock was harder than it'd ever been.

I needed to see her, needed to talk to her...I was getting obsessed with this girl.

But as soon as her boyfriend got home, I was going to have to go over there and destroy her life.

EIGHT

Gabriella

I TURNED THE SPRAY up high and hot and then climbed in. Showers are one of life's underrated pleasures. Mine have been known to go on for a half hour or more.

I started out with good intentions. I washed my hair and soaped myself up with strawberry-scented soap. And then....

And then I started to get distracted.

Maybe it was because of the window. Sometimes, if I'm in a certain sort of mood, I'll undress with the blinds open, right in front of the window. I mean, it's not like anyone can actually see me or anything, but it *feels* daring. I do it and I imagine I'm teasing a lover, that he's standing right there in the room, looking but not allowed to touch, and he's finding it more and more difficult to hold back.

A lover like *him*. The guy in the coffee shop with the black suit and the muscles who'd—I swallowed—caught my wrist. There was something about the way he'd held me, the fact that it was just *no effort at all* to keep me captured. It made me go a little weak. It felt as if he could have just hoisted me into the air, one-handed, and dangled me there while he kissed me.

I was sort of pressing my thighs together, now.

Kissed me with *those* lips. A little scrape from his stubble, then the hot softness of his lips meeting mine. He'd twist me sideways, encouraging me to open, and I would. His tongue would slip into my mouth, taking possession of me. He'd pull me closer and I'd feel the silk of his tie against my naked breasts. Closer still and my wet breasts would pillow against his shirt, soaking it through.

In my head, he was right with me, in the shower. Those big hands cupped my cheeks, taking total control of me, and then swept through my wet hair, tangling in it. He kissed me again and again, mouth open, both of us panting as he explored me: my upper lip, my lower lip, the line of my jaw. He laid a trail of hot kisses and each one left the skin aching to be touched again.

His hands slid around my bare shoulders and started to move down my back. God, they were so big—it felt as if they were completely covering me. And his fingers were so strong...he played piano scales down my back and then, as they reached the cheeks of my ass, he squeezed me hard, making me gasp. He started to alternate: first smoothing his hands over my gleaming, wet ass, enjoying its shape, then kneading it hard. I began to move my hips in response, grinding my thighs together in time.

He pulled me even tighter against him, my bare feet squeaking on the tiles. My groin mashed against his and, for the first time, I could feel the shape of him pressing against my thigh. Hot and hard and *big* and God, he was hard for *me*.... I was so close, now, that I had to tilt my head way back to be able to kiss him, my back arching. He ran his hands down the length of my back, following the curve of me again and again. Then, suddenly, he grabbed my hips and slammed me against the wall.

The tiles were cold for an instant and I cried out. But then his mouth was on me again and, as the heat of my wet body began to soak into the tiles, I relaxed. He filled his hands with my breasts and they felt *right* there. My boobs are on the big side but they matched his hands just perfectly and he knew just the right way to squeeze and rub, his thumbs making slow circles around the nipples, teasing me until I writhed and twisted. Only then did he work his way inward, stroking at the nipples themselves, breaking the kiss so that he could look down and see the effect he was having on me. We both watched as my nipples hardened under his touch. Through his soaked pants, I could feel his cock growing even harder against my leg.

I slipped my hands under his suit jacket and started to slide them over his pecs. His white shirt was plastered to him and I could see every line and detail of him through the translucent fabric, even his dark pink, dime-sized nipples. But it was the feel of him that was the biggest turn on. He felt as if he was carved from rock—throbbing and hot but just so solid, so *hard*. My hands went lower, molding the shirt to each ridge and valley of his abs. I wasn't normally so aggressive, even in my fantasies, but touching him was addictive. My fingertips toyed with his belt...and then my hands plunged lower, down into his pants, the soaked fabric tight against the backs of my hands, until I felt the throbbing root of his cock.

The instant I touched it, he caught his breath and gazed down at me with a new intensity. Suddenly, my wrists were captured and hauled upward, right up above my head, and he pinned them to the tiles with just one of those big hands, hard as an iron band.

The look he gave me said it all: *he* liked to be in control

He moved back for a second and, when I opened my eyes, I was staring right into those icy gray orbs. Again, I saw just that hint of blue, lust and maybe something more overpowering the darkness. But it didn't change the message those eyes sent: I was his.

He lowered his head and started to kiss down my neck, his stubble rasping lightly on the sensitive skin there, making me twist and gasp. I was burning up inside, the heat swelling and building, and every kiss soaked into me and added its heat to the fire. With my back against the wall, I was out of the main spray, but I had absolutely no chance of being cold. I wasn't sure I was ever going to feel cold again.

The water from the shower was thundering down on his head, streaming down over his face and hitting me, mixing with his kisses as he worked his way along my collarbone. Soft kisses, but possessive. He licked the water from the little hollow above my collarbone and I moaned. Then he lowered his head, pressing hard against me and—

I gasped and tensed as he bit my shoulder. Not hard enough to hurt, just hard enough to make me squirm. It was a lesson—that he could so easily hurt me, but he wouldn't.

And then he moved down to my breasts.

At the first touch of his lips against the soft skin, I pulled on my wrists. It wasn't that I wanted him to stop—just that I wanted to touch him, to run my hands down his back and feel his ass, to respond in some way.

My wrists moved all of a millimeter. Then he pressed them back, hard, against the tiles.

That did something to me. An unfamiliar, crackling dark heat that went straight down to my groin, like thick black oil shot through with lightning. I twisted my wrists. I knew they wouldn't move, and they didn't.

But it felt good.

I cried out as his tongue, hot and slick, lapped at my nipple. Water was cascading down off his forehead, bathing my breasts, and as he licked it was a non-stop mix of sensations: hot water, then a break of cool air as he blocked the water, then the quick, heated lash of his tongue against my aching flesh, then back to the water.

The pleasure built and built. Unable to do anything with my hands, I had to settle for crushing my thighs together harder and harder. The energy was pulsing and swelling inside me, getting ready to explode, and I had...to...contain...it....

He opened his mouth wide and took my breast into his mouth, enveloping nipple and soft flesh, and I went crazy, gasping and shaking, grinding myself against the wall. His tongue was pushing hard into the softness, drawing circles and then darting to flick across my nipple. His free hand started to work at my other breast and the pleasure expanded out of control.

I needed him inside me. My face was hot with how badly I wanted it. I jerked my wrists against his hand again but he held me fast. We were going to go at *his* pace and I had no say in the matter...other than to jerk my groin towards him to show him where I ached.

He responded. He lifted his head from my breast and looked into my eyes as his free hand slid down my stomach, interrupting the glossy sheen of moving water. It slid all the way down to my thighs, gliding over skin. Then inward.

God.... He was going to use his fingers on me there, tease me...that was too much, I needed *him,* needed him inside me—

I crossed my legs, one over the other.

He slid his hand between them like a blade and forced them open—*God,* so easily. Enough for him to slip a knee between them and then I was held open and defenseless. And I was hotly aware that part of me *wanted* to be defenseless, that the sensation of him opening me up was far and away the hottest thing I'd ever experienced. I was aware that I was twisting and squirming but not actually saying *no.*

And then his hand cupped me, hard fingers gliding over my lips, and I could feel how slickly wet I was. His fingers stroked *back* and then *forward*, rocking as much as rubbing, and little earthquakes of pleasure rippled out from my groin with every movement. I bit my lower lip, eyes tight closed, my breath coming as quick little gasps. I could feel the way I was opening to him, even though he was applying no pressure at all. My body was inviting him in.

He leaned towards me again, the hard buttons of his shirt pressing into my chest, a reminder that he was still fully clothed. I pushed with my wrists again but I was still trapped, helpless to resist as his mouth met mine, his tongue tracing the join of my lips and then plunging in as I opened. I groaned into his mouth as his thick finger parted the folds of my sex and slid up into me. And then I was thrusting back against him with my hips, shamelessly urging him on.

I was slippery tight around him and he pushed deep—*God,* those big hands, knobbly perfection.... I broke the kiss, sucking in breath—

And then he was pumping into me and my legs were instinctively bending at the knees, even though that meant taking my weight on my arms. He helped me, pressing his hips hard against mine to support me. I lifted my feet right off the floor, opening my knees wide for him and pressing the soles of my feet together, my toes wriggling against one another.

His hand pressed right up against me, his finger buried in me and his palm flat against my groin. He started to rock it against me and I could feel how wet I was, the lips engorged with blood, my clit throbbing and aching. He fucked me like that with his finger, palm grinding against my clit, and I gave myself up to it, getting wetter and wetter, hotter and hotter, the pleasure expanding to fill every part of me. The water was still rolling down his body and streaming onto mine, turning us both into shining statues, his tanned body between my pale thighs. His hand moved faster and faster, an insistent rhythm I couldn't fight and didn't want to. My legs drew up even further, my heels rubbing and circling—

He put his mouth right at my ear and spoke for the first time. The hot rush of air took me by surprise and then the words melted into my brain:

"Come for me." A low growl, the vowels drawn out by that heavy accent. Cold steel wrapped around a

white-hot core.

I exploded. My back arched, my breasts crushed against his chest. My head ground against the tiles, rolling from side to side, cushioned by my soaked hair. The climax rolled through me in waves and I felt myself spasm and shake around his pumping finger. I drew in big gulps of air as the pleasure carried me like a wave, leaving me floating in warm darkness. It was long seconds before I came back to reality and opened my eyes.

...to find myself on tiptoe, one arm stretched out above me, wrist firmly pressed against the tiles, the other hand down between my thighs. My shoulders and calves ached from holding the position for so long.

I cranked off the water and stepped out, my legs weak and shaky. I'd probably set a new record for the longest shower, even for me. And my brain was swimming with what I'd done. Where had all *that* come from, all that stuff about being...*pinned* and powerless. I wasn't into that. Was I?

I remembered his eyes.

Him. It had come from him. Or he'd triggered something deep inside me. I had no idea who he was or what he did—hell, he could be an accountant for all I knew. But it didn't feel like that could be true. He'd had an aura about him, one that was just as vivid in memory as it had been in person. A brutal power. Even as I thought about it, I felt a hot throb go through my groin.

I sighed. He was going to make good, slightly shameful fantasy material for months to come. It wasn't just the raw sexual attraction, it was that glimpse I'd seen—or thought I'd seen. That tiny hint of light amongst all the darkness. The idea of exploring that was even more enticing than the sex.

It killed me that I'd never see him again.

NINE

Alexei

SHE CAME back into the bedroom with just a towel wrapped around her. Her skin looked, if it was possible, even softer now. I could imagine the feel of her, warm and still slightly damp. I wanted to slide my hands under the towel and pry it free, let it fall to the floor and—

I caught my breath as she slowly unwrapped the towel. This time, I had a better view of her. I could see the dark brown hair at her groin, even the briefest hint of pink lips beneath the curls. She looked different, now, with her hair wet and pulled back from her face. Just as gorgeous and fragile, but more sexual. She was flushed and—Jesus, her nipples were hard.

She pulled on a pair of panties. Then a red nightshirt with a cartoon elephant on the front. I groaned because that meant she wasn't going out again tonight.

Maybe the hacker wouldn't come home. There'd

been no movement at any of the windows the whole time she was in the shower, so I was pretty sure he wasn't there. Maybe he was away for a few days or maybe he'd just been staying at her place for a few days and had moved on. There was a chance I wouldn't have to go in there at all.

For the first time, it really hit me how much I didn't want to burst in there. Not just because I didn't want to scare her, or take her boyfriend from her. The main reason was selfish: I didn't want her to see what I was. It wasn't that I had any illusions that we could be together. I wanted her—*Jesus,* I wanted her—but the thought of her innocence polluted by me—that was unthinkable. Even if, on some level, it was a turn on.

My phone rang. Nikolai.

"Why haven't you done it?" he asked immediately. He sounded edgy and annoyed, which was unlike him. My boss is a mean son of a bitch, but he's normally very calm. And how did he know I hadn't done it?

"The guy's not home yet," I said. "I'm waiting for him."

"Bullshit. That bastard's been in my computer in the last hour! What the fuck am I paying you for?"

I jumped to my feet. *Shit!* The guy had been there all the time. He must be in the room with the covered window. I pictured some fat fuck in a stained t-shirt, sitting at a computer—he probably barely moved from day to day. "It'll be done," I told Nikolai. "Five minutes."

In the apartment, the girl was sitting down and turning on the TV. My heart compressed down to a hard little ball of ice. I was going to have to kill him, right in front of her.

I couldn't imagine anything worse.

TEN

Alexei

ON THE WAY to the apartment, I dumped the rifle in the trunk and took out a silenced pistol instead, slipping it under my jacket. When I closed the trunk, Lev had twisted around in his seat and was giving me a *what the fuck?!* gesture through the glass. He tapped his watch meaningfully: I'd been in the office building almost an hour. I shrugged and crossed the street.

But he was right—this was taking too long. Had I really been waiting for the hacker to come home, or had part of it been delaying, putting off the moment when I'd have to show her who I really was? I didn't know anymore. Just the fact I was second-guessing myself was worrying enough.

I rehearsed it in my mind. Knock on her door. She'd probably put the chain on, but one good kick should snap it. Push her out of the way, three or four strides would take me to the door of the room where the hacker was. Open the door, two shots to the chest, turn, out through the door without even looking at her again. Then walk—don't run—away.

And then I was going to find the lowest, seediest dive bar I could, drink until I forgot about tonight and fuck until I forgot about her.

She'd be a witness. But a witness wasn't the worst thing in the world. The only important thing was stopping the hacker. Nikolai had told me, when he'd given me the job, that the bastard was trying to get into our bank accounts and suck us dry. He deserved everything he got.

As I entered the apartment building, I felt the calm descend. The adrenaline can leave you feeling like that, sometimes: sped up but serene, as if you're floating.

I knocked at the door of 1006 and then listened carefully. I wanted to know if he tried to escape onto the fire escape. But all I could hear were soft footsteps approaching the door.

Shit. I'd guessed it would probably be her, because the hacker evidently never got up from his computer. But I'd been hoping against hope that it would be him, and that I could do it at the door without her even seeing me.

I heard an intake of breath. She'd looked through the spy hole and seen me. I had my arms down by my sides, relaxed and unthreatening. I'd even taken a step back from the door—an old salesman trick to set people at ease.

The door opened a crack. I was right: she'd put the chain on. Those huge hazel eyes blinked out at me, uncertain and just a little excited.

She was pleased to see me. God help me, she was pleased to see me.

She was half-hiding behind the door, probably trying to conceal the fact she was in her nightclothes. But that meant I couldn't just kick the door open to break the chain—not without hurting her.

We looked at each other. I was desperately trying to think of a way to get past the door that didn't involve cracking it against her skull. I heard myself say, "Can we talk?"

I saw her shoulders lift as she took a long, slow breath. I could see the battle going on inside her, the little looks she was casting at my eyes, my suit, my neck—shit, could she see my tattoos?

Eventually, she bit her lip and nodded. Her eyes said, *don't let me be wrong about you.*

My guts twisted.

She unfastened the chain.

As soon as the door opened, I ran past her. The door to the mystery room was right where I'd imagined it. By the time I reached it, I'd already pulled out my gun.

I heard her give a strangled scream behind me.

I turned the handle and swung the door wide, the pistol coming up to fire—

The room was tiny. Barely room for a desk and a chair. And the chair was empty.

Everything clicked into place and I realized how incredibly fucking stupid I'd been.

I turned around just in time to see the girl running out of the apartment.

ELEVEN

Gabriella

This isn't happening. This can't be happening.

I was sprinting barefoot down the hallway. I wanted to scream for help but I needed all my air for running. At the same time, my lungs felt as if they were shutting down because I was going into full-on panic mode. For years, the apartment had been the one place I felt safe. Now, all the bad in the world had suddenly broken in.

I'd been forced out of my home and I had nowhere to run for sanctuary. To me, nowhere outside *was* safe.

I heard him behind me, long legs eating up the distance. He'd be on me in seconds.

I tried to go faster. I focused on the door to the stairwell at the end of the hallway—I knew I didn't have time to wait for the elevator. Another ten steps. Five. Three.

I put my hand on the door handle just as I felt his arm go around my waist.

I opened my mouth to scream and his hand clamped over it.

And then I was being dragged back down the hallway to my apartment.

TWELVE

Alexei

This isn't happening. This can't be happening.

I had one arm around her waist. Her back was against my front as I walked backwards, dragging her heels along the carpet, checking over my shoulder for any witnesses. My careful plan was gone. Inside, I was beating myself up over and over for my stupidity, but even that couldn't completely distract me from—

Her soft ass grinding against my crotch as she kicked and struggled—

That mass of walnut-brown hair, cool and wet against my neck—

Her open, panting mouth, lips soft against my palm—

I reached the door of her apartment and hauled her inside, kicking the door shut behind us. I dumped her in a heap on the floor.

She opened her mouth to scream.

I pulled out the gun and pointed it right at her face.

THIRTEEN

Gabriella

MY SCREAM died in my throat. I stared down the barrel of the gun and it seemed to expand to fill my vision, a black hole that was going to consume me. He was panting, though nowhere near as hard as me, and his eyes were wide. But the gun didn't waver at all.

I was sitting awkwardly, one leg bent and one straight, but I didn't dare move. I looked up into his eyes. The icy gray was there, colder than it had been in the coffee shop, colder than anything I'd ever seen. A merciless, machine-like gaze. But this time, I could see the other side of him, the flash of blue stronger than it had been before. He was battling with himself. My fate was being decided, right in front of me.

"You've got the wrong person," I croaked. "I'm nobody." I hadn't been ready for how the last two words made me feel.

He shook his head. Then he said, "You're the hacker."

And I suddenly realized what his accent was: *Russian*.

He'd been sent by Nikolai Orlov. Or one of the other Russians the Sisters of Invidia had hacked. We'd thought we were untraceable. And it had all happened so far away, on computers in Moscow...none of us had ever contemplated that these animals might catch up with us in the real world. "Oh Jesus Christ," I whispered. Which was as good as an admission.

His entire body was tensed and tight. I could see the corded muscles in his neck standing out and the white of his knuckles as he gripped the gun. And then I saw his finger start to tighten on the trigger.

FOURTEEN

Alexei

You have to.
What I wanted was irrelevant.
How I felt about her was irrelevant.
My entire career, I'd followed the rules: be distant, be disconnected, be a machine. And then she'd appeared out of nowhere and changed everything, made me break every rule.
And now I was paying the price.
One bullet. One shot between the eyes. One squeeze of the trigger.
That's all I had to do.
I'd never closed my eyes before. I'd always figured I owed them that, the people I killed. But I closed them now. *Just do it. You can pull the trigger and not open your eyes until you've turned away.*
It was worse, with my eyes closed. I could see her in the coffee shop, looking up at me. I could see her naked in the window. I could see her as she was now, in her nightshirt with the cartoon elephant on it.

How?! I screamed at myself. *How could you not guess it was her?* But I already knew exactly why: this girl had bewitched me from the very first moment we'd met. After that, my brain hadn't let me even entertain the possibility that the hacker might be female. She'd made me lose my edge and that was terrifying.

My finger tightened a little more on the trigger. All I had to do was move one finger. It shouldn't be this difficult.

Um... she said in my mind. We were back in the coffee shop and her wrist was so slender, so fragile in my hand.

I could smell her: strawberry soap and warm femininity. I heard a tiny, silken sound, right at the edge of perception, and realized it was the sound of her hair as she frantically shook her head.

I opened my eyes.

She'd started crying while my eyes were closed. Her cheeks were gleaming with tears and those big hazel eyes were scrunched up and brimming. I watched her cry and it was as if someone was crushing my heart in their fist.

The arm holding the gun suddenly dropped and I spun to face away from her. "*Chyort voz'mi!*" I yelled. *Damn it!* I called myself *zalupa* and *dolbo yeb* and a few other names beside as I cradled the gun in both hands, hoping that I could work myself up to it.

But I couldn't. I couldn't kill her.

I turned back to her and sat down on the floor with absolutely no idea what to do next.

FIFTEEN

Gabriella

HE SAT DOWN HEAVILY, his muscled body sending a shockwave through the floor. I didn't dare to move. Should I look at him? Not look at him? Which would be more likely to spur him to violence?

Everything I'd ever read or seen on the news about hostages and gunmen was blurring into one in my head, but none of it made sense. Those people were all crazy guys who picked up a gun and started shooting because something went wrong in their lives, or because there was something wrong with them. This guy was different. He'd marched into my apartment utterly efficient and without hesitation and he'd clearly been ready to kill me...until, suddenly, he couldn't.

He wasn't a crazed killer driven by emotion. He was a professional and emotion was the only thing keeping me alive.

He was sitting with his knees up and the gun

dangling between them, staring at the floor. The sheer size of him would have been intimidating even without the gun.

I had one leg bent under me and it was starting to cramp really badly. I *had* to move it. I did it as slowly as I could—

He didn't lift his head, but he raised his eyes to look at me. God, he was gorgeous. Those gray eyes were beautiful but, when they were filled with doubt and conflict as they were now, they were achingly sad. How could a man so strong, so physically brutal, have that much emotion inside him?

And why did I feel such an instinctual yearning to try to help him with the pain?

I slowly finished moving my leg. That left me sitting in the same position he was—on my ass on the floor, knees up, facing him. For a long moment we just sat there, barely breathing.

What the fuck am I going to do?

I tentatively leaned forward and put my hand on his ankle, just trying to make some sort of connection.

And that's when he grabbed me.

SIXTEEN

Alexei

HER FINGERS closed on my ankle and that snapped me back to alertness. All those hardwired instincts kicked in, the ones that had been forged in the mud and the rain with my commanding officer screaming in my ear. I *reacted*.

I grabbed her wrist and *heaved* and she flew through the air like a doll. She landed on the floor on her back, the air knocked out of her, and I was already on top of her. One hand was on her upper chest, pinning her down. The other held the gun, the barrel pressed to her forehead.

I was almost as shocked as she was. I'd done it on instinct, without conscious thought. But suddenly I was there, the gun cocked and ready—

Do it! Do it now!

Her eyes stared up at me beseechingly. I couldn't do it. But I couldn't let her go, either. The consequences of *not* killing her started to sink in. I had no idea what to do.

And as my mind spun, the rest of me was left to react in its own way. I started to become aware of things. Things like the scent of her, again, every breath I took drinking in more of her.

Things like the way her body felt under mine, so soft and warm. I was basically lying on top of her. One of my legs was outside hers, but the other was between them, our groins pressed together.

I glanced down at my hand. I'd just pinned her down, the way I would a man. But that meant my fingers were brushing her collarbone and the heel of my hand—

The heel of my hand was on the upper slope of her breast.

I could feel the warm softness through the thin fabric of her nightshirt. I remembered that she wasn't wearing a bra.

I looked down and saw that the nightshirt had ridden up when I'd thrown her. On one side, it was rucked up around her upper thighs. On the other, it was high enough that I could see her black briefs and even the skin just above them.

I could feel myself getting hard. My body's caveman reaction, a gorgeous woman powerless and spread beneath me....

No! Jesus, no! I wasn't going to take her by force! The idea sickened me. But that didn't change the effect she was having on me. I was rock hard, now. I knew she must be able to feel the bulge in my pants because it was throbbing against her thigh. And the head of my cock was right up against the front panel of her panties.

SEVENTEEN

Gabriella

Every breath I took made my breast rise and fall against his hand.

Jesus, he's going to—

No he's not.

I couldn't move, couldn't form a coherent thought. I just stared up into those icy gray eyes as they decided my fate. The gun was utterly motionless, the end of the barrel pressed right up against my forehead, holding me there like a butterfly stuck with a pin.

I was terrified and that was normal.

But...

No.

As I looked up at him, at those eyes—

No.

The way his chest bulged as he controlled me, the hardness of his body against mine—

No! This was wrong, utterly, utterly wrong.

It wasn't that I wanted him to do something. Not like *this*. It was the fact that just being this close to him, in this position, was affecting me. I was getting—

No! No, I'm not!

But it didn't matter how many times I denied it. My body was reacting and my brain had no say in it. It was pheromones or hormones or *something*. The feel of him, the sight of him, even the clean, masculine scent of him...it was sending hot currents swirling down through my body, joining together to make a dark vortex between my thighs. And his hard cock was right there, pressed against me. A few thin layers of cloth were all that separated him from...*me*.

It wasn't the situation. It was *him,* in spite of the situation. I knew I wouldn't have reacted like this with any other man.

He shifted his weight infinitesimally and I felt the head of his cock trace along the lips of my sex. I drew in a shuddering breath.

I wanted to scream. I wanted him to shoot me and get it over with.

But part of me just wanted him to lean down and kiss me.

We stared into each other's eyes, our breathing in sync and getting faster and faster—

There was a knock at the door.

EIGHTEEN

Gabriella

HE ROLLED OFF OF ME and sprang to his feet. I couldn't believe how fast he was, for such a big guy. I saw now how he'd caught me so easily in the hallway.

I lay there panting as he crept across the room, keeping the gun pointing at me the whole time. He put his eye to the door's spy hole for a second, then crept back to me. He leaned down and put his lips to my ear and, for the first time in what seemed like hours, he spoke.

"Get rid of him," he said, his accent turning each syllable into a rough-edged slab of steel, "Or I'll have to kill him."

I nodded dumbly. He allowed me to get up and walked with me to the door. Then he showed me how he wanted me to stand when I opened it—pressed right up against the edge of it.

I slowly opened the door. He stepped back, hiding behind it and watching through the spy hole. He put his hand on the small of my back, reminding me he was there. The heat of his touch throbbed through my nightshirt.

Standing in the hallway was my neighbor, Mr. Lazzari His white hair was poking out from under a Yankees hat—he must have been watching a game on TV. "You okay? I heard a scream."

I just stared at him for a second. Rescue was *right there.*

But the man with his hand on my back would kill him. Maybe, *maybe* he'd then show me mercy—if that's what had held him back so far. Maybe, if someone heard the shot and called the cops, I'd live. But Mr. Lazzari would still be dead. He had about sixteen grandchildren and he'd never hurt a person his whole life.

"I switched channels on the TV," I said. I was shocked at how level my voice sounded. "And I forgot I had the volume cranked way up, and there was a movie on and...wow! I nearly hit the ceiling." I forced a grin onto my face.

"Oh." He peered into the apartment behind me, but there was nothing to see, nothing knocked over or out of place. "You sure?"

The hand on my back felt as if it was burning through my nightshirt to touch my skin. "Uh-huh."

He nodded, a little embarrassed, and backed away. I swung the door slowly closed, turning as I did it. The man stepped forward from behind the door. And then we were staring at each other, our faces no more than a foot apart.

NINETEEN

Alexei

GOD, she was beautiful. Standing there in her apartment, close enough that we could lean forward and kiss, we could have been a couple of lovers. Me in my suit, just home from work and my gorgeous girlfriend greeting me at the door—

And then I felt the weight of the gun in my hand.

I'd screwed up everything and now my life was unraveling. I couldn't kill her but, if I didn't, they'd kill *me*. Disloyalty isn't accepted in the Bratva. And then they'd send someone to kill her, too.

One mistake. If I'd walked into that coffee shop two minutes earlier or later....

What the fuck am I going to do?

She must have seen my expression because she said, "You could just leave. I never saw you. I won't tell anyone, I won't go to the cops."

I shook my head.

She looked around the apartment. "You can take anything you want. Please!"

I shook my head again.

Her voice was rising in fear. "I won't go *near* Nikolai again. I'll delete everything I got. You can watch me do it!"

I sighed. I suddenly felt very tired—tired of the whole system I was part of. "It doesn't work that way," I told her.

"Tell me! Tell me what I need to do!"

I just shook my head. There was nothing she could do.

She'd started to cry again. "You can't just kill me! *Please!*"

"I don't want to!" I snapped. "But if I don't—"

There was another knock at the door. I checked the spy hole.

It was Lev.

I slowly opened the door. Lev had his hand under his jacket, ready to pull out his gun, but he relaxed when he saw it was me. He pushed past me. "What the fuck is going on?" Then he saw the girl. "Who the fuck is this? His girlfriend?"

I closed the door behind him. I thought about saying *yes,* but lying was pointless—unless I could produce a body, he'd figure it out. "She's the hacker," I said.

"*Her?!*" He looked her up and down in disbelief.

"Why did you come in?" I asked. Every muscle in my body was groaning and aching with tension. I'd never been so tightly wound in my life.

"Do you know how long you've been in here? And Nikolai called me, asking if it was done yet." He looked at the girl again. "Why haven't you done it yet?"

The girl and I exchanged a desperate look.

Lev saw. "Oh. You fucked her?" He looked at the girl's long, bare legs.

"No!" I snapped.

"You want to? Is that it? You want to fuck her before you do it?"

"*No!*"

"It's okay. Jesus, if that's what you want, just do it so we can get out of here." He looked at her legs again, then at the peaks her breasts made in the nightshirt. "We can both do her. Let's take her in the bedroom."

The girl was looking at me with huge, terrified eyes. I could feel everything sliding out of control. "No! Shut up!" I snapped.

But Lev didn't care what I wanted, anymore. He put his hands on her shoulders and spun her to face the bedroom. "Come on. I'll hold her. You can go first."

"*Don't touch her!*" I roared.

Everything stopped.

Lev blinked at me. "What...the fuck?"

I shook my head. "Just...go back to the car. I'll deal with this."

"You'll *deal with it?* Like you've dealt with it so far?" Lev shook his head. "What the *fuck* has got into you?"

"*Wait in the car!*"

"Christ!" He pushed the girl forward, away from him, and she went stumbling. "*I'll* fucking do it." He pulled out his gun.

"She could be useful," I said desperately. "She could work for us. Hack our enemies!"

Lev snorted. "Nikolai was crystal fucking clear. Kill the hacker. He wants us to destroy her computer, too."

And he raised his gun to fire.

TWENTY

Gabriella

I was staring down the barrel of a gun again, but this guy was different.

I'd known it as soon as I saw him, as soon as he'd leered at me. Meeting the second guy threw the first guy into sharp relief. He was smaller and slighter next to my huge guy. He was angry and jumpy where my guy was cold and controlled...and yet burning hot underneath. And this guy was leering at me with a crude, frat boy's lust where my guy....my guy seemed to *want* me on a much deeper, more powerful level...but was wrestling with himself, holding himself back.

I caught myself. *When did he become "my" guy?*

I looked over to where he was standing, my eyes wide and pleading.

The new guy cocked his gun.

I closed my eyes.

There was a quick, low sound that vibrated in my eardrums. I'd heard that sound in movies, the sound of a silenced shot. I waited for the pain, but it didn't come.

I opened my eyes to see the new guy slumping to the ground. Then I saw the big guy lowering his smoking gun. He was staring at it as if he'd never seen it before. He lifted his eyes to me and, just for a second, he looked helpless. Seconds passed.

"What have I done?" he asked.

I didn't have any words. I just shook my head.

Suddenly, he was running at me. He grabbed my upper arms and lifted me right off the floor and slammed me into the wall. *"What did you make me do?!"* he yelled. His eyes were wild.

I shook my head again, trying not to look at the body.

He pressed in closer, his abs hard against my stomach, his thighs forcing mine back against the wall. He grabbed my wrists and forced them up and out, pinning them beside my head. "This is your fault!" he yelled. "Why did you have to do this? Why did you have to steal from us?"

I felt my eyes widen. *"Steal?* I didn't steal from him! We don't steal!"

"You try to empty bank accounts!"

"No! I was looking for evidence!"

He frowned at that. "You're CIA?"

"No! I'm—" I was sobbing as I said it. It sounded so fucking stupid, saying it out loud. "I'm a...vigilante. I hack to get evidence against human traffickers!"

He frowned even deeper, then shook his head. "We don't do that."

"Yes! You do! Nikolai does!"

He thumped the wall beside my head, hard enough that I flinched. "You *stupid—"* He put his face right up to mine. "I work for Nikolai and Nikolai works for the Malakovs!" he told me. "They sell guns, not women!"

The size of him was terrifying, but, weirdly, I didn't fear violence from him the same way I'd feared it from the other guy. It didn't feel as if he wanted to hurt me. So I didn't back down. "Then Nikolai is doing some backroom deal," I panted, "because he's connected with a guy called Carl and he *is* a trafficker—one of the biggest."

He shook his head. But I stared right back at him. There were tears streaming down my cheeks but I lifted my chin defiantly. My whole life had changed, tonight, and I didn't know what the hell was going to happen, but I knew I was right about this.

He studied me, watching for any hint of a lie. I stared right back at him. After a few seconds, I saw in his eyes the first faint traces of doubt—doubt about the story he'd been told. He shook his head again, but he released my wrists and stepped back, cursing under his breath in Russian.

I figured he needed a moment, so I kept quiet and glanced around the apartment. That was a mistake, because I finally got a good look at the dead body.

Most of one side of his head was missing.

I turned and ran for the bathroom, reaching the toilet just in time. When I'd rinsed my mouth and come back into the living area, the big guy had just finished dragging the body out of sight behind the couch. I didn't know if he'd done it for my benefit, but I was insanely grateful either way.

"What happens now?" I asked when my stomach had settled enough to speak.

He looked at me with great sadness. "They kill us both."

TWENTY-ONE

Alexei

I FELT...lost. As if someone had pulled not just the floor but the whole world out from under me and I was falling through an endless black void.

I'd had the army, friends who felt like brothers, men I'd die to protect. My life had had structure and I was good at what I did. When I left the army, I'd been lost.

Nikolai had found me. He had work for a guy like me, he said. Work I already knew how to do. And so I found new brothers. A new family.

And now all that had been ripped away. After this, I wouldn't just be out of the Bratva, I'd be their target.

I looked at the trail of blood that led behind the couch and nausea rose up inside me. Lev had been an asshole but I hadn't wanted *this*.

But he'd been going to kill her.

I looked at the girl. She was white-faced and shaking and looked as if she might throw up again at any moment. And even in that state, she was the most beautiful thing I'd ever laid eyes on.

I knew I'd been wrong, when I'd had that momentary fantasy of the two of us together. I'd forgotten what I was—a monster. I didn't deserve her.

But right now, she needed me. Or she wouldn't last the night.

Staying close to her, but being unable to be with her, unable to make her mine...that would be pure torture. But to see in the headlines in a few days that her body had been found in a river or a garbage dump...that was unthinkable.

I'd done so much wrong in my life. I needed to just do this one thing right.

"I can help you escape," I said. "But we have to go right now." I looked at my phone. No call from Nikolai yet, but it would come. Or he'd call Lev's phone and wonder why he didn't answer.

She just stared at me. She was locking up, trying to blank it all out. I'd seen it before, when civilians see something like this. It's the brain trying to protect itself. It usually works in our favor, because it means witnesses can't give good testimony. But right now, it was going to get us killed.

I forced myself to move slowly and gently. I put my hands on her shoulders and said, "We must go. *Now.*"

She looked up at me, debating. I don't know why, but she must have decided to trust me, because she gave a single, quick nod.

TWENTY-TWO

Gabriella

I WALKED through to the bedroom. My legs felt numb, as if they belonged to someone else. I mechanically picked out some clothes and put them on—jeans, a tank top and a sweater—but it was like dressing a doll. *This can't be real. None of this is real.* The Russian Mafia couldn't really be after me. There couldn't be a body in the next room. And I couldn't be leaving—I couldn't *leave!* That meant going outside.

I started stuffing things into bags. Books. Computer equipment. I was going to need boxes or crates or something—

I heard a movement behind me and turned to see him standing in the doorway. "What are you doing?" he asked cautiously.

"Packing."

He shook his head. "We have to run," he said. "No time. No room. One bag."

"*One?* What about—" I indicated all my stuff.

"Leave it."

"Leave it?!" I glanced around in horror. It wasn't just about possessions, it was about...this was my *nest,* this was my one safe place. If I really had to leave it, I had to be able to recreate it someplace else.

"We must go," he told me.

I grabbed an armful of clothes and sneakers, my laptop and, as an afterthought, the portable hard drive that stores a backup of all my files. Nikolai *was* doing something with Carl, whether this guy believed it or not. I wasn't leaving that evidence behind. I threw in some toiletries from the bathroom and zipped the bag shut. That was it—my entire future life was in one bag.

"Ready?" he asked.

I blinked at him. Even without my...*issues,* just dropping everything you own and walking out would be a wrench for anyone, right? But he seemed to genuinely not get it. As if—

As if he didn't have anything in his life. As if he didn't have a home, just a place where he lived.

I nodded, grabbed my coat and we headed towards the door. *What the hell am I doing?* I was putting my trust in a guy who'd been sent to kill me.

But he was also the one who'd saved me.

As soon as I tried to step into the hallway, I knew we were going to have a problem. I tried to take deep breaths, but I could feel the panic starting to build. It got worse as we walked towards the elevators and worse still as we descended. I could feel the outside world, dark and huge and utterly unknown, opening up around us.

We walked through the lobby with him leading the way. Past the doors of the coffee shop, the furthest I'd been in over a month. He opened the door to the street and freezing air rushed in. And I stopped.

When he realized I wasn't with him, he turned and looked back at me. "What?" He looked towards the street, then back at me. "We have to go."

It's difficult to describe The Dread, as I call it. But I'll try.

First my legs locked up. The joints seemed to physically seize, aching and shrieking, as if my bones would snap if I tried to walk any further. The fear started to vibrate through me as if I was a bell being struck over and over again. My whole body started to shake and my guts began to churn and twist. And the further I shuffled forward, the faster the fear increased, until it was doubling with every millimeter, until I physically couldn't go any further

He frowned and walked back to me. "What?" he asked again.

My mouth was almost too dry to speak and I had to fight for air to make the words. "I'm *afraid*," I whispered. And I prayed that he'd understand that I didn't mean *afraid* in any normal sense of the word.

He did. I don't know how, given everything that we were going through, but he got it. I saw that flash of clear blue in his eyes, that shard of humanity and warmth. "What do I do?" he asked.

I stared at the door, which seemed to be a thousand miles away and getting further with each second. "*I don't know,*" I said, and started to cry. "*I don't know.*"

I knew it was useless. I knew anything he said to me, any rationalization he tried wouldn't work. I knew that, whatever his crimes, it was me who had caused all this. It was me who was going to get us both killed because I'd wanted to hurt the men hurting women and I'd been stupid enough to get caught...and now it was my fault again because I was such a fucking, *fucking* fuck up that I couldn't leave my building.

If you've never cried out of pure fear—most adults haven't—you don't know what it's like. I couldn't see. I was crying and I couldn't even wipe the tears away because I was frozen with terror. I felt myself retreating inward and downward, as always happened when things reached their peak. I let out a broken wail of loss—

A voice spoke in my ear, a voice made of granite and steel, but with a warmth I hadn't heard before. "My name is Alexei. What is yours?"

I answered in a voice that wasn't my own. *"Gab—Gabriella."*

A huge arm slid across my back and another slid behind my knees. "Close your eyes, Gabriella."

I closed them. And then I was being hoisted off my feet and carried, cradled in his arms. He rocked me towards him so that my head lolled against his chest.

It shouldn't have worked. I should have been terrified of him. But, instead, I flung my arms around his neck.

I felt us moving, his huge slow strides rocking me like a boat. I knew from the cold air that we were outside and that we must be walking down the street. But I just squeezed my eyes tight shut and focused on the warm, strong bulk of him.

I had a new safe place. And his name was Alexei.

TWENTY-THREE

Alexei

I walked for three blocks with Gabriella in my arms and her bag dangling from her back. She wasn't heavy.

Something had happened to her, when we'd reached the doors. I'd seen similar things in the army—men paralyzed by a sound or a feeling that triggered a memory. I knew some of the horrors that caused those problems in soldiers, because I'd seen some myself.

I had a pretty good idea what caused problems like that in civilians. And the thought of it made my hands tighten into shaking, white-knuckled fists.

I stopped only once, to take out all the cash the ATM would let me. Then I found a street with two cheap motels—down-market places that wouldn't ask too many questions. I paid cash and didn't put Gabriella down until we were in the room. When I sat her on the edge of the bed, she refused to stop clinging to me.

"It's okay," I said haltingly. The tone and the

sensation of comforting someone were unfamiliar...and yet they didn't feel completely new. They felt as if they came from a place deep down in myself, one I hadn't visited for a long time.

Very slowly, she started to unwind her arms from my neck. She opened her eyes and glanced fearfully around the room but her breathing was calmer, now, and her tears had stopped.

I reached out and tentatively stroked her hair with my hand. It was just as gloriously soft as I'd imagined it, but now I wasn't thinking about sex at all. I just wanted to look after her. I wanted to deliver her from everything that was happening to her and everything that was eating away at her from the inside.

She hugged her arms round herself and looked down at her lap, not meeting my eyes, so I took the time to look around the room. *One door, one window. Ambush point there. Bed could be pushed up against the door as a barricade—*

"I'm not a complete basket-case," she blurted. I turned and she was looking at me. "Not all the time. Most of the time I'm fine. As long as I stay in my...."—she flushed and looked at her lap again—"safe place."

"Your apartment," I said.

She nodded. She seemed...not back to normal, but better. Back to being *her*. "I'm sorry," she mumbled.

I laid my hand on her shoulder. "You don't have to apologize. Not to anyone." I felt clumsy saying it, but I meant it. The man who I suspected had done this to her...he was the one who should be sorry. My hands tightened again, longing for an arm to break, a neck to snap.

I don't enjoy killing. But that doesn't mean there aren't people I want to kill.

I indicated the room. "We can stay here for tonight. Until we work out what to do." My heart dropped down into the pit of my stomach as soon as I'd said it. As if there was *anything* we could do. For the first time in years I had no plan, no strategy.

She shuffled back on the bed and drew her legs up so that she could sit cross-legged. "We're going to have to run, aren't we?"

I nodded. "Run and hope they eventually stop looking."

She bit her lip. "You can't go back to them, can you? Your people. The Russians."

"The Bratva. No. Not after letting you go. Not after killing Lev. They could not allow that." That feeling of belonging to something, of being a part of something bigger than yourself, had been ripped out of me and I couldn't get used to the void it had left. It ached and burned in my chest.

"I'm sorry."

I nodded. I couldn't talk about it, not yet. Being cut off from the brotherhood was like being disowned by my family. I tried to change the subject. "We'll split up. Go far away, new lives."

I saw her shoulders tense at the thought. "I don't think I can do that." She looked right at me. "Not on my own."

And right in the center of that void inside me, there was a tiny flicker of warmth. The idea of being with her, of running off with her somewhere together...that almost made it all sound bearable.

Then I remembered what I was. Leaving the brotherhood didn't change that. The brotherhood hadn't made me what I was, they'd just found a use for my skills. I looked at her as she sat on the bed: so small, so delicate. So innocent—even her hacking had been well-intentioned. I didn't deserve to stroke her cheek.

Or cup her breasts.

Or slide my hands under that sweet, firm ass and draw her towards me, kick her legs apart and—

I turned away, walked over to the window, and pretended to check outside. Really, I just couldn't bear the torture of looking at her any longer without being able to have her. "It's late," I said. "Try to rest. We'll talk in the morning."

And then I stared fixedly out of the window at the darkened parking lot, making sure I looked through the dark glass and not at the reflection in it, where glimpses of long, pale leg and black underwear appeared as she undressed. I stood there and did my best not to watch as she slipped beneath the covers. And then I waited for whatever the night would bring.

TWENTY-FOUR

Gabriella

I'D STRIPPED DOWN to bra and panties. I hadn't had space to bring many clothes and I hadn't thought to bring a nightshirt—besides, the bed had thick blankets and a comforter and looked as if it was going to be pretty warm, even in October. I got in as fast as I could—a bed was familiar enough that, once I'd slid between the sheets, I could almost convince myself I was back home in my apartment. The Dread had subsided once we were inside a small, closed off room. That wasn't normal for me, especially after a freak-out of that magnitude. I knew some of the artificial calm was because he was there and the implications of that made my head spin. No one had ever been able to help me with it before.

I lay on my side, facing him, eyes half-closed. He stood at the window like a silent sentry, a colossus keeping me safe. God, his head came almost to the top of the door! How had he switched roles so quickly, from attacker to protector? From the first moment he'd realized that it was me he was meant to kill, he'd been reluctant. It felt like he'd already gotten to know me before he ever walked in.

He sat down in the room's only chair, his gun held across his knees, and switched off the light. Was he going to keep watch all night? Or was he just being a gentleman, since there was only one bed?

Should I offer to share the bed?

I was almost annoyed at the sudden hot rush that thought set off inside me. I was still recovering from my complete meltdown at the doors of my apartment building and I was on the run, fearing for my life...and now suddenly I was getting hot for him?

But deep down, it sort of made sense. Having a huge, strong man look after me—*literally* pick me up and carry me off—was kicking off all my primal, cavewoman instincts. I knew he'd killed—probably many times. He'd even done it right in front of me. But being scared of him didn't stop the feelings he stirred up. Especially now that it was clear he didn't want to hurt me.

This is nuts. The guy was a career criminal. A paid killer, from what he'd said. I should be running as fast as I could in the other direction but....

But I felt that *wrench* again, every single time I looked at him.

I didn't think I'd be able to sleep. But I'd underestimated how much the stress had taken out of me and my eyelids slowly closed.

TWENTY-FIVE

Alexei

THE ROOM was dark and still. She breathed so quietly that I had to go over to the bed a couple of times, just to check that she was okay. And each time I looked at her, with those soft pink lips slightly parted and her hair spread out across the pillow, it was more difficult to tear myself away.

As the streets outside grew quiet, the scene became familiar. I'd spent many nights sitting in the darkness like this, my gun on my knee, waiting for the owner of the house to come home. It was a good method, because you could get the job done as soon as they walked in the door—two shots and they went down, with nothing to alert the neighbors. Simple.

The opposite of my situation now. On the run, cut off from the brotherhood. They'd hunt me like a dog.

One of the skills they teach you in the army is to improvise. Another is to survive. As midnight came and went and I slid deeper and deeper into a black well of despair, my training began to kick in.

If we ran, what were our chances? Maybe I could slip away, get out of the country, and make it to Venezuela or Colombia, somewhere where the Bratva wouldn't find me and where they were plenty of jobs for men with my skills. But Gabriella? She'd last a few days, at most. Nikolai wanted her dead....

That thought nagged at me. She'd been convinced that Nikolai was involved in trafficking but I didn't believe it. No way would the family's leader, Luka Malakov, allow someone as senior as Nikolai to be involved in trafficking. He'd beaten a man almost to death, once, for running a brothel that used kidnapped and trafficked women. *No way.* And Nikolai wasn't stupid—he'd know he couldn't get away with doing anything behind Luka's back.

And yet...Gabriella had sounded so sure. And Nikolai had been so desperate to have her killed and her computer destroyed. He'd surely understand the potential benefits of having a hacker like that on our side. Why kill her, instead of persuading her to work for us? It didn't make any sense.

I pushed the thought away. Whether Nikolai was up to something or not, the result was the same: the Bratva would already be hunting us. I checked my phone and there were four voicemails from Nikolai, each one more worried and angrier than the last.

I looked over at Gabriella. She was as good as dead, on her own. Or I could stay with her and try to protect her and maybe we'd last a few months before they caught up with us. It would be harder to hide with two of us—I was used to disappearing but she wasn't. And every day, I'd have to wake up and see her and know that we'd never be together...Jesus, it would be worse than hell.

And when they did eventually catch up with us, it would be a slow, traitor's death for me. For her? Even worse. My stomach turned. Luka's people were honorable but, if a price was put on our heads, there was no telling which lowlife scumbags would chase us down. They'd find us in some cheap motel room like this one, throw Gabriella on the bed and—

I closed my eyes.

And my training kicked in with an answer. There was a way out of this, a simple way. A way that would put everything back how it was. I could contact Nikolai and say that there'd been a mistake, make up a story about Gabriella killing Lev and taking me hostage. I could rejoin the brotherhood and life could return to normal.

All I had to do was one little thing.

I drew in a long, shuddering breath and opened my eyes.

It was the only thing that made sense. It was what I'd been told to do, after all, what I was good at. The *only* thing I was good at.

I stood up and walked silently over to the bed.

I looked down at her as she slept. She was on her back, one arm down by her side and one arm thrown out over her head. She'd rolled in her sleep and her head was in the gap between the two pillows. The covers had fallen down to just below her bra. She was indescribably beautiful.

I picked up one of the pillows, taking care not to wake her.

Then I positioned it above her face and prepared to push down.

This is right, said a voice inside me. *This is what you do. This is all you do.* I was a monster, after all.

And the monster doesn't fall for the princess: he kills her.

I lowered the pillow until it was almost touching her nose. I couldn't see her face, now, just that spray of soft, walnut-colored hair spread out across the sheet. That made it easier.

I prepared to press down, bracing myself for her struggle and panic. It would be over in less than a minute. I took a deep breath—

And smelled her scent. Honeysuckle and strawberries and *woman,* the first thing I'd noticed about her. I froze, the pillow just brushing her nose.

This is right! The voice inside my head was screaming, now. *You can put everything right! You can have it all back!*

But I didn't want to. Didn't. Want. To.

How many have you killed? What difference does one more make?

But it was *her.* I imagined her slumbering face beneath the pillow: that soft skin, those perfect lips. The way she'd said *Um* when I'd grabbed her wrist in the coffee shop.

Do you think she'll ever love you? You can't have her! Not a man like you!

I knew that.

But I felt something rise up in myself. A stubbornness, a resistance to following orders. It was something I thought had been beaten out of me a long time ago, back in my army days, but now I realized it was like a block of lead, absorbing each blow, but getting a little harder each time. It had been hammered for years, and now it was hard enough to bore through a planet.

I lifted the pillow up and away, revealing her face.

I was a monster.

But I was going to do this *one thing* right.

I could never have her. But maybe I could save her.

Very gently, I reached down, lifted her head with one hand, and slipped the pillow underneath so that she was comfortable.

She half-woke, smiled and murmured, "Thank you."

TWENTY-SIX

Gabriella

WHEN I WOKE, there was a moment of panic as I realized I wasn't in my own bedroom. Then the weight of everything that had happened the day before slammed down on me and I groaned.

"Good morning." A low rumble from behind me. I rolled over.

He was still sitting in the same chair. God, had he sat there all night? I sat up, remembered I was still in my underwear and tugged the comforter up as well. "Hi."

We looked at each other. Then I glanced down at the pillow, frowning as I remembered something. "Did you put a pillow under my head in the night?"

"Yes. You'd rolled off it." He looked embarrassed.

"Well...thank you." I nodded at the chair. "Didn't you sleep?"

"I can sleep sitting up. I take shower now, though." The slightly mangled grammar, combined with the accent, was a reminder of just how different he was, how far away he came from.

He ambled past the bed to the bathroom, closing the door behind him. He must have been waiting for me to wake up, so that he didn't wake me.

I slipped out of bed and went over to the window. The curtains were still drawn but the sun was blasting around the edges. I sneaked a peek around the edge....

A street I'd never seen before. Another motel across the street. An utterly new place, without familiar anchor points—

I felt that *slip* as the panic started. It's like when you unexpectedly slip on ice, but with your soul and mind instead of your body.

I wasn't sure I could find my way home.

I quickly pressed the curtain against the wall and turned away. I wanted to shower before I put on fresh clothes so I was sort of stuck until Alexei had finished in the bathroom.

Alexei...just the shape of it felt weird on my tongue. I'd come across plenty of Russian names since Lilywhite put The Sisters of Invidia together and invited me to join, but they'd always been just letters on a screen. I never thought I'd actually meet one of the Russian mafia...let alone be thinking so much about him.

I took a look around at the room—I'd been too freaked out, the night before, to really take it in. A TV, its remote held together with Scotch tape; white walls with a big water stain on the ceiling and a big, creaky bed. One bed. Two people.

How long were we going to be here? Was he going to sleep in the chair every night?

I couldn't get a handle on this thing between us.

He'd seemed into me in the coffee shop, then he'd been ready to kill me, then he'd saved me and now...now I didn't know.

At that moment, I heard the bathroom door open behind me and spun around. He was done *already?* I was used to showers taking a half hour, but he'd been in there two minutes! Then I saw him and all conscious thought stopped.

He had his pants on but was still doing up his shirt. I got a glimpse of his naked chest and *holy hell,* even my shower fantasy hadn't done him justice. He wasn't pumped-up and veiny like a bodybuilder, he was just *big,* like he'd been born that way. *Mighty,* like some hero peasant blacksmith who'd won a battle with only his sledgehammer. I hadn't been ready for the way his pecs stood out: it looked as if you could hurl cinder blocks at those hard slabs of muscle and the blocks would shatter into dust. Or as if you could put your head on them, as you lay next to him, and be very comfortable indeed.

I pressed my palms against my hips. I was getting an almost uncontrollable urge to run my hands over that chest, just to see what it felt like.

The other thing I hadn't been ready for were the tattoos. I'd almost forgotten about glimpsing the very tip of his ink over his shirt collar. Now, I could see the full thing: a scorpion, its claw open menacingly. And the tattoos continued on his chest: a rose and a snorting, charging bull. I knew they had meaning: it was an entire story, written in a language I couldn't understand. It should have been terrifying and it was, in a way. But I was drawn to it, as well. This stuff was raw and real and darkly exciting.

"Seen enough?" he asked. And I looked up to see

him looking right into my eyes.

Which was when I remembered I was standing there in my underwear.

I wondered how much looking *he'd* been doing while I stared at his chest. Had he been checking me out? A deep, hot throb went through my body as I looked into his eyes. I could see the traces of lust still fading.

He *had* been checking me out.

And there was something else there, as well, beyond the coldness and the lust. Something lighter than his ruthless efficiency, more human. Determination.

"Go have a shower," he said. "Then we eat."

I grabbed a blouse and my jeans and hurried in there, closing the door behind me before either of us did something we regretted.

***

Twenty minutes later, we were sitting in the diner. I'd been twitchy and nervous on the street, but the inside of the diner wasn't as bad: maybe because it was stereotypical, with its squeeze-bottles of ketchup and its booths. I hadn't been to a diner in years but, thanks to movies and TV, I felt right at home.

I knew it was going to be a different matter when we went further from the motel and tried to actually run. The world outside was huge and dangerous. Stepping outside felt like stepping out of the shallow end in a swimming pool, your feet flailing for a floor that's no longer there.

I tried to think of something, *anything* else. I looked at his food. "Oatmeal?" I asked. "Seriously?"

He looked down at his bowl. "What's wrong with oatmeal? In Russia, we have *kasha*—like this, but with butter." He spooned some up. "I eat this every day since I come here."

I blinked. "Every day?"

"Every day."

I pictured him, hulking over the table at some diner every morning, or in his apartment, eating oatmeal. "You like it that much?"

He looked at me as if I was crazy. "It's good for you. It gives you energy."

"So you don't care about the taste?"

He frowned and then shrugged. "It doesn't have taste. It's fuel."

"But don't you ever want to eat something you *enjoy?* Don't you enjoy food?"

He tilted his head slowly to one side as if he was studying a strange new species.

My food arrived then. Juice and coffee, two eggs, bacon, toast and a few hash browns. The hash browns were so fresh off the griddle, they were still hissing. A truly glorious smell wafted up. I felt hungry for the first time since all this had started. It also brought home what I'd been missing out on, cooped up in the apartment. You can cook a big breakfast at home, but it's not the same as a diner breakfast.

Alexei watched me eat. His eyes went from my plate to my body. Eventually, he blurted, "Is it trick? Are you hiding it under table?" Most of the time, I'd noticed, his English was pretty good, but just occasionally, when he was in a hurry, he'd mangle his grammar.

I swallowed my last mouthful, then looked down at the huge plate and my small form. "I have a lot of nervous energy," I told him.

And just for a second, I saw a flicker at the corners of his mouth. It was gone again immediately, but I knew what I'd seen.

Alexei had nearly smiled.

***

I felt better when we'd eaten, pleasantly buzzing from caffeine and glowing from the carb rush. Alexei walked me back to the room, then said he was going out. "I need to call my boss," he told me. "I need to find a payphone."

"There's one in the office," I said, pointing.

"One that's not here. But close."

"Why?"

"I want to see how much trouble we're in."

TWENTY-SEVEN

Alexei

THERE WAS another motel across the street, which was perfect. First, I walked down the street to a bank and emptied my bank account—it wasn't much, but it would cover us for a while if we lived cheap. Then I walked to the motel across the street from ours, picked a room that had its curtains closed, and hammered on the door until I was sure it was empty. Like our motel, there was a payphone in the office. I dialed Nikolai and he picked up on the second ring.

"It's me," I said. "I'm alive."

"What the *fuck* is going on?" yelled Nikolai "I sent people to the hacker's apartment. Lev's dead."

I wanted to gauge how much he knew. "The hacker stabbed me and then shot Lev and escaped. I had to get to a doctor, but I'm okay. I'm tracking him down."

Nikolai's tone changed. "Bullshit. We searched the place. We know it's a girl."

Shit.

"She's with you, isn't she? Why are you protecting her?"

"We can use her, Nikolai. She could hack our rivals—"

"Jesus *Christ*, Alexei, just kill the bitch!" Then he managed to calm himself a little. "Just...finish the job."

I took a deep breath. "I can't do that, Nikolai. Not this time."

"You killed Lev, didn't you? That *wed'ma* sucked your cock and made you turn on your own."

"I had to kill him. I didn't want to." It was important that he knew it was me. If they caught us, I didn't want Gabriella taking the blame.

I could almost hear Nikolai shaking his head. "You pathetic, traitorous bastard."

"Look, I just want to walk away. Both of us. I leave and she never bothers you again."

There was a long pause. I could hear him sucking in air through his nostrils, *fuming,* trying not to scream at me. Finally, he said, "I want her questioned. I want men I can *trust*"—he emphasized the word—"to talk to her. I want to know that she gets the message."

"I won't let her be hurt."

"We won't hurt her. We'll talk to her. And then the two of you can fuck off to Mexico for all I fucking care." I could hear something else in his voice, now. *Worry.* This whole situation had Nikolai scared and *nothing* scared my boss.

"We're in a motel," I told him. And I gave him the number of the empty room. Then I walked back to our motel, my stomach churning. I was sure, now, that Nikolai wanted both of us dead. In minutes, we'd find out how badly.

TWENTY-EIGHT

Gabriella

Alexei told me to grab my stuff. I threw everything into my bag and then joined him at the window.

No more than five minutes after Alexei had returned, a car pulled up across the street and four men approached the other motel. They went straight to one particular room—

I stifled a scream as all four of them pulled out guns and started firing through the window and door. It wasn't just bangs, it was a continuous roar. *Machine guns.* They were absolutely guaranteeing that anyone inside was dead.

"Oh Jesus," I whispered, looking at our own room's flimsy door.

The men didn't stop until the window, door and the room beyond were utterly destroyed. Then they kicked in the remains of the door and checked inside. They were out in moments, one of them already putting a cell phone to his ear.

I looked at Alexei. From the expression on his face,

it was even worse than he'd thought.

"We have to go," he said. "Right now."

My stomach tightened at the thought of the world outside the door. But this place wasn't safe anymore. I felt like a mouse, scurrying between hidey holes.

As soon as the men had driven away, Alexei led me down to the parking lot. I leaned against a wall, trying not to panic breathe, as he looked at the cars. It was only when I saw him draw back his elbow, ready to smash a car window, that I came alive. "Wait!" I said quickly.

He hesitated. "What?"

"*That's* how you steal a car? Smash the window and then...what, twist some wires together?"

For a second, he looked abashed. Then he lifted his chin. "So?"

This whole time, he'd been looking after me and that left me with nothing to focus on but my fear. The chance to *do something* was exactly what I needed. "Oh, for God's sake. Move out of the twentieth century!" I pulled out my laptop and looked around. "There. See that car?" I hunkered down beside it. "Wireless everything. *Including* door locks and ignition." I started keying in commands. "But it's one of the early models and the security was weak, so unless the owner's updated it—which they never, ever do...."

Alexei gave a sort of grunt of disapproval. But after a few seconds, he came to stand behind me, looking over my shoulder at my screen. "I don't trust this stuff," he muttered.

"Hacking was how I found out your boss was up to no good," I said without turning around.

"And how you got caught."

I typed in a final command and looked at the car. There was a very satisfying *click* as the doors unlocked and then a roar as the engine started up. I climbed into the passenger seat and waited, trying not to smirk.

"My way is faster," Alexei muttered. But he walked around the car and got in beside me. As we drove off, we could hear police sirens coming down the street.

We passed the other motel, where people were already congregating to look at the ruins of the motel room. My stomach churned as I saw the hundreds of bullet holes. "We can't just run, can we?" I asked.

Alexei shook his head. "Nikolai wants you dead...but it's more than that. I thought he just wanted to kill the hacker, to send a message. But he sounded worried. He's scared of what you know and scared you've told me. He's not going to let us go, ever." He turned into an alley and parked, then turned to me.

"Do you think he's doing something with that trafficking guy, Carl?" I asked. "Some deal the big boss—Luka, right?"—Alexei nodded—"Some deal Luka wouldn't approve of?"

Alexei shook his head. "Anything big and Luka would find out. If it was small, it wouldn't be worth the risk. But he *is* doing something, or planning something." He stared at me with new respect. "I think you stumbled on it when you hacked him. Now he's worried I'll find out what he's doing and stop him."

"Can't we just go to Luka and tell him something's going on?"

"No one in the Bratva will even talk to me now. They'll shoot me on sight. Word will have passed round that I'm a traitor." He almost spat the word. "They will not listen to accusations."

"So what do we do?"

He thought. "Work out what Nikolai is plotting. And then stop him. If he really is doing something against the family's code, we would be heroes, not outlaws. All this would be over." He nodded at my laptop. "Can you find out what he was doing? A name, somewhere we can start looking?"

I stretched my fingers and went to work. I had Nikolai's email archive on the portable hard drive, plus some of his bank records. All of it was in Russian but, with a lot of backtracking and cross-referencing, I started to piece things together.

We went to a drive-thru and got fried chicken for lunch, eating in the car. I wrinkled my nose at Alexei's choice. "Chicken?" I asked. "*Just* chicken? No bread, no fries, no slaw or beans or salad? *Just* chicken?"

"Protein," he grunted.

I shook my head and focused on my own food. It was some mom and pop place and the fries were amazing, crispy on the outside and meltingly fluffy on the inside. I munched through half a bagful of salty goodness and then took a long pull on my soda—

And noticed something in the reflection in the windshield: he was looking sideways, watching me.

I pretended I hadn't seen. Eating takeout food had to be the least sexy thing to do in the world, right? So why would he be watching me?

When we'd wiped our sticky fingers, I went back to work while Alexei kept watch, sitting still as a statue. I got the impression he could do it for days at a time, if need be.

Eventually, I sat back, stretched my aching

shoulders and pointed at the screen. "There." It was an email sent from Nikolai to Carl, one of the most biggest human traffickers we knew of. Lilywhite had been after him ever since she'd set the Sisters of Invidia up, but so far we hadn't been able to track him down. The email said simply, "Payment sent to Semnadtsat." That same day, $150,000 had left Nikolai's private bank account, destined for a numbered Swiss account. "What's *semnadtsat*?"

"It's 'seventeen.'"

"You think he *is* doing trafficking after all? Seventeen women?" My guts twisted. "Jesus, 'seventeen years old?'"

He looked at my screen. "It says *to* seventeen. And it has capital letter, like a person."

"Who's called 'seventeen'?"

"I don't know. But I know someone who will." Then he pressed his lips together, tracing the shape of the steering wheel with his fingers as he thought.

"What?"

"We will have to go into *my* world." He shook his head. "It is not a place for you."

"For me, a woman?"

He turned and looked at me and I saw that flash of blue in his eyes again, the fierce fire of emotion under all that cold. "For *you*."

"I'll be okay," I said, with more confidence than I felt.

He considered, fingers drumming on the steering wheel. "What about...?" He indicated the outside world through the windshield.

"Better than staying on my own."

He looked at me again, this time for longer. Eventually, he seemed to make his mind up. "OK, then. But you do just what I say and you stay *right the fuck* beside me."

I nodded quickly, trying to ignore the building fear inside.

And I tried to ignore something else, too: the fluttering in my chest when he'd turned all protective of me. "Where are we going?" I asked.

Alexei started up the car. "Little Odessa."

TWENTY-NINE

Alexei

LITTLE ODESSA. A little bit of Russia, right in the heart of Brooklyn. It had always felt like home...but I knew that would already be changing as word got around of what I'd done. By tomorrow, it would be hostile territory...and that tore me up inside.

We pulled up outside a place called *Soblazn*, with a broken neon sign of a cocktail glass and a heavy, steel-reinforced door. I'd been there twice, when Nikolai wanted something delivered to Vadim, the owner.

I looked between Gabriella and the door. "Stay *right beside me,*" I told her. "Okay?"

She nodded. Then said, "Why? Who's in the bar?"

"It's not a bar."

I led her up to the door. We were still a few feet from it when one of Vadim's thugs filled the doorway. He seemed to have no neck, just a line where his chin met his muscled chest, and he was rolling a lollipop from one side of his mouth to the other. "Alexei," he growled. It could have been affectionate or threatening—he made it deliberately difficult to tell. "Business?"

I nodded. "Is Vadim in?"

The guy clacked the lollipop a few times against his teeth, looking at Gabriella. "Artur is in."

Artur was Vadim's number two. We could start with him. I nodded and the doorman stepped back out of the way.

There was another guy, sitting behind a Plexiglas window with a pay slot at the bottom. He didn't ask us to pay the cover fee, but he nodded at Gabriella as she passed. "She here to audition?" he asked with interest.

I squeezed Gabriella's hand a little tighter. "No." We pushed through a door and I heard Gabriella gasp in surprise. I think it was the fact it was broad daylight outside, as much as anything. She must have imagined these places only operated at night.

Soblazn means "temptation."

We'd stepped into a world lit in purple, pink and blue. The room wasn't big, but every bit of space was used, the tables and chairs deliberately arranged so that you had to spiral around to get anywhere. It made movement predictable—you could see where someone was heading long before they got there. That made it easier for the security guys to spot trouble and easier for the women to home in on customers.

There were two working the poles, one of them a long-legged blonde who looked as though she might be Polish, the other a curvy redhead who was probably Russian. A third woman, dark-haired with long legs, was stripping on a small stage while Artur watched. *She must be auditioning.*

Gabriella squeezed my hand. I turned to see her

gazing around in horrified wonder, her eyes going from naked breast to shaved pubis to the floor and then back again.

There were plenty of customers in the place, even in the middle of the afternoon. Businessmen enjoying a "long lunch," a few people who'd been out all night and didn't want to go home, or were starting tonight early. Everyone except for Gabriella was Russian and male.

Gabriella swallowed and then whispered to me, having to put her mouth right to my ear to be heard over the throbbing dance beat. "Are these women...do they want to be here?"

"They aren't trafficked. It's a job. They get paid." I looked around at the seedy surroundings. "But *want* is strong word."

I could see a few of the customers start to notice Gabriella. At first, they just looked up in surprise and there was even a quick flash of guilt, as if all women were connected and she might be a hotline straight to their wives or girlfriends. But then they glanced over at the dark-haired woman Artur was watching and, when their eyes returned to Gabriella, they slowly slid down her body. They were making the same assumption as the guy behind the pay window. They assumed they were going to be seeing her naked in a few minutes.

I walked her quickly over to Artur. Vadim owns the club but he lets Artur run it for him so that he can focus on more important things, like getting drunk and fucking his mistresses. Mistresses plural.

Artur was sprawled in a chair, intimidatingly close to the stage, his eyes fixed on the woman who was auditioning. The club lights painted his close-cropped blond hair purple and lit up his pale skin blue and, with the complex, winding tattoos on his arms and chest revealed by his tank top, he looked like some war-painted warrior.

"What do you want?" asked Artur, barely looking up.

I opened my mouth to speak, but he put up his hand to stop me. "Who's she?"

I looked around at Gabriella. "A...friend. She's okay."

But he shook his head and gestured her away. He wasn't going to talk with a stranger around.

I sighed and turned to Gabriella. "Go get a drink at the bar. Stay where I can see you."

She nodded nervously and walked off, still glancing in amazement at the dancers.

I hooked a chair with my foot and dragged it over beside Artur's. "I need to see Vadim," I told him. "Urgent."

"It's always urgent." He raised his voice, speaking to the woman on stage. "Bra off." He dropped his voice again. "What does Luka want now? Or is it Nikolai?"

"It's...personal."

For the first time, Artur turned properly around and looked at me. "Personal? You don't *do* personal." He frowned. "Is it 'personal' to do with her?" He nodded at Gabriella.

"It's personal and private," I said. I didn't know who Nikolai had spoken to, so I didn't know who was still on my side. The fewer people I talked to, the better.

Artur looked back to the woman on the stage. "Take your panties off, now."

She slowly complied.

"Can I see him?" I asked Artur.

He glanced at me for a second, then sighed with resignation. "Because it's you," he said. "But you owe me one."

I nodded.

"He's in the steam bath," said Artur. "You know the place."

I got up, clapped him on the shoulder and we briefly embraced. I liked Artur. He could be a mean fuck, but you always knew where you were with him.

I turned towards the bar and lifted my hand to wave Gabriella towards the exit.

But she was gone.

THIRTY

Gabriella

I STILL couldn't believe I was in a strip club, or that all this was going on: naked women writhing around poles, half-drunk men throwing dollars at them—when it was broad daylight outside. I'd always imagined these places only faded into existence in the early hours of the morning and vanished by dawn, like the magic shop in a story.

I went to the bar, as Alexei had instructed. With my non-existent social life, it had been literally years since I'd had alcohol and I figured starting now would probably be a bad idea. The bartender seemed as surprised by the request for a mineral water as he was by the sight of a woman with her clothes on. But he poured me one and I stood by the bar sipping it while desperately trying to fit in.

Having Alexei close by was helping to soothe the panic a little, but this place—this whole area—still felt very alien. As I stood there listening to the chatter around me, it started to sink in that everyone else in the place was Russian. I knew rationally that I couldn't be all that far from my apartment, in terms of miles. But it felt as if I was in a different country. And even the thought of my apartment didn't calm me. It had been violated—literally stained with blood. It wasn't safe anymore.

My only safe haven now was with the huge, muscled Russian across the room.

I tried to focus on the dancers to distract myself. God, they were beautiful—tall and long-legged and glamorous in a way I'd never be, with perfect boobs—maybe too perfect to be real, but men didn't care, right? I watched the way they slunk around on their podiums, lithe as cats and untouchable as goddesses, yet always with that sultry, heavy-lidded look of promise: another dollar, another twenty dollars, another hundred dollars and I can be yours. What would it be like, to dance like that for men, or just for one man?

What would it be like to dance like that for Alexei?

A bolt of heat stabbed straight down to my groin, unexpectedly powerful and urgent. I remembered the way he'd looked at me in the car, even when I'd been doing something as unsexy as eating. How would he look at me if I did *that:* lean back against a pole with my arms above my head, arching my back and thrusting my breasts out? Or *that:* sliding down to my knees, the pole between my thighs as if it was a lover who was—I blushed and looked away. But the heat in my groin didn't fade.

A group of men approached the bar, all wanting to be served at once. Alexei had said to stay right there, but I didn't want to be in the center of a group of drunk Russians so I moved away a little, deeper into the club. There was a quiet, shadowy area where I felt a little less exposed so I stood there, my eyes still glued to the dancers. Why *did* Alexei keep looking at me in that way? I was nothing special...and he'd seen what a fuck-up I was.

"*Vy mogli by.*"

I spun around. The man was standing beside me, so close that my elbow knocked against his, but he didn't seem to notice. I hadn't heard him approach over the music. "What?"

"American?" He blinked, then recovered. His Russian accent was heavy and I could smell the alcohol on his breath. "Not many Americans, here. I said: you could."

"I could what?"

He smiled and nodded at the nearest dancer, the one I'd been staring at. It took me a second to realize what he meant and then my eyes widened. "Oh! Oh, no. I wasn't—"

"You have body for it. Good tits. Good ass."

I felt my face flush red. The man grinned again. He seemed half drunk, his tie was missing, and his collar was unfastened. But he didn't sound as if he meant to insult me. He sounded as if he was trying to pay me a compliment.

"...thank you," I said at last. "But I wasn't—"

"*Ona pozzhe?*" A new voice, on my other side. I turned to see a similarly drunk businessman, ignoring me and talking directly across me to his friend. Then he grinned at me and I realized he was talking *about* me to his friend. The first man shrugged and laughed. "He asked if you were on later," he told me.

"No, I'm not a dancer. And I'm not auditioning!"

The men looked at each other, frowning, then back

at me. "You like the girls?" the second man said. His Russian accent was even heavier than the first. "You like to..."—he mimed rubbing his body up against another person's. The mood was still friendly, jokey. They were being a little drunk and coarse, but I didn't feel threatened, just embarrassed.

"What? No! I'm here with a...friend." I looked for Alexei, but the men were between me and him, now, and they were both big enough to block my view.

"A boyfriend?" the first man asked.

I hesitated. "No..."

"So you're single?" The men's grins got wider.

I was about to speak when Alexei barged between them. He looked panicked, which was something I didn't think was possible. It clicked that, just as I hadn't been able to see him because of the two men, he hadn't been able to see me. "Come on," he said brusquely.

The first man said something in Russian, a half-hearted plea.

Alexei ignored him and reached for my hand.

The second man made an appeal, nodding at me and then at the club.

Alexei suddenly turned, grabbed the man's shirt and hauled him up into the air. Then bellowed and threw the man at his friend. Both men went crashing to the floor. I gave a yelp of horror and grabbed Alexei's sleeve.

The entire club stopped to watch.

Alexei pulled out of my grip and marched over to the men, his face twisted with rage. He snapped something at the men and got a hastily groaned apology.

The man he'd sat down with a few minutes earlier,

the one who'd been watching the stripper, ambled over. He looked tiredly down at the two men on the floor. "Perhaps you and your friend should be leaving, Alexei," he said mildly. A couple of security guys were walking towards us.

I ran over to Alexei and grabbed his sleeve again. "Come on!" I said. "It's okay! Leave them!"

I studied his face as he stood there glaring down at the two men. I'd never seen him so angry, even when we'd been back in my apartment. He looked as if he'd almost lost control, something I didn't think was possible.

Then he grabbed my wrist and stalked out of the club, forcing me to hurry to keep up. We were in the street before he spoke. "I told you to stay by bar!" he snapped.

I gaped at him. "I—What? I couldn't! A whole load of guys came over and—"

He pulled on my wrist, spinning me around to look at him. The anger was bubbling up inside me, scalding hot, and I was ready to yell at him for being so unreasonable—

And then I saw it: underneath the anger, the concern. And I remembered the look of panic on his face. He was worried about me. And he didn't know how to do that, didn't know how to be concerned about someone other than to rage and shout and hit people.

I just stood there and stared at him, shocked, while he glared and panted and...

...*looked as if he wanted to wrap me up in his arms and kiss me.*

"Are you okay?" he said at last, his eyes burning into me.

I wasn't capable of speech. It felt as if my heart had ballooned in my chest, blocking my voice. "*Mm-hmm,*" I managed. *Alexei!*

"You need to be more careful," he muttered. And with that he got into the car and slammed his door.

I quickly got in beside him. He pulled away immediately and I waited a few minutes for him to calm down before I asked, "Did you find out who *Seventeen* is?"

"No, but we're going to see a man who will." He was gradually relaxing and something else was replacing the anger. "He'll see us, but...."

"What?"

He swallowed. "Something I need to tell you, about place we're going...." He was looking very determinedly out of the windshield, avoiding my eyes. Was he...was Alexei *embarrassed?*

"What?"

For just a second, he glanced at me. Yes, he was embarrassed and...something else. A hint of excitement he was trying hard to hide. "We won't be able to wear any clothes."

THIRTY-ONE

Alexei

Her first reaction was to grin. Then she realized I was serious. "No clothes?"

I nodded. And tried to keep looking at the road because I was worried she'd see how excited I was at the possibility of seeing her naked again.

Idiot! All I was doing was torturing myself. I still couldn't stop thinking about how she'd looked through the sniper scope. This would be up close and in person. Close enough to...touch.

Except I could never touch her. I could never even let her know how I felt about her. I couldn't start something because, with this girl, once I started there was no way I'd be able to turn back. I wouldn't be able to stop until I'd kissed every inch of her sweet flesh, until I'd plundered her body in every conceivable way. But the thought of her innocence, ruined by my sins, didn't bear thinking about. I had to get her out of this thing, alive and unharmed, and give her back the life she should have had. Let her go back to that civilian world where things are safe and warm and comfortable.

A little voice inside me asked if that was true, if she'd ever really lived in that world...or if she'd been eking out an existence in a kind of limbo, holed up in that apartment with no contact with anyone. It asked me if maybe, she was just as lonely as me.

I crushed the voice down. Even no life was better than the one I could give her. She shouldn't have the hands of a killer—

Running down her back, over her ass—

Cupping her breasts, thumbs stroking her nipples—

My hands tightened on the steering wheel. *Stop thinking like that!*

The more I got angry with myself, the more I found myself back in the strip club. *Come on,* the drunk guy had said. *She belongs here.*

Even as I'd tensed with rage, the second guy had joined in. *She'd look great up there.*

I'd lost it. I *never* lost my temper and now I'd done it twice in as many days. I'd wanted to pound them both into the ground, render them just stains on the carpet for even daring to suggest that Gabriella belonged in that filthy, criminal place.

But not all of the anger had been directed outward. I'd been kicking myself for ever taking her there, and for leaving her alone, and for one more thing....

The image the men's words had conjured up in my mind. The idea of the gorgeous, soft-skinned Gabriella up on a podium in *Soblazn*, her innocence the perfect counterpart to the seediness of the place. The men had been drunk idiots, but they were right about one thing: she had the perfect stripper body, with her full natural breasts and flaring hips. Thinking about her stripping, revealing that glorious body inch by inch...it was the definition of purity corrupted.

And it had me hard as a rock in my pants. Just like the thought of fucking her.

Her innocence was utterly captivating and it made me fiercely protective of her...but the dark parts of me wanted to see her spread and arching under me, hear her calling out my name as I buried myself in her. I wanted to knead those silky-soft breasts until she begged for my mouth and then stroke the hardened nipples against my lips. I wanted to take this angel and make her into my own, personal succubus.

And that's exactly why I had to keep my distance. She was too fucking tempting for me to ever stop, once I got going, and I couldn't drag her down to my level.

And that's why the next half hour was going to be exquisite torture.

I pulled up outside the baths. "We're here."

You would never find the place if you didn't have the address. There was no sign, just a plain wooden door in a nondescript stone building that must have been a hundred years old. I led Gabriella inside, through the maze of different businesses. She stared at them as she passed: dressmakers and cell phone repair companies and people riveting Gucci logos onto handbags.

We went down two flights of stone stairs, the street noise fading away and the air growing steadily warmer and moister. When I opened the next door, the temperature rose by a good ten degrees. An unsmiling woman with ferociously red hair looked us up and down from behind her desk.

"We're here to see Vadim," I told her. "Tell him it's Alexei."

The woman stomped off down a corridor and I heard her speak to someone in Russian—probably Vadim's bodyguard. She returned a moment later and nodded. "You know the way?"

I nodded and led Gabriella by the hand. I'd noticed that I'd started to do that—take her hand whenever we were moving together, even when it wasn't strictly necessary.

We went through a door and the temperature shot up again, to the point where clothes started to feel uncomfortable. We were in a small tiled room lined with big metal lockers—there couldn't have been more than twelve in total. A basket of white towels sat in one corner.

I turned to Gabriella. "Okay," I said. "Take off your clothes."

THIRTY-TWO

Gabriella

I STARED DOWN at the tiles beneath my feet. They were a complex mosaic of black and white swirls and looked very, very old. "Um..."

"It is rules," said Alexei. "Sorry."

I wondered if he was really sorry. He looked sorry, but in the car I was sure I'd seen a hint of something else. A flash of raw lust at the thought of seeing me naked. All the moments we'd shared so far came back to me: his hand on my wrist, in the coffee shop; him on top of me, in my apartment; the way he'd been so protective of me, in the strip club.

He took his jacket off and I saw the holster he wore underneath. I gulped—I'd known it was there, but seeing it was still a shock. I'd never even seen a gun, in real life, until he'd pointed one at me, but Alexei just took the holster off and laid it in his locker like it was nothing at all. Then he rolled up his pants leg and there was another holster there, with another gun. *Jesus.* I just stood there staring like a moron. I could see faint hints of his Bratva tattoos through his shirt—and then, as he started to unbutton it, the harsh, black ink of them. *He's so completely different to me. He lives in a whole different world.* I knew I was staring and I could feel he was aware of it, the tension building and building. I wanted to say something, but I had no idea how to even process something like this.

And then something happened that I *could* react to, a chance to delay things: he took out his phone.

"*That's* your phone?" I blurted.

He turned and frowned. "What is wrong with phone?"

It was an ancient Nokia, a thick block of plastic with actual buttons you pushed and a one inch screen. "Please tell me it's a retro-cool thing." I stared at his uncomprehending face. "Oh God—it isn't, is it?"

He shrugged. "It is simple. I like simple."

I took my own phone out of my purse. "But new phones have cameras. And apps! And email and... I can even track this on my laptop, if it gets stolen, and find out where it is. What do you do if you lose *that?*"

He looked blank. "Buy another one." Then he nodded at my clothes. "You should get undressed."

I swallowed. So much for delaying things.

The idea of him seeing me naked terrified me. I barely knew him! And yet, at the same time, it sent a scarlet ribbon of heat twisting down my body, finishing at my groin. I glanced around, but there were no cubicles, nowhere to hide.

I settled for turning my back. I opened a locker and concentrated *very very hard* on the empty interior as I began to take off my clothes. My sweater, first—that was easy enough. I mean, I wouldn't even be wearing that if it wasn't so damn cold outside. I stripped it off over my head and put it in the locker.

Next, my blouse. Well, he'd already seen me in my underwear, back at the motel. So I unfastened it all the way and took it off. Then my sneakers and socks. Then, with shaking hands, I unfastened my jeans and bent to push them down my legs. I folded everything up and put them in my locker, surprised to find I was a little light-headed. *I probably straightened up too quickly.*

Now I was about to cross a line. This was the most of me he'd seen.

I reached back and felt for the clasp of my bra. Usually not a problem but—dammit, it was stuck—why wouldn't it—

Warm hands suddenly took the straps from my fumbling fingers. My whole body went tense. The hands effortlessly unclipped the bra clasp and then retreated.

I swallowed. "Thank you," I said in a strangled voice. Every beat of my heart seemed to reverberate throughout me, as if I'd turned into one giant kettle drum. The vibrations filled my ears and throat, shuddered outward through my breasts to ache and tingle at my nipples. They throbbed downward through my legs and back up to my groin, leaving me trembling.

I hooked one shoulder strap off me, then the other. I held onto the bra until the last possible moment and then tossed it into the locker along with everything else. And then I was standing there topless, my back to Alexei. *How much can he see?* I wasn't certain. My breasts are on the large side so they weren't hidden completely by my body. Even if I was *precisely* angled away from him, he could probably see some side boob.

I glanced down at my panties—simple black briefs. I hooked my thumbs into them and—

He'd stopped moving.

Sometimes, you aren't aware of a noise until it stops. I realized now that I'd been hearing little movements and rustles of clothing behind me...but now they'd suddenly ended.

He was standing there, watching me.

You don't know that.

Yes I do.

My heart seemed to speed up ten-fold. I was panting and I couldn't pretend it was just due to the heat and humidity. I felt drunk on adrenaline, every square inch of revealed skin throbbing, so much more alive than ever before. I felt like—

I felt like one of the strippers, back in the strip club. Stripping off for men.

Stripping off for *my* man.

I can't do this. I wasn't that sort of woman. *I can't just—Not with a man I barely—*

And then I remembered that I had to. And if I didn't have a choice...well, that was okay, wasn't it?

I bent at the hips, nowhere near as graceful as one of the strippers and very aware of how my breasts swung forward and hung down. I slid my panties down my legs—

--I heard an intake of breath behind me—

--and stepped out of them. I could feel his eyes on me, roving up my naked calves, up my thighs, up between my legs—

I knew I had to do it fast, or I'd never do it. I spun around to face him.

And realized I'd made a colossal error: I'd been so busy obsessing about taking off my clothes that I'd forgotten that *he* would be naked, too.

The first thing I saw was—no, not that. Not yet. I'd just turned around and my eyes were staring right at his chest. I'd glimpsed it when he'd taken that shower but now there was no half-closed shirt to get in the way. I could feast my eyes on those broad, powerful muscles, a solid wall of strength. His pecs flowed into massive shoulders. I thought of cannonballs: not just the shape of them but the heavy, hard mass. If you'd made a statue of Alexei, you would have had to cast it from iron. It was the only material that could possibly do him justice.

His tattoos were fully visible, now: the vicious-looking scorpion, the delicate rose and that big, muscled bull. Then those rows of hard, piano-key abs with the deep center line between them, defined but also *big*. The broadness of his chest made his waist look small by comparison so it was only when you got up close to him, as I was now, that you appreciated how big he was all over.

All. Over. My eyes dipped down below his waist and—

My brain went *fzzt* and refused to process, skipping to his legs.

He didn't look like an underwear model. He was too big, too sturdy—he looked as if he'd crush an underwear model into the mud. He reminded me more of photos I'd seen of soldiers: muscles that were actually used for something, thick and hard and powerful. His calves seemed as big as my thighs—he looked as if he could stand firm in a hurricane.

And then I'd reached his feet and my gaze went automatically back up to—

O. M. G.

My first thought was that he was big.

My second thought was: that doesn't make sense, because it looked as if he was only halfway hard.

Then my brain put those two together and it very nearly went *fzzt* again.

His cock was hanging down the side of one of those marvelously strong thighs. The skin was a soft tan, just a shade darker than the rest of him. The head was a blunt-nosed, purple-pink fruit hanging ripe at the end. Ripe and...*swelling*.

The shaft was thickening and hardening, right before my eyes. Hardening as he looked at—

I looked up into his eyes. There wasn't a trace of embarrassment or guilt there. He was far past that. He held my gaze for a second and then I saw his eyes drop and rove over my naked body and I imagined his cock hardening and hardening, lifting to press against that washboard stomach. I didn't dare look down at it again. My whole body was throbbing and pulsing, the tension between us building towards a screaming, nerve-shredding peak. I wanted to run and hide; I wanted to hurl myself at him and feel his hard body against me...*inside* me—

Alexei drew in a shuddering breath and twisted away. "We should go," he said. And turned towards the door, plucking a towel out of the basket on his way. His ass was tight and hard, dimpling hypnotically as he walked.

I hurried after him, grabbed a towel and tried to brace myself for whatever was next.

THIRTY-THREE

Alexei

Jesus, she's naked. I could feel her right behind me, hear the slap of her bare feet on the tiles, smell that intoxicating scent. As we stepped through the door into the actual baths, the temperature rose again to stifling levels, but it barely registered next to the raging, thrashing heat inside me. All I wanted to do was turn, grab Gabriella and slam her up against the tiled wall. I wanted to kiss her so hard we both forgot what I was, then spread her thighs and make her mine.

And I knew that all of this was on show—at least, if I turned around. She'd already seen how hard I was for her and soon she'd see again. My cock was harder than I ever remembered it being before. God, I needed her.

The walls here were tiled and wet with steam. The lights were low and it was so quiet we could hear our own breathing. Before us was one final door and it was quite different to any we'd gone through before. A simple oblong of dark wood planks as old as the building—old, and very small. The top of the door barely came up to my shoulder. It wasn't a good seal, either—steam and heat was billowing out around the edges, which was why the whole place was so hot. A glass door with a rubber seal would have done a much better job and saved a huge amount of energy, but that wouldn't be traditional...and Vadim Andreyev was all about tradition.

I took a deep breath, swung open the door to the steam bath and ducked inside.

Vadim had run things from Russia for many years before finally making the move to the US. Originally, he'd come here for cancer treatment after years of cigars had left his lungs infested with creeping darkness. Then, cancer free and having secured one of his nurses as his latest mistress, he decided that perhaps the US wasn't so bad after all. Now he flew back and forth, king of a good chunk of Little Odessa and a significant chunk of Moscow. His wasn't the most powerful Bratva group, by any means. But they were the best connected. Vadim had made his fortune by doing deals, not burying his opponents, and he knew everyone and everything that went on.

He sat hulking in the darkness, on the big tiled bench at the rear of the room. He was almost spherical, not fat so much as *rounded*—when he wore a pin-striped suit, his back looked like a globe complete with longitude lines. His body was still powerful—he'd been in the army, many years ago, and had the strong shoulders and chest to show for it. Still good-looking, too, though he was in his late fifties now and his hair was almost completely silver.

Like me, he was utterly naked, his tanned body

shining with sweat. The room's only lights were a handful of dim bulbs above our heads, which turned the scene into a mixture of deep black shadows and gleaming flashes of skin. Steam hissed from ancient copper pipes somewhere near the floor, the air so saturated with water that moving felt like swimming.

Vadim pinned me with a gaze as soon as I entered. "Artur called and said you needed to see me—something private and urgent." His gaze fell to my cock. "I see now what he meant," he deadpanned. "But I do not play for that team."

Three sides of the room were lined with benches. I sat down carefully on the bench to Vadim's right, easing myself onto the scalding tiles.

Gabriella entered, holding her towel uncertainly in front of her.

Vadim shook his head. "The towel is for mopping your brow," he told her, demonstrating. "There are no clothes in here, no secrets."

That was indeed the tradition in these places, but these days his words had another meaning. With everyone naked, it was impossible for anyone to wear a wire or sneak in a camera. Vadim had conducted most of his business meetings in the steam bath for years. He boasted that the constant steam was the secret to his youthful looks.

I nodded to Gabriella that it was okay. Her throat bobbed visibly as she gulped. Then she lowered the towel and my hands gripped hard at the front of the bench—

I'd drunk in her appearance in the changing room but now it was even better. The dim lighting painted her pale, soft body in light and shadow, accentuating its curves and highlighting the textures. I could see the silky-smooth skin of her breasts and the delicately crinkled skin of her areolae. I could see the soft curve of her stomach where it hollowed around her navel and the firm swell of her hips and ass as she turned towards the bench to sit down. I was *transfixed*.

Vadim was, too. His eyes were all over her, and followed her to the bench. When she was finally sitting down across from me, he said, "Now I can see why you are..."—he nodded again at my cock—"what did we used to call it in the army? *At full readiness.* Who is this enchanting lady?"

Gabriella's breasts rose and fell as she panted, unused to having to work so much just to breathe. "Gabriella."

Vadim nodded respectfully and then turned to me and said reproachfully, in rapid-fire Russian, "You'd better be fucking this one, Alexei."

I mumbled something non-committal and shrugged, hoping Gabriella didn't guess what he was saying.

Vadim sighed. "Youth is wasted on the young," he said. Then he switched to English for Gabriella's benefit. "So why am I being visited by two such visions of youthful vigor?" He beamed at Gabriella and she broke into a shy smile. There was a reason Vadim had women flocking around him, even at his age. He was old enough that I didn't mind his flirting with her, but I knew that having her sitting there, naked, was going to make it difficult for me to focus.

I did my best. "Do you know anyone called Seventeen?"

Vadim frowned, suddenly serious. "I know one man who goes by that name."

Gabriella leaned forward excitedly. Her breasts

swayed and bounced and my cock throbbed almost painfully. "A human trafficker?"

Vadim shook his head. "No. A competitor to *you,* Alexei. A killer."

He hadn't said the word unkindly—it was simply what I was. But the word still seemed to echo around the tiled room. I saw Gabriella tense and her fear drove an iron spike into my heart.

"Who does he work for?" I asked.

"Mostly, Konstantin Gulyev."

I drew in my breath.

"Who?" asked Gabriella.

Vadim turned to her and spoke kindly. "You know who Luka Malakov is?"

"Loosely," she said. She glanced down for a moment and I could tell she was thinking about her uncovered breasts. "Alexei's boss's boss, in Moscow?"

"Correct. Konstantin is the equivalent—a rival who controls most of St. Petersburg. Like Luka, he spends some of his time here in New York."

Gabriella nodded, absorbing it all. The movement made her long brown hair dance and sway and I caught just the faintest hint of her scent, carried on the steam-filled air. I had to grip the bench to keep from launching myself across the room at her.

"Who does Seventeen answer to?" I asked. "And where is he?"

Vadim waved his hand dismissively. "Last I heard, Seventeen was with some two-bit gang that Konstantin uses for dirty work. They're run by Petrov Denakin, here in New York...but I don't know where."

I stood and slapped him on the shoulder. "That's more than enough. Thank you, Vadim."

I nodded to Gabriella, indicating that she should

leave first. She stood up, breasts bouncing in a way that made my breath catch and—

A pool of shadow cast by her body had hidden her groin from view...but now, as she rose, I saw the small triangle of dark, glossy hair at the juncture of her thighs, little jewels of water clinging to it. God, she was beautiful.

She thanked Vadim over her shoulder. Then she was opening the door, the sweet peach of her ass towards me—God, almost brushing my erect cock as she stepped back to swing the door wide. I swallowed, hypnotized by her.

And then she was gone and the door was swinging closed behind her. I stepped forward to leave but Vadim's voice stopped me on the threshold. "I meant it, Alexei. She's special. Don't let her get away."

The words reverberated through me as I hurried after her. They seemed to echo louder with every step I took down the hallway, my long strides eating up the distance between us. I couldn't take my eyes off the sight of her swaying ass in front of me, the heat inside me building faster and faster, reaching boiling point. Just as she reached the changing room door, I caught her. She stepped back, as before, to swing open the door...and this time I was so close that she backed right into me: her back against my chest, the shaft of my cock momentarily between the cheeks of her ass. She yelped in surprise.

I grabbed her arm and spun her around, pushing her back against the dripping tiled wall.

THIRTY-FOUR

Gabriella

SUDDENLY, he was right up against me, my ass squashed against the slippery tiles and my breasts pillowed against his chest. I couldn't move.

I didn't want to.

The tension had been building and building inside me ever since we met. Inside him, too—I was sure of that, now. And all of that energy was thrumming and pulsing in both of us, drawing us together. My nipples rasped against his pecs and I groaned at the contact, the sensitive buds tightening until they were hard as pebbles.

Both of us were dripping with sweat and water, slippery as eels, and our bodies were super-heated. Every touch of hot, wet flesh was scalding and divine, sending tremors of pleasure radiating through me. I felt as if my body had been sleeping for years and was suddenly awake for the first time. I drew in long, shuddering breaths, the air so hot it nearly burned my throat. I felt as if I was drowning in warmth, enveloped in it and filled with it.

I gave myself up to it.

I could feel his cock hard between us, throbbing and ready, the head of it hard against my stomach. I went weak at the feel of it, at the thought of that length and thickness inside me.

His hands were on my hips, powerful fingers digging into the soft flesh, holding me pinned there. It was dark in the hallway, and quiet. *God, we could just do it, right here!* The realization made me feel as though I was teetering on the edge of a cliff, looking down into the darkness. Was that what he wanted? Was it what *I* wanted? *Jesus, he's a killer!* I was already immersed in a world I barely understood. And I barely knew him and—

At that instant, he shifted slightly and I felt the hard muscles of his thighs press against me. All my qualms evaporated in that instant, God, he was so powerful...all he'd have to do was to insert a knee between my legs and I'd be helplessly spread for him. Helpless...and willing. I thought of his hard, muscled ass and the way it dimpled as he walked. Of how it would look as he thrust into me, driving up into me—

I closed my eyes and tilted my head up for his kiss.

THIRTY-FIVE

Alexei

I MOVED IN to kiss her, drawn inexorably in by those soft, satin lips. Every beat of my heart seemed to shake both of us, we were so tightly pressed together. Every breath she took made her chest swell and those exquisite breasts push against me a little harder. This was it. I could take her, make her mine. She moved a little and I twisted, following her lips as I closed the distance between us. I was so close I could feel her breath on me. Her silky hair was brushing my shoulder and, down between us, I could feel the soft hair of her groin against my thigh.

I closed my eyes.

Our lips touched.

And I froze.

Every cell in my body was screaming at me to do it—to push her legs apart, slide up into her and fuck her until she screamed my name. To pinch and lick her nipples until she thrashed and bucked from pleasure and pain, to bring her to climax after climax and then spin her around, shove her face-first against the wall and do it all over again from behind.

But she was so innocent. She came from a completely different world. The only reason I'd even met her was because I was sent to kill her. If I started something between us—where would it end? What could I possibly offer her? I wasn't going to take her on dates or buy her presents—I didn't understand any of that stuff. I understood killing and fucking.

I'd never worried about losing a woman before. All I'd ever known was one-night stands. But with Gabriella...once I'd had her, I'd want to keep her. *Forever.* And that was impossible.

I tore myself away from her and stalked across the hallway. There was a small alcove there with a shower for after you'd been in the steam bath, and I cranked the ancient metal lever all the way to the left for ice-cold. The water crashed down on my shoulders, like being tossed head-first into an arctic lake. I stifled a gasp, gritting my teeth and bearing it. Punishment was what I deserved for losing control like that.

Across the hallway, Gabriella was opening her eyes and looking around in bewilderment. When she saw me in the shower, her eyes grew wide with confusion...and then hurt.

I'd hurt the person I most wanted to protect.

I let the water sluice away the sweat and then purge the heat from my body. I became ice and then granite and then freezing, unyielding iron. I'd hurt her because I was weak. I wouldn't be weak again.

I strode out of the shower and hauled open the door to the changing room. "Take a shower if you want to," I told her. "I'll meet you outside."

THIRTY-SIX

Gabriella

When I emerged, fully dressed, into the hallway with the reception desk, Alexei was waiting for me. His suit was immaculate, his face set like stone. There was no sign of the Alexei who'd pushed me up against the wall, who'd finally confirmed how he felt about me.

I'd taken a shower, flinching when I discovered how cold he'd set it and turning the lever to warm. Why had he suddenly pulled away from me? Why had he felt the need to punish himself? Maybe because he'd been tempted by me...and then remembered how damaged I was?

That hurt more than anything. If he'd merely not been interested in me, it would have been what I'd expected. But to have all that tension and then for him to change his mind at the last minute because he'd remembered my freak outs—it made my stomach twist into a hard knot.

This place hadn't been too bad. Maybe it was the

gloom and the heat, but it had been almost comforting—womb-like. I'd even been shocked by how I'd reacted to the nudity. I'd been embarrassed, sure, but the feeling of Alexei's eyes on me and the sight of *him* naked had overridden all that. Even Vadim looking at me hadn't been as bad as I'd expected, because he wasn't at all leery or pushy, just appreciative. I'd actually walked out of the steam bath with a new-found confidence.

Right up until Alexei pushed me away.

It hurt...and I realized I wanted answers. If it was because of *me*, because of this thing I carried around in my head, I wanted to know. So, when he started to turn away to head out to the street, I stood my ground.

After a couple of steps, he realized I wasn't with him. He turned back, maybe expecting to see me freaking out again. But I was just standing there defiantly.

He tried to stare me out.

I crossed my arms.

He cursed in Russian under his breath and walked back to me. "We have to go," he said, his voice neutral.

"Why?" I asked.

"We need to find that gang," he hissed, one eye on the receptionist. He reached for my wrist.

I pulled away from him. "You know *goddamn well* what I meant!" I snapped. My voice was loud in the quiet hallway. The receptionist, to her credit, kept her eyes on her desk. "Why did you do *that?*"

I studied his face desperately, trying to glimpse some clue. At first, all I got was that icy gray in his eyes, the cold-hearted killer. But as I kept staring, I finally saw a hair-thin crack in the mask, a tiny hint of blue. And as I felt my own gaze soften, his softened in return, until it was as if a dam had burst: he was still locked down and in control, but I could now see the humanity inside him.

"Let me buy you something to eat," he said at last.

"Eat?" I echoed.

"And..."—he wrestled with the next word, as if it was an alien concept—"...talk."

I nodded and followed him out to the car.

The panic started up again when we began to drive—that feeling of getting further and further from any place of safety. But Little Odessa didn't seem to bother me as much as the area around my apartment had. The streets there had been familiar—American brands and signs, American voices around me—and yet I'd been lost and exposed. It was that combination: a place that should be safe and familiar and yet wasn't—that seemed to be most triggering to me.

A shopping mall, for example. I gave a physical shudder at the thought.

But Little Odessa was so alien, with its weird little businesses and restaurant menus in Russian, that it didn't trigger me anywhere near as much.

That, and the fact that I had my own personal safe place sitting next to me. Even now that he'd pushed me away, the fact that Alexei was with me made the panic bearable.

We stopped just a few streets away from the steam bath, at a cafe. He led me inside and I saw that everyone was sitting at long, communal bench tables. Men and women, some in suits, many in uniforms. It was four in the afternoon, a weird time to be eating, but the place was pretty much full.

"Two jobs," said Alexei. "They eat here, then go to the other one. Or they work shifts and eat here and then sleep."

I sat down across from him, between a man in a fluorescent crossing guard uniform and a man in janitor's coveralls. It was the first time I'd thought of Little Odessa as an actual community, not just a place where the Bratva were based.

"Don't we need to order?" I asked.

He shook his head and pointed to a chalkboard on the wall. The words were in Cyrillic. "One menu. No choice." He looked as if he approved of that concept.

"You live around here?" I asked sullenly. I still hadn't forgiven him.

"I don't live anywhere," he said. "Russia. New York. An apartment or motel. I go where they tell me."

"But you must have a home. Where do you keep your...*stuff?*" I thought of my own apartment, every cupboard bulging with things I'd acquired over the years.

He rubbed the back of his neck as if embarrassed. "I have bag," he said. "It's still in the car, across the street from your apartment."

"A bag? Your entire life is in a bag?"

He put both hands flat on the table. "I don't have a life," he said simply. He looked me right in the eye and I knew it was true.

A woman in an apron who must have been at least eighty hurried past our table and swept up the two five dollar bills that Alexei offered. I was still trying to process what Alexei had just said. To buy time, I asked, "What do we get for five dollars each?"

"Fed." He reached out and took my hand in both of his and, immediately, the heat of him spiraled up my arm, blossoming in my chest. "Gabriella..." He sighed. "*This is what I am.* All my things in a bag. Going where they tell me"—he lowered his voice—"*killing* who they tell me."

I felt myself tense up again at that word *killing,* just as I had in the steam bath. "Go on," I muttered.

"This is not a life you should be part of," he told me. "You're a...civilian."

"I'm a *hacker.*"

He sighed again. "You sit at home and"—he mimed typing. "You are...safe."

"Not *that* safe. They sent you to kill me."

He looked at me seriously. "I didn't mean you *were* safe. I meant you *are* safe. Safe to be around." He paused. "I am not. Not safe to be around and not good to be around."

"Who decides that? You? You saved my life!"

"I tried to kill you. I nearly did."

I grabbed his hands with my free hand and squeezed. "But you didn't. You've protected me ever since. That first night, you sat in a chair all night just watching over me!"

He looked ashamed for a moment. Then, staring down at the table, he said, "I am trying to protect you. That is why I should not have done...what I did at the steam bath. I am"—he stopped as if to taste the unfamiliar word before he said it—"*sorry.*"

"*That's* why you pulled away, because you were trying to protect me?" I leaned forward. "And you think that's why I was hurt...because you nearly kissed me? Alexei, I was hurt because you *stopped!*"

He stared at me with such an intense look of lust, I thought he was about to haul me over the table and fuck me right there. But before he could speak, soup plates were set in front of us.

"*Borst,*" said Alexei, by way of explanation. It seemed to be a purple-red soup. Neither of us knew what to say, so we both started to eat.

It was several spoonfuls before I'd worked out a speech. "Alexei...you used to be that man. The Bratva made you into him, but you're free of them, now."

He shook his head.

"What? What does shaking your head mean?" I was starting to get frustrated with his icy-cold, you-don't-understand-my-problems thing. "You're still that man? The Bratva didn't make you that man? Or you're not free of them?"

He looked at me with the saddest eyes I'd ever seen in my life. "All three."

We finished the soup—which was delicious—before he spoke again.

"I was...what I am...long before the Bratva found me. I was in the army. Killing was the only thing I was ever good at."

"But you can change—"

"Maybe I don't want to!"

He sounded defensive, more than angry, but the force in his voice was still enough to make me flinch. "B—But...You've left the Bratva, now. Aren't you exiled or disavowed or whatever the fuck they call it?"

He leaned in towards me and his voice grew softer. "Because of what I did, they want me dead. But if you are right about Nikolai, if we expose him, if they forgive me...."

My jaw dropped open. "You'd go back to them?"

He shrugged. "They are my family."

And everything reversed in my head. I'd been thinking of him as a reformed criminal, a gangster who'd seen the error of his ways and turned on his employers. But that wasn't it at all: he wanted to prove his loyalty by exposing a bigger traitor, and was praying they'd take him back.

We weren't on the run together. *I* was on the run and I'd towed him along with me. I'd forced him to choose between me and his family and he'd picked me. But if he could set things right, he'd go back to being a killer for hire in a heartbeat. He'd go back to the Bratva and I'd never see him again.

I felt sick. I suddenly understood why he'd pulled away and now I wished I'd never asked. If it *had* been my fault, that almost would have been easier.

The soup plates were whisked away and two fresh plates were set in front of us. Each one held four bony, meaty things wrapped in white that I didn't recognize at all. "What are those?" I asked hoarsely.

"Pig's knuckles," he said.

Which gave me the excuse I needed to run for the door. When he caught up with me outside, dry-heaving into the gutter, I blamed the food. It was only when we were back in the car that I said, "I'm sorry."

"For what?"

"For messing up your life." I shook my head. "This whole time, I've been thinking about me—leaving my apartment, being chased...but it's *you*. It's you who's had their whole life ripped away."

He started to shake his head.

"If you'd burst in and I'd been a guy, you'd have shot me, right? You'd have shot me and carried right on with your life."

He wouldn't meet my eyes. I could see him wanting to say *no*.

"You spared me because I was a woman," I said.

He finally looked right at me. "I spared you because you're...*you.*"

Which might just be the nicest thing anyone had said to me in my entire life. I felt my eyes filling with tears and looked away, out of the side window.

I never should have tried to get him to talk. From now on, I had to accept things as they were—a partnership of necessity. Most likely, the Bratva would catch up with us and we'd die together. But if by some miracle we did figure out what Nikolai was doing and expose him...my protector would disappear back to his old life and I'd be alone again.

"Drive," I said. It sounded rude, but my voice was cracking and I could only manage one word.

He drove.

THIRTY-SEVEN

Alexei

SHE WAS STARING out of the window and I knew she was silently crying. I just didn't know what to say to fix things, or if that was even possible.

I felt like a rhinoceros, trying to figure out the mechanism of a Swiss watch by nudging it with my horn.

All I knew for sure was that, whichever way this ended, I couldn't have her. Either we'd both wind up dead or I'd go back to my old life—I couldn't see any other way out. I didn't know any life except killing.

I risked a sideways glance at her. God, even like this, red-eyed and tear-stained, she was the most gorgeous thing I'd ever seen in my life. I'd never had to comfort a crying woman—never been deeply enough into a relationship to be in that situation. But even I knew I was supposed to take her in my arms and hold her close.

And I couldn't. That would set everything in

motion again, undoing the fragile stability we'd found. The best thing I could do—the *only* thing I could do—was to keep her at arm's length. "This gang—Petrov's gang, the ones who Seventeen works for. Can you find them with your hacking?"

"I can find *anyone,*" she muttered.

I nodded and drove on for a while, giving her space. At last, she turned back towards me, blinking away the last of her tears. "The university," she said. "Their sociology department runs a criminology course and its network has a gateway into the NYPD database. Much easier than breaking in directly." She looked me up and down. "But first, you need some new clothes. You'll need to look like a student."

We found a clothes store that Gabriella declared was suitable. I stared dumbly at the racks while Gabriella picked out cargo pants, sneakers, a t-shirt, a shirt and a jacket. We threw in a backpack to put my suit and shoes in.

"I feel stupid," I muttered when I came out of the changing room.

"You'll pass," she told me. "If anyone asks, you're a Russian grad student."

We walked back to the car with me adjusting my pants every few steps. I couldn't get used to not wearing a suit.

It wasn't difficult to sneak into the sociology building. With her laptop under one arm and her jeans and sneakers, Gabriella looked like any other student. I still felt ridiculous, but I walked alongside her and tried to blend in.

"Don't look so damn purposeful," she said after a while. "Just...stroll."

I looked down at my feet and tried my best. She

was right: the students moved differently. They slouched around, takeout coffee cup in one hand, Macbook under the other arm, listening to music on their headphones. They moved as if they had all the time in the world.

This is the life she should have, I thought. A student, with friends and a whole world of possibilities. Not an empty existence in that apartment.

If we fixed things, if things could go back to the way things were...would she go back to that solitary life? Was that her future, when we parted? She deserved better. She deserved—

She deserved a man. That thought tore me in half, because I didn't want to think of her alone. But I couldn't bear the thought of her with someone else, either.

"So, what do we do?" I asked impatiently. The sooner we got the information we needed and got out of there, the better. I was way out of my element.

"Their network has WiFi so I can login from anywhere in this building, but I need a username and password."

"How do we get those?"

"Well, I've never done it like this before. Normally I'd do it from my apartment: I'd find a criminology student on Facebook and befriend her and get her to install some game Yolanda had tinkered with on her laptop. The game would be malware—"

"What wear?" I didn't understand any of this stuff. I didn't trust technology—technology was the preserve of the government, the police. Messing with it was a good way to get caught. That, and I'd never had anyone to teach me.

Gabriella bit her lip, trying to find a way to explain it. "Malware is like...like the inside man on a bank job. That would let me take over her laptop and use the network as if I was her. But we don't have time for all that, so we'll have to do some social engineering."

"Some what?" I was feeling steadily more and more stupid.

"We have to get someone's password from them."

Finally! Something I understood. A male student with a lip piercing and bleached blond hair was just walking past me. I checked no one was watching and then grabbed his shirt and dragged him towards the men's room.

"Hey! Shit!" He flailed and kicked, so I lifted him off the ground and carried him.

"Um..." said Gabriella, sounding worried. She hurried after us.

I crashed through the door to the men's room and slammed the guy up against the wall. "What is password?" I snarled.

"What?" he squeaked.

Gabriella burst in. *"This wasn't what I meant!"*

"What is password?" I snarled again, putting my face right up to his.

"Your password for the network!" Gabriella said quickly. "And your username!"

"What?" The guy's voice was going higher and higher. "Are you *serious?*"

I grabbed his hand. "I break his fingers," I said, and gripped the first one.

"ARGH! SHIT! km425 and my password's *giraffechewing* with '3s' for the 'e's!"

"You tell anyone, I come in night with knife and slit your throat," I told him.

He looked as if he was going to throw up, but he managed to nod. I let him go and he fell to the floor, scrambled to his feet and fled.

When I turned around, Gabriella was staring at me in horror. "What?" I asked, genuinely confused.

She shook her head and refused to meet my eyes.

"He's okay," I said defensively. "He's not hurt."

She shook her head again. "You can't just...." She raised her hands helplessly in the air and indicated the whole scene in the men's room. Then she lowered her hands and grabbed mine, squeezing the fingers that had wrapped so easily around the student's knuckles.

I'd only done what I'd always done. Hurting people, scaring them— that was part of what I did. I hadn't really thought about it—compared to the killing, it seemed like such a small thing.

But for the first time, I saw it through her eyes— through the eyes of a civilian. And suddenly it didn't seem like such a small thing at all. We were even more different than I'd thought: it wasn't just the killing, it was the whole way I interacted with people. I nodded, to show I understood, and she released my hands and turned away. But I stood there for a second before I followed. I'd just realized the gulf between us was even wider than I'd thought.

Gabriella led me to a quiet corner of the building, then fired up her laptop. I prepared to keep watch, but it only took her a few minutes to find what she needed.

"Petrov's gang," she said with satisfaction. "They operate out of a ship in the harbor."

I looked at her, sitting there with her laptop—so small, so fragile. I hadn't dealt with Petrov's men, but

I knew their kind. Not civilized men, like Vadim and even Artur, but foot soldiers. Thugs. The thought of men like that, around a girl as beautiful as Gabriella, made my guts twist. What had happened in the men's room had reminded me I was a monster, but it had also shown me how unprepared she was for dealing with people like me. She was innocent...and defenseless.

I couldn't leave her behind—by now, word might have got around of my treachery and there might even be a price on our heads. She'd be an easy target, sitting on her own in a car. I had to keep her close.

But I could at least make sure she could hurt the bastards, if anything went wrong. "Does this place have a gym?" I asked.

"Sure. Why?"

"There's something I need to teach you."

THIRTY-EIGHT

Gabriella

IT WAS evening, by now, and the gym building was open but mostly deserted. The hallways were empty and echoing and I found myself walking closer to Alexei, fighting the rising panic. I could smell floor polish and nothing looked familiar and—

"You okay?" Alexei asked.

"Yep," I lied.

We slipped into an empty yoga studio. Alexei pulled a wad of mats from a pile and threw them on the floor, pushing them with his feet until they formed a thick pad. He stepped onto it and gestured for me to do the same.

"What is this?" I asked.

He looked down at his feet as if embarrassed. When he met my eyes again, he said, "I want to teach you how to hurt someone."

"You mean like self-defense?"

"No. Not like self-defense." He stepped closer. Close enough that I had to look up at him. "Self-defense is for getting away...so that you can run. Like with a guy in an alley."

I swallowed. Fear was starting to churn in my belly. "But?"

He was reluctant to answer. "But with the people we have to deal with, you may not have any place to run. You may have to hurt them badly enough that they can't hurt you."

I shook my head. "I can't do that. I'm..." I looked down at myself: not just much shorter than him but smaller in every dimension. "I'm...*me*."

"You can do more than you think." He squared up to me. "Most men will try to grab you. To pull you close." He paused again. "They'll want to—" He looked into my eyes and I could see he didn't want to say it. It wasn't just that he didn't want to upset me—I could tell he detested the idea so much that he didn't even want to give it voice.

"I understand," I said, hoping I sounded braver than I felt.

"They'll expect you to pull away. But you will pull them *towards* you. And then choke them."

I felt my eyes go wide. "*Choke* them?!"

"I will show you." He lifted those big hands towards me, then froze. "Gabriella...you know I would never hurt you?"

That hadn't even crossed my mind. I hadn't tensed, when I'd seen those hands coming—in fact, just the action of him reaching for me had made my whole body come alive with anticipation. I knew he wouldn't hurt me...but hearing him say it was a thousand times more powerful than I would have dreamed. "I know that," I managed.

He put his hands on my shoulders. I tried to ignore

their warmth, tried to resist the urge to snuggle into them.

"Grab me around the neck with both hands," he told me. "You're going to pull my head down, hard."

I hesitantly reached around that massive body and grabbed the back of his neck with both hands. He was so warm, so strong under my fingers, with a dusting of fuzzy hair I wanted to caress. I tried to pull his head down, but it was like trying to coax a bull to move. *This is ridiculous!*

"Step back suddenly as you do it," he ordered. "Pull me with you. And bring your knee up hard, knee me in the chest. Then I'll have to bend."

I stepped back uncertainly, the gym mat squishy under my feet. I brought up my knee and, just as he'd said, he had to bend at the waist to cushion the impact. His upper body swung down, the top of his head brushing—

I felt his breath, hot against my stomach through the thin cotton of my blouse. "You want the top of my head to be on your right...breast."

I nodded. I didn't miss the little hesitation. I pulled his head down until it was in the right position and tried to ignore how it felt.

"Now bring up your right arm. Put your wrist against my windpipe."

I brought it up and nestled it there, careful not to push too hard.

"No. Turn your wrist sideways. Use the bone."

Feeling uncomfortable, I turned my wrist and felt the hard edge of it push up against his soft, gristly windpipe.

"Now push me down with other hand. And *hold on* because I'll fight. Keep going until I go limp."

I mimed doing it, my squeamishness increasing.

He got me to do it several times before he said, "Good. Now do it for real."

I looked up at him and grinned, delighted. *Alexei made a joke!*

I should have known better. I looked at his stony face for several seconds and my grin crumbled. "Not *really* for real, though?"

"You have to know what it feels like."

"But not *really*...not until you pass out!"

"If you're not used to it, you might stop too soon."

"What if I stop too *late?!* I could kill you!"

He thought about it. "Then don't stop too late." He moved back and prepared to come at me again.

I put my hands up to stop him. "Wait. I'm not sure about this." I looked around. The gym and even the corridors around us were completely deserted, now. If anything went wrong, there'd be no one to help.

He shook his head. "You have to. You need to be able to do this. It might be the only thing that saves your life."

"Wait—"

He pinned me with a look, letting me see just a fraction of that cold menace he used on other people. It was like someone running a freezing steel pipe between my shoulder blades. Despite everything I knew about him, everything we'd shared together, I got *scared*. Just as he wanted.

And then he came at me, big hands reaching, clawing, huge and powerful and *male,* ready to tear—

—tear—

—tear my clothes off and—

I reacted. I grabbed him around the back of the neck, stepped back and brought my knee up hard, feeling him *oof* as it drove into his stomach. The edge of my wrist came up and dug into the gristly tube of his windpipe and, this time, I pushed his head down until I felt his windpipe give. He started to struggle and thrash, his big arms swinging at me, and I had to dodge out of the way as I held on. It was an eerily intimate sensation, holding him pinned like that. He thrashed and thrashed and the nausea rose inside me, but it still felt unbelievable that a huge beast like him could be felled by someone like me. *It's okay. He's just pretending, to make me feel good. He's not really—*

His body went suddenly heavy. *Really* heavy. His arms stopped swinging and he keeled forward, almost knocking me over. I panicked and rocked him the other way, trying to let him down gently, but he was way too big for me to control. He slumped to the pile of mats, his head bouncing off of it—he probably would have cracked his skull, if we'd been on concrete.

"Alexei?" My voice was shrill with disbelief. He wasn't faking. "*Alexei?*"

He just lay there, huge and warm and silent. My one safe place: gone. *Shit!* Was his chest moving? It was difficult to tell. I put my ear to his mouth and, after a few seconds, I thought I could detect breath, but it was weak and raspy.

I shook him. "*Alexei!*"

He opened his eyes, licked his lips and coughed, then rubbed at his neck. Then he said something in Russian.

"What?"

"I said *good*. Well done."

I couldn't help it—I threw my arms around his neck and hugged him tight, pressing myself as hard as I could against him. Then, as soon as I could bear to let him go, I sat down next to him and punched him in the arm. "Jesus! You scared the hell out of me."

He sat up, looking a little unsteady. "Now you know. Now you can do it. Make a man pass out...or even keep going and kill him."

I shook my head. "I don't know if I could."

He nodded as if he had absolute faith in me. "Yes you could. You just don't want to believe that you could."

I swallowed and looked away, not meeting his eyes. I knew he was right. I was becoming more like him. I just hoped that he was being over-cautious, that the ship wouldn't be as dangerous as he feared.

It wasn't. It was much, much worse.

THIRTY-NINE

Alexei

Things started to go wrong almost immediately.

By the time we reached the docks, the sun had fully set, and the place was a treacherous obstacle course: coiled ropes, chains hanging diagonally from boats at neck level, pools of water and spilled oil. It was the sort of place where an outsider was at a disadvantage: if we had to run, we'd either have to slow right down or trip over something—either way, Petrov's gang would catch us easily.

We had the name of the ship, but finding it amongst all the dark shapes took a full half hour. Eventually, Gabriella spotted it: an aging cargo ship painted in cheap gray paint. I parked as close as I could, reversing the car in so that we could drive out fast, but there was still far too much dark, cluttered dockside to navigate for my liking.

We didn't have a choice, though. Word spreads fast in the underworld. By morning, word of my rebellion against Nikolai would have made it around all the

Russian gangs in New York and that would make things a thousand times more difficult. I just had to hope word hadn't already reached Petrov.

There were only two guys standing watch on the deck of the ship. That was bad, because Petrov's gang weren't stupid: there must be more than that. We just couldn't see them, yet.

I checked the gun in my holster one last time—I'd put my suit back on, which felt fantastic after those stupid student clothes, like coming home. I got out and motioned for Gabriella to do the same, approaching the ship slowly and openly, hands where they could be seen. We'd almost reached the gangplank when a voice rang out from behind me.

"Alexei Borinskov. What brings you all the way out here?"

I spun around, but found myself looking straight into a narrow, sun-bright circle of light. A man—Petrov, I guessed—was standing on top of a shipping container and he had us pinned in the beam. I knew it wouldn't be just a torch. It would be a tactical light attached to the top of a gun. He had us right in his sights and I couldn't see a thing.

I tried to brazen it out. "I just want to talk business."

There was a metallic click off to my left as someone cocked a gun. Another click off to my right. They had us surrounded. They must have seen us as soon as we'd entered the docks.

"Word is," said Petrov, "you went soft on some girl and turned on Nikolai. Disloyalty, Alexei, is never good. I'm sure Nikolai would be very grateful if I cleaned up his mess for him."

Shit. "That's not what happened," I said, trying to

sound angry.

"Then what did?" The circle of light moved to Gabriella and she flinched, throwing up her hands to shield her eyes. "She's alive, isn't she?"

Suddenly, I knew exactly what I had to do. They'd heard rumors, but they weren't sure—if they were, they would have shot us by now. They knew me by reputation—everyone did.

All I had to do was become *that* Alexei again. The one who'd walked into Gabriella's apartment. As soon as I thought it, I could feel my old ways coming back to me. It felt right, even though I knew it was wrong. It felt as good and familiar as when I'd put my suit back on.

I grabbed Gabriella by the waist and hauled her up against me, her ass to my groin. And then, as she squirmed in shock against me, I ran my hands up her body and over her breasts. *God*, the feel of them in my hands at last, even through her blouse. I could feel myself getting hard, despite the situation.

"Why the fuck do you think she's alive?" I snapped. "Look at this body! I'm having some fun with her, before I shoot her in the head."

FORTY

Gabriella

I PANTED FOR AIR as Alexei mauled my breasts, his huge hands just as warm and powerful as I'd imagined. I was reeling in shock from what he'd just said, but that didn't change the effect: blazing ribbons of pleasure rippled out from my breasts, making my hips jerk and my groin ache.

The light that had been on Alexei switched back to me. This time, it didn't stop on my face—it stroked lazily down my body, illuminating his hands as they fondled me, tracing over my waist and hips and then down my legs.

Then it switched off, as if a decision had been made. I heard boots on steel as Petrov climbed down off the shipping container. My eyes were still throbbing and burning from staring into the light so I couldn't see him until he was right up close, pointing his gun at us.

His face was all hard lines with no hint of softness, as if his skin was slightly too tight on his skull. His lips were pressed together into a thin, straight line, as if he was permanently on the edge of rage. It made me shy away from him instinctively and he laughed when he saw that.

"So she's your plaything?" he asked Alexei.

"She's my plaything," Alexei growled. His thumb found my nipple through my bra, stroking it to erectness. It didn't matter that I was terrified—his touch was a direct hotline to my groin, a twisting, thrashing heat I couldn't control. I'd been waiting so long for this....

And it wasn't just his touch. To my horror, the words burrowed down inside me, right down to the secret places we never admit exist. I was his *plaything*.

"Does she do as she's told?" asked Petrov. He still had his gun pointing at us, but it was wavering a little.

Alexei leaned in and licked my earlobe. I yelped and instinctively tried to pull away because, however much I loved it, doing it as a display for Petrov felt wrong. But Alexei held me tight against him and now I could feel the throbbing hardness of him against my ass.

"Mostly," said Alexei. "I punish her when she doesn't." His hand captured my breast again and, this time, he pinched my nipple through my bra with his thumb and forefinger. I cried out, arching my back and squeezing my thighs together, silver pleasure and white-hot pain mingling together.

I knew it was a trick. I knew Alexei was just acting. I knew we were in a very, very dangerous situation. But none of that mattered to the dark places that had suddenly started glowing, deep down inside me. *I'm his plaything. His captive, tied to the bed in some hotel room while he uses me however he wants....* I twisted and tried to pull away from him and it wasn't acting—I was trying to fight against my own reaction.

Petrov chuckled and lowered his gun a little. He sounded considerably more relaxed, now. Relaxed and...something else my brain was too addled to decipher. "So you and Nikolai are okay?" he asked.

"Nikolai and I are just fine. The cheap bastard just didn't pay me in full, so I yelled at him and he got mad and now he's bad-mouthing me. I'll finish the job once he pays up. But in the meantime, I'm going to fuck this one over and over and over." He rolled his hips against my ass and I wailed...and went mushy inside. *God, what's wrong with me?!*

I heard movement in the darkness off to our sides. Men lowering their guns.

"Fucking Nikolai," said Petrov, lowering his gun completely. Alexei had him on his side, now—everyone understands getting stiffed for a fee and everyone understands sex. "So why are you here?" He sounded as casual as an old friend...but there was still that edge in his voice—excitement? "You said you had business. Or did you just come here to show off your sex toy?"

Alexei did something I'd never heard him do before: he chuckled. A dark, lusty sound that made me feel as if I was being wrapped up in dark smoke. I closed my eyes and shuddered, feeling the heat turn to slick moisture inside me. "She's worth showing off, isn't she? But I need to talk, too. Some things for Nikolai, for when he pays up."

"Fine," said Petrov after a moment. "Come inside. It's too fucking cold out here." He started towards the gangplank.

I went limp against Alexei. *Thank God.* Now we'd get the information we needed. And hopefully, I could make Alexei believe that my responses had just been play-acting. He grabbed my shoulders and steered me along behind Petrov so that I was sandwiched between the two big men.

"I'm taking a turn at her first, though," said Petrov casually. "You don't mind sharing your plaything, do you?"

And suddenly I understood that edge of excitement in his voice. I turned and tried to run, expecting Alexei to be doing the same.

But Alexei caught me and shoved me forward, sending me staggering into Petrov. "Of course not," he said with a shrug.

FORTY-ONE

Gabriella

MY EYES WENT WIDE and I had time for a single scream of fear before Alexei clapped his hand over my mouth from behind, his huge palm killing all sound. His other arm wrapped around my waist and he began to walk me along behind Petrov, using his hips to swing mine and lifting my feet clear of the ground when I resisted. "She's not used to others," he explained. "Yet."

My insides had turned to ice water. It had all just been an act...hadn't it? Was this just part of it, or....

Or was this going to be the cost of getting out alive? To convince Petrov I was really just Alexei's sex toy, was I going to have to....

I thrashed and twisted but Alexei held me easily while Petrov watched and chuckled. We entered the ship—metal bulkheads and harsh overhead lights. My desperate grunts and the kicking of my feet on the metal floor made men poke their heads out of doors. They laughed when they saw the scene. Everyone understood what was happening: a thrashing, kicking woman being force-walked towards their leader's room.

Is it a trick, or is this really going to happen? All the dark arousal I'd been feeling at the idea of being Alexei's plaything had evaporated. The idea of Petrov....I didn't even want to think about it. I twisted around and looked at Alexei, but he was grinning at Petrov. *How far is he going to let this go? All the way?*

Petrov opened a heavy steel door and led us into a room. There was a desk covered in papers and a buzzing overhead strip light. Petrov waited until we were inside, then slammed the door. Once it was shut, the room was quiet as a tomb save for my desperate panting.

"Get her on the desk," said Petrov.

No!

But Alexei lifted me like a doll and placed me on my back on Petrov's desk, my legs hanging off the end. He kept his hand over my mouth the whole time.

Petrov grinned and reached down, undoing the button of my jeans. As I tried to kick at him, he began to peel them down my legs.

No!

Something red flashed across the room and Petrov sat down, hard, on the floor. An instant later, my brain registered a metal *clang*.

The hand lifted from my mouth. I sat up. Petrov was shaking his head, dazed. Next to him on the floor, still spinning, was the fire extinguisher Alexei had hurled.

Before Petrov could get to his feet, Alexei was on him, punching him once in the face and once in the guts, his face contorted with fury. Then he lifted Petrov off the floor, hurled him into an office chair and pulled out his gun, pointing it at Petrov's head.

Petrov spat blood onto the floor and glared at Alexei, but he'd gone pale.

"You okay?" Alexei asked me without looking at me.

I shakily pulled my jeans up my legs and stood up. "Yes," I said in a small voice.

Alexei still didn't look at me, didn't dare take his eyes off Petrov even for a second. "Sorry," he said at last.

Petrov shook his head in disgust. "So the rumors were true. You *have* gone soft for a girl. We should have killed you on sight, and all of us fucked her."

Alexei hit him across the face with his gun. I flinched at the violence, but a little part of me cheered.

"Seventeen," said Alexei. "He works for you. Who is he?"

"What the fuck do you want with Seventeen?"

Alexei moved the gun from Petrov's forehead to his balls. "I'll blow one off," he told him coldly, "then the other. You'll bleed to death before they can get you to a hospital."

Petrov set his jaw and glared at Alexei. It turned into a battle of wills—which of them could be the most intimidating?

Petrov never even stood a chance. After just a few seconds, he wilted. "Slava," he said. "Seventeen's real name is Slava Federoff. But I don't know where he is. He left a few days ago and I haven't seen him since."

Alexei cursed. We'd been right: Nikolai had secretly lured Seventeen away. Everyone thought he still worked for Petrov, who in turn worked for

Konstantin. But really, Seventeen was now doing Nikolai's bidding.

"You have no idea who you're dealing with," Petrov said. "That guy is *insane!*" He shook his head at our stupidity. "Do you even know why they call him Seventeen?"

"He's killed seventeen people," Alexei guessed. He sounded unimpressed at that number.

"He killed ten," said Petrov. *"By the time he was seventeen."* He let that sink in. "It's not just work, to him. There's something wrong with him."

I felt the hairs on the back of my neck prickle, as if someone was standing right behind me.

"Seventeen will kill you," Petrov told us. "Or the rest of the Bratva will find you first. They'll hunt you down and shoot you. And *she'll* end up on her back, with her legs—"

Alexei hit him with the gun again, this time hard enough to knock him out. He finally turned to me, the first time he'd been able to look at me since he'd put me on Petrov's desk. His hand slid across my cheek, his fingertips burying themselves in my hair. "You okay?" he asked again. I could hear the pain in his voice, the fear that he'd hurt me.

I nodded. I was so overcome with relief, I thought my legs were going to collapse and dump me on the floor. And with the release of all the tension, something else came back to me—all those rogue thoughts I'd had about being his sex slave. I flushed. "Now what?" I asked.

"We walk out of here. But you need to look—" He stopped, embarrassed.

"Yes?"

"Like you've been...fucked." He was trying to keep

his voice neutral, but I didn't miss the note of lust on that last word.

I looked down at myself. "How do we—"

He grabbed the front of my blouse with both hands and ripped it savagely apart. The sides gaped open almost to the waist, exposing my bra. But that wasn't enough: he shoved the blouse and my bra strap down off one shoulder.

"Take off your jeans," he said. His voice had grown thick and heavy, almost a growl.

I quickly stripped off my jeans. He took them from my hand and carried them, along with my sneakers. The hem of my blouse barely covered my panties.

"Now..." he said, and stepped closer. He put one hand behind my head to stop me moving. Then he rubbed his thumb roughly across my lips, smearing my lipstick. Despite everything, the feel of him doing it made me close my eyes. My groin tightened and my toes dug into the floor. I wanted so badly for him to just lean his face down to me and—

"There," he said, stepping back.

I opened my eyes and my gaze locked with his.

"Now you look like you've been fucked," he said. There was no mistaking the fire in his eyes and I remembered the feel of him, hard against me, as he'd pulled me onto the ship. This had all been an act, but part of him wanted it to be real. Part of him wanted me to be his plaything.

And part of me did, too.

He grabbed me by the wrist. "Act like you're hurt," he said, his mouth twisting a little in disgust at the idea. "Make me drag you. But hurry."

He opened the door and walked out, pulling me behind him. I stumbled along, giving him what I hoped were sullen, hate-filled glares.

Men were lining the hallway, laughing and jeering. I felt their eyes on my bare shoulder, on the exposed skin of my upper breasts and on my legs. A lot of them made comments in Russian and I was glad I couldn't understand them.

"Where's Petrov?" asked one man.

"Recovering," said Alexei. "He wore himself out."

The men thought that was hilarious. A few of them started reaching for my blouse, trying to pluck it from me, and I pressed myself closer to Alexei. As if I had Stockholm Syndrome, as if this man who'd abducted me and made me his sex slave had become my protector. They thought that was even funnier.

Only I knew the truth. I pressed myself up against Alexei's muscled body and I knew he'd get me out of there. I knew he'd never hurt me and I knew he'd die to protect me. The feel of him, the scent of him, was the only thing that let me make it through that hallway without breaking down completely.

I felt air on my face and then we were through the final door and making our way down the gangplank. The car was thirty feet away.

A shout went up from inside the ship.

"They found Petrov," snapped Alexei. "Run!"

We sprinted for the car, but we had to keep slowing to pick our way around crates, ropes and other obstacles in the gloom. Twenty feet. I tripped on a chain and nearly went down. We could hear boots clattering on metal inside the ship and there were shouts all around us in the darkness. The guards on the dockside had been alerted.

Ten feet to the car. Five. The first gunshots rang out. Alexei got the door open and almost threw me into the passenger seat, then ran for the driver's side. He was getting in when there was an echoing sound like the crack of a whip. A hole appeared in the driver-side window.

"Jesus!" I ducked down, trying to get my head below the level of the windows.

Alexei just sat there.

"Go!" I was panting with fear. "Drive!"

He looked down at himself, frowning. He put a hand to his chest and it came away dripping. Then a flashlight beam lit up the inside of the car and I saw the spreading red stain on his shirt.

FORTY-TWO

Gabriella

WE LOOKED at each other. I opened my mouth—to scream, I think—but he cut me off, grabbing my arm. "Are you hit?"

I just stared at his chest.

He shook me. *"Are you hit?"*

He'd been shot and he was thinking of me. I shook my head dumbly.

Footsteps were approaching the car and more flashlights were lighting up the interior. Alexei pulled out his gun and fired through the driver-side window, shooting blindly towards the lights. The recoil of each shot made him grit his teeth, his other hand pressed to his chest. The rest of the glass shattered and fell and someone outside screamed. The footsteps stopped but more shots rang out. Holes appeared in the hood and in the windshield and I screamed and ducked down. They were going to make sure we were both dead before they came any closer.

Alexei lifted his hands to the wheel but winced and

dropped them again, panting. Firing the gun had taken the last of his strength. "You have to drive," he told me.

Oh shit. Not that. "I can't!"

"Lean across. Take...wheel." The red stain covered the whole front of his shirt, now, and his words were growing hoarse. "I'll do pedals."

He doesn't understand! But I leaned over like he said. My nostrils filled with that Fourth of July smell: cordite, from the gunfire. I tried not to look at his chest. I gripped the wheel...but nothing happened.

"Put it...in 'drive'," panted Alexei. His eyes were half-closed.

I looked around at the levers sticking out of the steering wheel, even the buttons on the dash. I finally found the gear lever and just stared at it. "I don't know how to drive! I never learned!" *Oh Jesus Gabriella you fucking* moron! There were tears in my eyes. More bullets hit the car and I heard one slam into the seat just above my head.

Alexei started to say something but then the pain overcame him and he closed his eyes completely. He reached out one hand towards me, pleading.

It's just like figuring out a video game. I stared at the gear stick through a haze of tears. *D. D for drive.* I tugged it into position just as the rear window exploded and showered us with glass. Alexei stamped on the gas and we shot forward—

Straight for a shipping container.

I was almost hysterical, now, tears streaming down my face. The only thing that kept me going was the knowledge that he'd die, if I didn't figure out how to do this. I turned the wheel hard and the car slewed wildly to one side. We missed the shipping container but now we were heading for the water.

I spun the wheel the other way and we swung back. Alexei kept his foot on the gas and I aimed for where I thought the ramp up to the street was, the car fishtailing wildly. We crashed through some piles of crates and at one point we came within an inch of hitting a concrete post, but then we were on the ramp.

As the gunfire fell away behind us, Alexei grunted, "Smaller movements."

I tried moving the wheel less and that helped. My arms were aching from gripping the wheel so hard.

Alexei groaned, showing his teeth as he arched his back in pain. "How do you not know how to drive?" I got the impression he was trying to distract himself.

"It isn't a skill you pick up in an apartment!" I stopped to concentrate as we went around a corner. Luckily, there was nothing coming the other way.

Alexei had both hands pressed to his chest, now, but I could see blood oozing between his fingers. "What about school? Driver-Z?"

I knew he was just talking to take his mind off the pain, but the questions were driving me crazy. "They home schooled me, after it happened!" I snapped.

And then realized I'd said too much.

"We have to get you to a hospital," I said.

He shook his head. "No hospital. First place they'll check."

"You'll die if we don't!"

He started to say something, but then his head lolled and his body went limp.

I felt the Dread start to build. I'd been okay as long as he was by my side but now it was back. It was on every side of me, seeping into the car from the darkness outside, where anything could be lurking.

Rushing towards me from the vanishing points—the distant road junction ahead, the streets stretching off to the sides. Everything was too big and safety was much too far away.

It was the most total fear I'd known since leaving my apartment. I'd been lulled into a false sense of security by having Alexei as my own mobile safe place. I'd thought the Dread had gone, but it had been hiding inside me, biding its time.

Alexei's foot had slipped off the gas. The car rolled to a stop and I sat there, in the middle of the street, paralyzed with fear. I was on my own, in the middle of a strange area of the city, and no one was going to save me.

I felt myself *slide*. I could feel myself getting smaller and smaller in my seat, until it felt like I was going to shrink right down into it.

No one was going to save me. No one was going to save me and he was going to come. He was going to come and take me and—

A horn blared behind me. I was blocking the street.

I knew what would happen now. I could see it unfolding in my head like a movie. Another few seconds and the driver behind me would get impatient and stomp around to my window to see what the hell I was doing. They'd see an unconscious man bleeding in the driver's seat and a near-catatonic woman beside him and they'd call the police. And somewhere between the emergency room and prison, Alexei's people would find him and kill him.

He was going to die unless I did something *right now*.

The Dread screamed at me, telling me how tiny and insignificant I was. But the fear of losing Alexei was even stronger.

I took three more panicked breaths and then climbed out of my seat and slid onto Alexei's lap. I gripped the steering wheel, found the gas pedal with my foot and stamped on it.

I knew what I had to do.

FORTY-THREE

Alexei

I half-opened my eyes. Bright lights. Was I in heaven?

Then I heard the yapping of dogs. Lots of dogs. Maybe all dogs *did* go to heaven.

I opened my eyes a little further and then I knew I was dead because an angel was before me. A soft-skinned angel all dressed in white, with hair the color of walnuts. I was lying down and she was bending over to kiss me—

She didn't kiss me. She pushed a metal thing into my chest and I felt a dull, faraway ache.

I blinked a few times and my eyes started to adjust. There was a dazzling lamp right above me but the rest of the room was in darkness. I could make out cages and each one had a dog in it. That explained the yapping.

I looked down. I was on a vinyl-covered table. No, *two* tables, pushed together.

Gabriella followed my gaze. "They were made for

dogs," she said. "I had to get creative." Her voice was raspy, as if she'd been crying.

It took an effort to make my tongue work, but I managed to ask, "Where am I?"

She looked exhausted but relieved. Triumphant, even. "A veterinarian's office. I figured they'd have all the stuff we needed."

I tried to look down at myself but I was too weak to lift my head that far. "It doesn't hurt," I said.

"That's because I shot you up with enough morphine for a horse." She held up a vet's dosing chart. "Literally." She reached into my chest again. "The bullet must have clipped the door frame because it shattered. Good news—that slowed it down enough that it didn't go too far in. Bad news—it made a lot of holes, which is why you bled so much. And I have to get the bits out." My shirt had been cut away and there was a green cloth over me with a hole through which she was working. The white coat she'd put on, the cloth and—I looked down—the floor were all stained with blood.

"How do you know how to do this?" I grunted.

She glanced to the side.

For the first time, I saw her laptop, the glowing screen facing her. I swore in Russian. "Please tell me you're not learning this from internet."

"I found a site for army field medics," she said. She actually sounded excited. "It's not all that hard. The hardest part is keeping the patient alive while you operate. Luckily for us, you're built like a rhino." She dropped a piece of metal into a bowl. "There. I can't guarantee I got every little bit, but I got all the big ones." She put down the forceps and raised a needle and thread. "I'm going to sew you and then use adhesive sutures as well, because I want it to hold together and you're not going to be able to lie here and rest." She looked off to the side, where there must have been a window. "The sun'll be up soon."

I nodded weakly. "Good plan," I rasped. I could feel myself getting light-headed. I didn't know how much all the blood on the floor and my shirt and her coat added up to, but it must have been a lot. I started to doze off as she sewed me. Each time the needle entered, there was pain...but the morphine blunted it to a dull throb.

"Gabriella?" I said as I drifted off.

"Hmm?"

"Well done."

FORTY-FOUR

Gabriella

THANKS TO the blood loss and the morphine, Alexei spent the next few hours in a dreamy, hazy half sleep. I managed to wake him just enough to get him off the table and back into the car, then returned for my laptop. The examination room was a wreck. There was blood on the floor and table and the vet's coat I'd thrown on to protect my clothes was covered in it. Packaging from the drugs and syringes and bloody gauzes littered the place. Even if I cleared everything up, they were going to notice the missing drugs and the broken door lock and report it to the police. At this point, though, that was the least of our problems.

I was in a pair of medical scrub pants and flip-flops I'd found in the vet's office and my blouse. My jeans and sneakers were still somewhere on the dock—Alexei had dropped them when the shooting started. I was glad now that I'd brought a few pairs when I fled my apartment.

I'd figured out driving a little more, on the mad dash to get Alexei to the vet's. By now, though, the car was pretty much a write-off: two windows were shattered, it was full of bullet holes, and almost every surface was dented from me hitting things. We'd have to steal another one tomorrow.

I caught myself. When did stealing cars become so normal? Bar the hacking, I'd never even broken a law until a few days ago.

I found a cheap motel, got a room, got Alexei and our bags onto the bed and then drove the car a few streets away. I left the keys in it in the hope that someone would steal it, but it was such a wreck that it seemed unlikely.

By now the sun was up and it had started to drizzle. I hunched up my shoulders, wrapped my arms around myself and walked back to the motel, shivering and exhausted. I realized I'd been on my feet for almost twenty-four hours. I'd been to a diner and a strip club and a steam bath and a college and a ship and done surgery and—The weight of it all hit me and I had to force my feet to go on. We had Seventeen's real name, now. Would that be enough to track him down and figure out what was going on?

I staggered through the door of our room and sat down heavily on the bed. God, I was sick of motels.

Alexei stirred, roused by the moving bed. He muttered something, still halfway between sleep and waking. I put my hand on his forehead but I couldn't decide if he was running a fever. I'd shot him up with antibiotics but I was still worried about infection.

"Mhuhhh....Gabriella?"

"Right here," I told him.

"I'm sorry for falling...." he drawled.

"It's okay. Fall asleep. Sleep is the best thing for you, right now." I needed to sleep, too. I kicked off my sneakers and lay down on the bed next to him.

"I'm sorry for falling...in love with you."

I sat bolt upright. "What?"

But his breathing deepened and he slipped into sleep.

FORTY-FIVE

Alexei

I WOKE UP and it was morning. But not the morning I expected. The wound on my chest had changed from a searing pain to a throbbing ache and my muscles were stiff—far stiffer than they should have been after just a few hours. I sat up—which hurt—and frowned.

Gabriella was sitting cross-legged at the end of the bed, watching me. And she was smiling in a way I'd never seen before.

"It's Saturday," she said by way of explanation. "You've been asleep for three days and nights. Well, mostly asleep. But you were pretty groggy even when you were awake because I was keeping you dosed with morphine. And I've been feeding you soup. Do you remember that?"

I frowned. "No." The last thing I remembered was the vet's, and even that was hazy. There was a fresh dressing on my chest and, when I cautiously peeled it back, I seemed to be healing well. As she'd said, the wounds had been bloody but not deep.

She shifted closer on the bed and gave me that smile again. "Hungry? There's a diner next door and they're still serving breakfast."

I frowned at her, trying to work out what was going on. She was acting *weird*. "Yes," I said at last.

She helped me get dressed. My white shirt was a ruined, blood-stained rag so I had to wear the shirt we'd bought for the university. It was blue and I stared at it in the mirror, unable to get used to it. I'd never worn anything but a white shirt with my suit.

"It looks good on you," she told me. And smiled.

Walking around hurt a little, but it wasn't too bad—the three days in bed had healed the worst of the damage. In the diner, Gabriella handed me a menu but I shook my head and tossed it down. "Oatmeal," I said.

"But there's so much choice!" That smile again. Why was she so excited?

"I always have oatmeal. You know this."

"Exactly. You *always* have oatmeal. Alexei, maybe it's time for food to be more than fuel."

Someone else in the diner had ordered bacon. I could smell it as it passed by our table on a waitress's tray. It did smell good. But taste, enjoyment, *choice*...those were all civilian luxuries. Things that made you lose your edge. I shook my head.

She leaned across the table towards me. She was wearing a low-necked red sweater I hadn't seen before and I tried not to stare at her soft, pale cleavage. "Your body needs to rebuild itself. You need protein for that. Eggs are protein."

There was definitely something strange going on. She was suddenly so relaxed around me. *Closer,* somehow. I didn't understand it. I couldn't help it—I found my eyes dropped to those full, mouth-watering breasts and I felt my resolve weakening. "I do need protein," I mumbled. "Maybe some eggs."

"And some bacon, because it goes with eggs," she said.

"...and some bacon, because it goes with them," I said, defeated.

She sat back in her seat and grinned like a delighted child. What the hell was going on? I could still feel all the tension I had before: my lust for her, fighting against the need to keep away. But for her, it all seemed to have disappeared.

We ordered and, when the food came, it was amazing. Soft, creamy scrambled eggs and crispy bacon that melted in my mouth. Coupled with the glorious sight of Gabriella across the table, it was the most enjoyable breakfast I'd ever eaten.

"What's our next move?" she asked when we'd finished.

I thought about that for a while. Petrov had given us Seventeen's real name but I'd been hoping to get a location as well. Tracking him down was going to be difficult. And the way that Nikolai had quietly tempted Seventeen away from his employer made me uneasy in a whole new way. I was starting to get the sense of something really bad brewing.

"I should probably rest a few more days," I said. The food had made me feel a lot stronger, but I knew I wasn't up to a fight.

She grinned as she paid the bill. "Just the two of us, in the motel room? I can live with that."

And she squeezed my hand. Not in a comforting way, more like—

I looked down at our joined hands and then frowned at her. "What's going on?"

She looked confused. "What do you mean?" She led me outside, heading back towards the motel.

I broke free of her grip. "All morning, you've been...*weird.*"

She gaped at me. "Weird?"

I cursed in Russian. "Different!"

She frowned at me and then slid her arm around my waist. The nearness of her, the scent of her, had me instantly hard...and my heart seemed to swell in my chest—

I broke away again. Why was she suddenly throwing herself at me, when all I'd done was push her away? "What are you doing?"

This time, she didn't try to approach again. She just stood there with her mouth open, as if *I'd* done something wrong.

"You know it's not like that," I told her.

"But...it *is* like that," she said in a small voice.

"It's not."

"But...before. When you—"

I shook my head. "In the steam bath, that was—" I hated to lie, but I couldn't let her know how deep my feelings ran. "That was me losing control, because you're so beautiful." I forced myself to harden my heart. "But that's all it was."

"No, I meant—when you...." Shit, she had tears in her eyes. She stared at me beseechingly.

I became aware of something right on the fringes of my memory, a ghostly fragment that wouldn't get any clearer no matter how hard I concentrated on it.

I gently shook my head, not understanding.

She turned from me and stormed down the street

to our motel room, slamming the door as soon as she got inside. When I got there, I realized she had the only key. I lifted my hand to knock, then let it fall again. Better that I give her some time to cool off.

What the hell had I done wrong? I sat down with my back against the door and reflected that I'd never, ever understand women.

FORTY-SIX

Gabriella

lilywhite > He did WHAT?

diamondjack > He apologized...for falling in love with me

yolanda > OMG!

lilywhite > *squee!*

diamondjack > But now he's denying everything. It's like it didn't happen. He's gone back to strong and brooding.

I'd avoided contacting the others until now. I didn't want to draw them into it and I'd had no idea what to say. But I couldn't keep everything bottled up any longer.

yolanda > Where are you now?

diamondjack > crummy motel. A *new* crummy motel. I'm so sick of crummy motels.

lilywhite > I want to know how Nikolai knew where you lived

I'd been wondering that myself.

yolanda > You took all the normal precautions, right?

diamondjack > duh.

yolanda > Then how the hell did he find you?

lilywhite > No clue. But diamondjack knows her stuff. Nikolai couldn't have traced her on his own. Don't go near his computer again until we figure it out.

diamondjack > I won't.

yolanda > So what now?

diamondjack > I searched for this "Seventeen" guy - Slava Federoff - but there's nothing useful online.

lilywhite > So your Russian's going to have to beat his location out of someone?

diamondjack > He's not *my* Russian. At least, not as of this morning :(

yolanda > So what now?

She sounded so helpless. Both of them did. They were doing their best, but this whole thing was way outside any of our scope of experience. We dealt with virtual threats, names on a computer screen, not actual violence.

diamondjack > Let him heal and then track down Seventeen and try to put this whole thing straight.

yolanda > I meant you and him.

I stared at the screen for a while.

diamondjack > I have no idea. Look, I have to go. Need to think.

lilywhite > Yell if you need us. Or if you need to get out of the country. I can get you passports.

I blinked at that. She was good with government databases but actual, physical passports? I wondered how much I didn't know about lilywhite.

diamondjack > OK thanks.

I cut the connection, lay back on the bed and thought. After my breakthrough in the car, when I'd overcome the Dread for a little while and saved Alexei, I thought I'd made some sort of huge forward leap. And then, when Alexei declared his feelings for me...God, I hadn't been ready for *how much* that would affect me. All of the feelings that had been building inside me had swelled up...but then I'd had to wait, because he was still in too much of a stupor.

I'd spent three long days and nights nursing him, the anticipation growing and growing. He'd slept most of the time, waking only to drink the mugs of soup I brought him. That morning, when I'd finally stopped the morphine and he'd fully awoken, I'd imagined us talking and kissing. I'd imagined all sorts of things...except what actually happened. I'd never dreamt that he'd just deny saying he was in love with me.

He'd been in a drug-induced haze when he said it. Maybe he remembered saying it and was regretting it, or maybe he plain didn't remember. Either way, he clearly didn't feel that way about me *now*. I'd been ecstatic all that morning, following him around in a lovesick haze...and then it had all been ripped away from me.

I was sick of this whole thing. Sick of running, sick of dirty clothes and living in motels, sick of being afraid for my life.

There was a knock at the door.

I knew I couldn't just leave him out there. We had to work together until we resolved this thing, however awkward it was. Well, at least I knew where I stood, now.

I opened the door. He stood there staring at me, eyes sad and confused.

I stepped out of the way so that he could come in, but he stayed out on the step. "Come with me," he said.

"Where?"

"A quiet place I know. I've been thinking. There's something else I need to teach you."

The last thing I wanted, right then, was more time alone together. I would have happily just sat in the motel for a few days watching TV while his wound healed. But we had to work together.

"Fine," I told him in an *okay-but-I-don't-have-to-like-it* voice. I grabbed my coat and laptop bag and stalked out to the parking lot. He went inside the room, grabbed something from his own bag and followed.

This time, there weren't any cars around with wireless control systems so Alexei got to demonstrate his method: an elbow through the side window, a kick to the steering column to break open the plastic casing and then a jerk of the wires to tear them loose. Two wires touched together, a few sparks and the engine was running. It *was* quicker than my method. In the real world, simple brutality won out over subtlety and technology every time.

I climbed in beside him and sat in sullen silence for the whole journey. Alexei glanced at me a few times as if wondering whether to say something, but eventually just sighed and gave up. I pushed myself down in my seat and tried not to think about how big the sky was. Big and gloomy—storm clouds were rolling in and we were heading in that direction.

We drove way out of town and pulled up outside a junkyard. Not an active place, with machines crushing cars and eco-friendly recycling going on. More like a place cars went to die. They were piled up into mounds three stories tall. Almost every car had had its headlights removed, giving them the appearance of empty-eyed skulls. The tires were gone, too, and the glass had been removed or broken. The paint had peeled off and all that was left were the rusting metal bones, sometimes with a few shreds of rotting upholstery. An alien place—too alien, thankfully, to trigger me too much, especially with Alexei there. Since the night of the vet's, I'd been a little better, as long as we stayed away from big places with lots of people in them.

"No one here on weekends," Alexei told me, getting out. "No problem with noise."

"Noise?"

He showed me what he'd brought with him from the motel—a small, stubby black handgun.

I put my hands up defensively. "No. No way. I don't want to shoot guns."

"You need to. It'll give you a better chance, if they find us. I usually carry this here"—he pointed to his ankle—"as my spare. I want you to have it. But you need to know how to use it."

We were interrupted by a long roll of thunder. The clouds were close and getting closer.

"I'm not a gun person! I can't!"

"You couldn't choke a man, a few days ago."

"I don't know if I could now!"

"You already have, remember? You did it to me. You'll be able to do it again, if you need to." He hefted the gun, weighing it in his hand. "Same with this."

I sighed and gingerly took the gun. "You're not going to ask me to shoot you, are you?"

Despite everything that had gone wrong between us that made a smile twitch the corners of his mouth for a second.

He took a takeout menu from his pocket and jammed it under the hood of an old junker so that it hung down over the radiator. Then he walked back to me and the lesson began.

He showed me how to load a magazine and how to chamber the first round. He showed me where the safety catch was and how to take it off. He taught me how to hold the gun in a two-handed grip, and how to aim down the sights.

"Now try it," he said.

I wrapped my finger around the trigger and s-q-u-e-e-z-e-d. It was like trying to burst a balloon with a pin: I tensed up more and more, my eyes half-closing, bracing myself for the explosion....

There was a bang and the gun kicked up into the air. I have no idea where the bullet went, but nowhere near the car. My ears rang and my wrists ached.

"Good," said Alexei.

"Liar."

"You're over the fear, now. Try again."

My second shot was no better than the first. My third was even worse. I was too tense, too *afraid*.

Then Alexei stepped up behind me. His chest pressed against my shoulder blades and his arms wrapped around me. He covered my hands with his much bigger ones and my anger at him just evaporated. He hunkered down so that he could put his mouth to my ear, the stubble on his cheek brushing me ever so gently in a way that made me catch my breath. I was suddenly aware of how quiet it was in the junkyard: there were no birds here, no trees to rustle. It was as if we were the only living things in the world.

He spoke to me in that accent like crashing rocks and the vibrations shot straight down to my groin. It didn't matter that he'd hurt me. My body responded to that sound like a goddamn tuning fork. "Relax into it," he said, and I had to fight the instinct to relax into *him.* "Do you trust me?"

I thought about it. I wanted to say *no* and yell at him. But I told the truth. "Yes."

"It won't hurt you. *Know* that, inside."

I needed something else to concentrate on or I was going to go nuts, having him pressed so close against me. So I focused on what he was saying. I *believed* that the gun wouldn't hurt me and, for the first time, it felt a little less scary.

He put his hands on my shoulders, his thumbs tracing down the sides of my neck, and it was all I could do not to tilt my head to the side and push my cheek against his hand. "Pull your head down towards your shoulders," he told me. I did. Then he skimmed his hands down the length of my arms, his size letting him reach easily. "You should be firm here, but not tense."

I relaxed my arms a little. I felt him look down at my feet and then he moved against me, pushing me to adjust my stance. A breeze had gotten up, blowing my hair into his face and—

I suddenly felt his cock against the back of my thigh. He was rock hard under his pants. When he spoke again, I could hear the tension in his voice.

"Don't think about pulling the trigger. Think about your target. See the bullet in your head, going right through it."

My whole body was aching with anticipation. He seemed to completely encase me from behind, wrapped around me. All I had to do was turn around....

I took a long, shuddering breath...and squeezed the trigger.

A hole appeared in the dead center of the takeout

menu. I didn't even register the kick and the bang until afterwards.

I lowered the gun and turned to him, but he didn't step back in time. As I turned, my breast brushed his arm.

I looked up into his eyes and the cold, distant gaze I'd been seeing all day was gone. The fire was back, those hot flashes of blue beyond the ice.

"You—" I started.

And then he grabbed me.

FORTY-SEVEN

Alexei

MY BODY knew what I wanted before I did. My cock had been hard as soon as I pressed up against her. When her hair blew in my face and I smelled her scent, every muscle tensed. I was *aching* for her.

The warm, soft touch of her breast against my arm was all it took to tip me over the edge. My hands grabbed her waist and pulled her up against me even as my brain asked *what the fuck are you doing?*

The tension between us had built until I was past the point of reason. The soft, warm world of beauty that was Gabriella pulled me forward and everything else—my past, my life, the knowledge of what I was—pulled me back. I felt as if I was going to rip in two....

And then I saw the faintest hint of a tear in her eye, her fear that I was going to pull back again, hurt her again. And I'd be damned if I was going to let anyone hurt her, even me.

I finally broke free...and kissed her.

FORTY-EIGHT

Gabriella

IT WAS the kiss I'd been wanting since the very first moment I laid eyes on him, as if the shockwaves of it had rippled backward in time and hit me even when I'd been in the coffee shop. He slid one hand under my back and stroked the other along my cheek, burying his fingers in my hair. Then his lips were coming down on mine and it was like we'd been made for each other, our bodies twisting and moving exactly in rhythm.

It started with a gentle press, almost as if he was savoring it after so long wanting it. Just a brush of our lips against each other, our hot breath mingling as we both began to pant. Two soft little kisses and then the third was hard, his mouth twisting to force mine open and I welcoming him in with a groan. His hands moved to my back as the tip of his tongue touched mine and then he growled, a low rumble through the kiss, and his warm palms closed on my cheeks to hold me fast. His tongue started to dance with mine, our lips crushing together. I could feel the strength of him through the kiss: the way he tilted my head back, the way he controlled my body. I melted into him, molding myself to his chest and he groaned again.

He broke the kiss abruptly and stepped back. I opened my eyes and saw the conflict on his face.

"Don't fucking say you're sorry," I panted.

He stared at me, then shook his head. "I—Remember," he said. He was panting as hard as me.

"Remember what?"

"Remember telling you I'm in love with you."

And suddenly the whole day rewound back to waking up that morning and everything was clear and bright and rich with possibilities. I reached out and grabbed his shirt, pulling him against me, and I kissed him so fast our teeth clacked together. My breasts squashed against his chest as I pressed against him and he kissed me even harder than before, his hands tangling in my hair. Then he scooped one hand under my ass and lifted me clean off the ground, pulling me up to his level and kissing me there, my feet dangling in the air. He gave a groan of pain and I broke the kiss, wincing, remembering his wound. But one look at his expression put me straight: he was in pain, but he wasn't going to let that stop him. He wasn't going to let *anything* stop him.

I kissed him again and again and soon I was lost, carried on a pink cloud of pleasure, the heat throbbing steadily upward through the fluffy stuff. I wanted to spin around and around, I wanted to dance with this guy. *He was in love with me!* But every kiss was taking me closer to the place where I just wanted him to tear my clothes off.

Amongst all the warm pleasure, a frosty spot

appeared. It was right on my scalp, a circle of cold that really shouldn't be there. I ignored it, but then another one appeared on the other side of my head and slid down over my ear. I realized it was starting to rain.

I broke the kiss and looked up. Yep, the gray clouds were right overhead now and fat drops were starting to hit the ground all around us.

Alexei followed my gaze and then, without words, he grabbed my hand and ran with me. We found an old sedan—no wheels, no glass in its windows, but the seats were intact. He hauled open the rear door and we dived inside, lying full-length on the seat with him on top.

The rain really started to fall, then, thumping off the roof above our heads. It was like being in a gazebo: we could hear it, look out and see it, feel the cool air against our faces, but we were dry. Everything stopped for a second. He brushed the droplets of rain from my hair with his fingertips, shaking them off like little jewels.

"I'm sorry," he said.

I started to protest, but he put a finger on my lips.

His voice dropped to a low growl. "Sorry I didn't do this sooner."

A deep, hot throb radiated out from my chest and hit every single part of me, before coalescing in my groin. I'd never known love and sex so perfectly mingled.

I was in the least sexy outfit imaginable—my back-up jeans and sneakers, a tank top and a deep red sweatshirt. I'd changed out of my sexy red scoop-neck sweater while I was in a huff with Alexei. And yet when he looked down at me I felt sexy as hell. He didn't undress me with his eyes; he gazed at me as if my clothes didn't matter at all because he was looking at *me*.

Then he was kissing me again, his shoulders and chest hulking over me as he bore me down on the seat. His hands ran up and down over my hips, growing warm from the friction of the denim, as if he was teasing both of us before he went higher. I started to buck and wiggle under him, flexing my ass against the cream vinyl seats, wanting his hands everywhere. It was only when I broke the kiss and gasped that he finally slid his hands up.

My sweatshirt was thick and there was my tank top, too. But when those big palms slid up my sides, it was as if I was utterly naked. They rubbed in slow circles, leaving my breasts for later and concentrating on the sensitive skin of my sides and stomach. I felt a thin sliver of cool air as my clothes started to hike up my body a little, but the warm press of him and the fire he was stoking inside meant I wasn't cold for a second.

He was still kissing me—not just my lips, now, but my cheeks and the line of my jaw and then down to my earlobe and neck. It was just like in my shower fantasy but a thousand times better. He wasn't just the big, powerful stranger anymore, the guy who could pin me down and make me his. He was the guy I'd utterly fallen for. Every touch of his lips gave me another little rush of pleasure and a fresh burst of heat until I was groaning and thrashing under him, ready to tear our clothes off just so I could feel him naked against me.

He worked his way down to my collarbone, the lowest point he could reach thanks to the neck of my sweatshirt, and then he sat back—as much as he could in the cramped back seat. I lay there panting, staring up at him, and he gazed down at me, his eyes hooded and burning hot. They didn't look gray, anymore. They looked sharp, blazing blue. I realized he was recording the moment in his mind, freeze-framing an image of me, and I did the same. God, the sight of him, his size even more outrageous in this small space. His shoulders, under the black suit, were so wide, so *solid,* it looked as if he could just stretch the metal of the car to make space for himself if he'd wanted to. I could see the sculpted slabs of his chest moving under his blue shirt. His lips were slightly parted and trembling ever so slightly—his breathing was shaky, he was so turned on. He flicked his tongue across his lower lip, remembering the taste of me, and I saw him brace his hands against the ceiling of the car, as if holding himself back. As if there was one part of me he'd wanted for so long, but he was making himself wait before he sampled it.

His eyes roved all over my body but settled on my breasts.

The heat inside me twisted and pulled tight. I pressed my thighs together, my groin aching for him and my breasts suddenly super-sensitive under the layers of cloth. I'd seen him looking at them, had felt him react to the touch of them, but I hadn't realized how much—

And then he almost launched himself across the car at me, unable to resist any longer. His hands scooped my breasts through my clothes as if gathering precious treasure and I groaned. My boobs are on the large size but his hands were the absolute perfect size to capture them and squeeze, fingers teasing the soft flesh while his palms covered my nipples. I could feel them hardening against his touch. He let out a long, low hiss of satisfaction, as if he'd been imagining this moment as much as I had, and the thought sent a shiver of lust right down my spine.

He began to circle and knead them with just the right amount of roughness, while his mouth found mine again. We kissed, open-mouthed and hungry, as he ran his hands over and over me, alternating between skimming my shape and squeezing. I started to rub one leg against the other, my toes dancing, desperate for more.

He broke the kiss again and lifted himself from me, panting. "I have to see you," he told me. And suddenly his hands were on the hem of my sweatshirt, bunching it up along with my tank top and lifting. He did it slowly, following the fabric with his mouth, kissing a line up my stomach. I arched off the seat to help him, taking my weight on my shoulders. My clothes slid higher, higher, until they reached the bottom of my bra. Then, with a sudden tug, he pulled the bunched fabric up under my arms.

Alexei looked down on my bra-clad breasts with such a look of scalding lust that I actually let out a tiny whimper. It felt as if he was already touching me, his eyes roving over my soft skin like a caress. And then he slid his palms all the way from my stomach up to my shoulders, lifting my breasts and letting them bounce back again, luxuriating in the feel of them. He muttered something in Russian.

"What?"

"I said you have the most beautiful breasts in the world." He stroked the upper slopes of them with his thumbs, his palms rubbing circles on my nipples, and

I gasped and quaked, closing my eyes. Then he was reaching beneath me and unclasping my bra and then tugging the whole bundle of clothing off over my head.

I gasped as my bare back flopped onto the seat, but our bodies had already warmed it. My breasts throbbed in the cool air. It felt scandalous to be so exposed: thanks to the lack of glass, I could feel every breath of wind against me and even the occasional splash of rain. The feeling of being outside only added to the spiraling black heat inside me. I grabbed Alexei's shoulders and pulled him down on top of me.

He gathered my breasts in his hands, smoothing his palms over my nakedness and then ducking his head to take one nipple in his mouth. I twisted towards him, rising up on one shoulder and wrapping my arms around him. His tongue flicked over my hardened bud, teasing the edges and then lashing across it again and again until I was moaning and pressing towards his face. His hands traced down my back and I mimicked him, pushing under his suit jacket and following the hard bulges of his muscles through his shirt. We explored each other as we lay there, silent except for the sounds of his mouth on me and our panting breath. He'd slid down my body to reach my breasts, so with his long arms he was able to reach my ass and upper thighs, smoothing over my curves as if sculpting me from clay. I could only reach down to his mid-back, so I had to settle for running my hands over those powerful shoulders, feeling them flex as he moved. When he started to kiss his way down my stomach, I tangled my fingers in his hair, urging him on.

When I felt his fingers on the button of my jeans, I let out a strangled moan. Both of us sensed the subtle change in mood, that point you reach when you know with certainty that this is no longer just *kissing-that's-got-out-of-control,* when you know that unless you stop, right this instant, it's definitely going to happen.

Neither of us even contemplated stopping.

There wasn't a lot of room and he was still wincing sometimes when he moved, but he was determined. He got the zip down and I wriggled my hips and then my jeans and panties were sliding down together. I felt his eyes burn a trail down over my pubis, through the curls of dark hair and down to the pink lips beneath. I could feel myself getting hotter, wetter, responding to his gaze.

It was too awkward to get my clothes off my legs so he left them there, bunched around my ankles. He slid off the seat and knelt on the floor of the car so that he could lean over me and—

I grabbed the edge of the seat and the headrest as his mouth made contact. Kisses, first, around the little triangle of hair and on the soft skin of my inner thighs, getting closer and closer. Then he was burying his nose in my hair and licking the edge of each lip. I opened my knees to make it easier for him, but we were so short of space that it was hard to get it to work. His tongue parted my folds, hot and quick, then slipped inside and I groaned as he tasted me. But I could tell he was getting frustrated: he wanted me spread and available to him, wanted to be able to ravish me completely.

Suddenly, he pulled back. Grabbing me by the hips, he flipped me over. "Kneel up," he said hoarsely. "Chest down."

It wasn't a request. I had a momentary flashback to his words outside the ship, the idea of being his plaything. *She does what she's told, or she's punished.* An unexpected shudder of heat went through me, pitch black and powerful enough to take my breath away.

I knelt up. Chest down.

He put his palms on my shoulders and then ran those big hands all the way down my naked body, describing the shape he wanted. I arched my back like a cat, thrusting my hips back and up. I felt the seat move as he knelt behind me and then gulped as his knees nudged mine apart. I could feel my moistened folds open for him.....

Facing away from him meant I couldn't see and *that* meant that he could drive me crazy with anticipation. As soon as I felt his breath on me, I started to grind my hips. When I felt the first touch of his tongue, I closed my eyes and pressed my cheek to the seat.

Now I knew why he'd been frustrated before—he was good at this. An expert. His gentleness, as he began to feather his tongue against me, was all the more incredible because of his size. He teased me and teased me, circling closer and closer to my clit so that the energy inside me built in a twisting, tightening spiral, but deliberately stopping short of release. I could feel myself getting wetter and wetter, rocking back against him, begging him with my mind to enter me but not wanting to stop the sensations. Thunder crashed outside and I was dimly aware of the rain growing heavier, droplets splashing up and hitting the sides of the car. There were bright flashes, too, visible even behind my closed lids, but I barely registered them: the world outside seemed far away. Everything that mattered was in the car and at the center of it was the crackling silver energy that was coiling tighter and tighter, ready to whip me over the edge into my climax.

His tongue left me for a second and I had to hold back a moan of loss. I'd never felt wetter or more ready.

Then I felt something warm and firm pushing at my super-sensitized lips: two of those thick, strong fingers—

I groaned as he plunged them all the way up inside me. Then his tongue started circling my clit and any last shreds of control I had slipped away from me. I pressed my cheek hard against the seat, swirling my hips and grinding back against him as he began to thrust, feeling how wet I was around him. I had my mouth open, panting out my need. Then I felt his hand on my back, stroking all the way down the length of my spine, making me arch and tremble. My walls were slippery around him as his fingers moved faster and faster and—

I rocketed over the edge and screamed. My cry echoed around the car and was swallowed up by the storm as I spasmed and clenched around him, my knees trying to press together, to trap him inside me. I bucked helplessly, pushing back against his expert hand and tongue, and he smoothed his palm over my back and growled dark, hard-edged words in Russian the meaning of which I could only guess at.

When I came back to myself, I barely had the strength to lift myself up and turn over. I managed to flop onto my side, my jeans still around my ankles, and sat there panting and wide-eyed, staring at him. I knew what was coming next, but I'd been waiting for it—fantasizing about it—for so long that I couldn't believe the moment had really arrived.

He lowered himself down onto the seat next to me, lying on his side so that we were face to face. I scooched back on the seat as much as I could, pressing my back against the seat back. He smoothed his hand over my cheek, pushing my hair off my face. "I am going to fuck you, now," he told me.

I drew in my breath. And nodded.

He began to unfasten his shirt and I helped him, undoing the buttons from the bottom while he worked from the top. More and more of that magnificent chest appeared and soon my hands were finally on those hard abs I'd stared at so many times. We met in the middle and as one we pushed his suit jacket and shirt back and off his arms.

I almost threw myself at him, kissing the smooth wall of his chest, running my hands over its curves and delighting at its hardness. I skirted around the dressing that covered his wound, secretly proud that it had stayed in place so well. My fingers swept over each tattoo in turn. I wanted to know the story behind every one of them.

For now, I kissed him. I couldn't get enough of his lips—exactly the right combination of hard and soft. I kissed my way across his mouth and then down the line of his jaw, both of us twisting and panting as we fought to take control. He worked his way across my cheek to my ear and I flexed and ground my whole body against him in response. I found his lips again and sucked the upper lip into my mouth, nibbling on it, and he groaned. I never stopped running my hands over his muscles—God, he was so hard against me, as if he was carved from sun-warmed granite.

My hands skimmed over his abs and brushed his

belt. He shifted on the seat and we locked eyes.

And suddenly my hands were working at his belt, pulling it frantically through the loops. I needed him as naked as I was.

Together, we shoved his pants and boxers down his thighs and then the heavy, hot length of him was in my hand. I'd seen it a few times, now, but it was the first time I'd touched it: satiny-smooth and throbbing with need. The size of it, now I held it, made me go weak. I ran one hand up the shaft and there was room for my other hand to easily wrap around beneath it.

I wasn't sure how we were going to manage it, in such a confined space, but he gave me the answer by simply picking me up and placing me down again so that I was sitting on the back seat, right in the middle. Next, he stripped the wad of jeans and panties off my ankles and tossed it out of the way, along with my sneakers, so that I was completely naked.

He knelt on the floor facing me, shoving his feet under the front seats. Then he pulled me forward, opening my legs and lifting my knees. Now I was sitting on the very edge of the seat, but tipped back until my shoulders rested on the seat back to support me. That brought my groin right to the edge.

I put my feet down on the edge of the seat, my knees wide apart. My gaze was locked on his erect cock as he grabbed a condom from his wallet and rolled it on. He rose up on his knees, his cock bobbing as it moved closer. He was perfectly lined up to—I gulped.

He brushed his fingers along my cheek and ran them through my hair. "I've been thinking about this for so long," he told me. He ran his thumb across my lips. "My beautiful Gabriella."

My breath came faster and faster as he moved his hips between mine. He was so achingly hard that his cock pointed upward, along his stomach, and he had to gently draw it down to nestle the head between the lips of my sex. The thought of him inside me, so hot and so hard, had me wetter than I'd ever been.

There was a flash of lightning outside that lit up every muscle, every vein—he was a perfect marble statue, so hard and smooth and...*big*. I grabbed his forearms, squeezing his biceps as if they were the safety rails on a rollercoaster.

He must have been able to see my nerves because he looked deep into my eyes, waiting until I nodded, before he began. He kept looking into them as the blunt, arrow-shaped head of him opened me up, my widening eyes mimicking the sensation. He went slow, gliding into me, groaning at my soft tightness, and the feeling of him spreading me was like steel easing past silk. He slid up inside me, his hips coming closer and closer between mine, and I closed my eyes as I felt myself gloriously filled.

I'd always been in awe of his size, but feeling him there brought it home to me. It was something about my position—it wasn't like being on my back, where I could flex and buck and wiggle. I had to stay still, to support myself, and with my knees open wide for him I felt like I was offered up to him—the virgin princess, made the prize for some conquering champion. I had to be passive, while he would just...*take* me. That thought, coupled with the solid heat of him inside me and the sight of him looming over me...it triggered all the same things that the idea of being his plaything had.

He slowly drew back out of me, but I knew it

wasn't going to stay slow and gentle for long. The pain in his chest wasn't going to hold him back. *Nothing* was going to hold him back. My eyes flicked over the solid muscles of his thighs, the power in his abs and hard ass.

We weren't going to fuck. He was going to fuck me. And God, I wanted it.

He started a rhythm: a slow push into me and a quick pull back. Immediately, twin currents began to surge and flow inside me: the silvery pleasure of it, building rapidly, and the glorious, fluttery feeling, halfway between lust and panic, as I looked down and saw more and more of him entering me with each stroke. *God, I can't—He can't...I am. He is.*

The silvery pleasure started as delicate threads, a delicate filigree spanning out from my groin, but the threads quickly twisted together to become cords and then ropes, coiling around me and jerking my limbs like a puppet. I pulled my legs wider, bracing my heels on the edge of the seat. I wrapped my arms around his neck, urging him on. At the same time, the nervous excitement I was feeling at his size had me heady and weak, tossing my head against the seat back.

I was his, now, a slave to the sensations he was unleashing in me. He moved closer to me with each thrust and I wanted him right up against me, buried in me, wanted to feel those hard pecs press against my chest. I looked down, my eyes half closed, and saw him go steadily deeper and deeper and—

Ah!

He was in me to the root and I'd never been so completely filled. My whole body seemed to throb and pulse with pleasure—moving would be almost too much. There was no pain, just the sensation of being utterly his.

My hands slid down his muscled back to his ass, clutching him there as our bodies locked together. He was panting, his mouth close to my ear. "I've needed to do this for so long."

Then he began to move. Slowly at first, relishing every millimeter of my tightness. Each movement made the pleasure flare and brighten, until I was grasping and clawing at his shoulders, my toes dancing on the seat. Each inch he moved out of me was like a physical loss—I wanted the friction but I wanted him *back*. The lightning lit him up again and his face was set, jaw hard and teeth bared. Almost a snarl. It sent a deep, dark thrill through me, that image of him again as the conqueror, taking me how he wanted.

And then it clicked that his strained expression was from holding himself back. He was trying to stay gentle with me. *This was him being gentle.* And the dark thrill doubled.

He started to thrust, his toned ass and solid thighs like a machine, pumping into me. The pleasure whipped back on itself, taking my breath away. My eyes were locked on his, on that blue glint of lust in the growing darkness. I could see his control slipping away. What he really wanted to do was to take me, hard and fast.

I swallowed and ran my fingertips over his shoulders, tracing the muscles. Doing that gave me the courage to ask for what I really wanted. I craned forward and put my mouth to his ear, but it was three more slow thrusts before I dared to whisper, "*Do it.*"

He drew back from me and stared into my eyes, checking to see if I was serious. But I saw the gleam in his eye and felt the accompanying twitch of his cock inside me.

I nodded.

He stared at me a moment longer and then a look of such powerful lust crossed his face that it alone brought me right to the brink. Then his huge hands slammed into my shoulders, pinning me back against the seat, and he drew back from me—

ohmygod

He grunted as he filled me and immediately started a fast, unforgiving rhythm that made me moan. The sound of our coupling filled the car, drowning out the rain: pants and gasps and the slap of his body against mine.

I felt like a kite caught by a force-ten gale. The silver pleasure, once so delicate and sensual, was replaced with something rawer, darker and more primal. Every forbidden fantasy came snaking out of the depths, all the stuff we're not supposed to want. I could feel my orgasm looming ahead of me, rushing towards me faster than I could think.

His hips were rising and falling between mine, pounding me, each flash of lightning freeze-framing him in a position of power, like some oil painting of a warrior and a helpless maiden. Despite the cold outside, both of us had started to sweat, a fine glossy film across our bodies. It made him gleam, every muscle hard and visible. He took me like that for long minutes, until I was thrashing and arching under him, my climax hovering on the very brink.

His thrusts got steadily faster, hammering into me, my nipples scraping against his chest with each stroke. I swirled my hips, circling around him, and we groaned together at the slick friction. He put his mouth to my ear and as his cock drove into me hard and tight, he hissed in Russian all the things he was going to do to me. My mind ran wild, imagining what they might be, and that sent me over the edge.

I felt myself tighten around him and I gasped—and then the starbursts were going off throughout my body. I still couldn't move my hands, so I hooked his ass with my feet and clutched him to me as I shuddered again and again. He growled and pushed *deep* and then he was coming too, a hot throbbing I could feel even through the condom.

When he eventually lay still atop me, he brushed my hair away from my ear and whispered. "You are the most incredible woman I've ever met."

Only then did he release my hands and draw himself from me. My arms dropped limply to my sides. He put his arms around my waist and turned and lifted me so that he was lying on his back on the seat, his knees pulled up to allow him to fit, and I was straddling him. I collapsed forward on his chest. Too late, I remembered his injury and jerked my head up. But he stroked my hair and pressed my head down again.

"Doesn't it hurt?" I asked.

"A little," he said, which in Alexei-speak probably meant *a lot*. "But it's worth it."

It was a half hour before we moved again, my back growing cold but my front kept delightfully warm by his body. When I started to fidget and shiver, he helped me get my clothes back on and then he put his on, too. Then he spooned me from behind, his body against mine and his strong arms wrapped around me. The storm clouds had made it as dark as night and, with the rain pattering outside and no other sound, the car became a private, intimate place.

After a long time, he said, "What did he do to you?"

I knew exactly what he meant, but the shock of the question, coming out of nowhere, made me stall for time. "Who?"

"The man who hurt you."

I twisted around to face him. It was awkward because the seat wasn't all that wide and, however much he squashed himself against the seat back, he still took up most of it. I had to press myself up against him or risk falling off the edge, so our faces were very close. "Why now?" I asked in a small voice.

"You don't have to tell me." He meant it. I could see it in his eyes. He was already regretting asking, having heard the tension in my voice. And that made me feel guilty about not wanting to talk about it, which I knew wasn't his intention. The whole situation was twisting back on itself, turning into something that would come between us.

"Why now?" I repeated.

He stared into my eyes for a moment. "Because I've wanted, ever since I first saw you, to protect you."

"You can't protect me from the past. It's done."

"Is it? I think that man is still hurting you. Every time you panic." His hands tightened on my back, pulling me even closer. "I want to protect you from everything. Even the things that've already happened."

I pressed my lips together into a tight line, deciding. I loved that he could be so gentle when he needed to be, loved that he wanted to help. I wanted to tell him but I wasn't sure I could. I sure as hell couldn't do it while I looked into those eyes, so full of concern that they were already making me well up with tears.

I turned away from him and then nestled back against him as tightly as I could. He cuddled me into his arms. I lay there in the gloom for a long time.

Everyone has that place inside them, the dark cave mouth that leads down and down, down to where the worst memories live. I didn't dare to venture inside, normally. Too cold and too dark. But the warmth of his arms around me gave me strength. It was like a fire in the mouth of the cave, providing just enough light for me to find my way back again.

I went deep.

And I started to tell him.

Helena Newbury

FORTY-NINE

Gabriella

People get it wrong.

They think trauma is like an injury, like a broken bone. Something awful happens and you break, and then eventually, if you have the right help, you heal. Maybe you're always a little weak after that, in one particular spot. Or maybe you don't get the help you need and the bone sets badly and leaves you in constant pain, and someone has to come along and fix you—which might mean causing you more pain as they help you dig down to get to the problem.

A lot of trauma is like that. I know people who've been hurt like that and healed like that.

But that's not how it was with me.

Sometimes it grows. Something awful happens and hurts you, like getting cut with a knife, and you get help and the wound closes up and it looks okay to everyone. Maybe it even looks okay to you. But what you don't know is, the knife was dipped in poison. Deep inside you, where no one can see, something black and fetid grows and grows until it controls your entire body and your entire life.

Its slow progress means you can't ask for help because that awful thing happened years ago and it would be crazy to be affected by it now. And, besides, everyone thinks you're okay and your parents are so proud of you and you don't want to let them down. So you pretend it's something else. You blame kids at school or teachers and you nod and agree when doctors say it's *social phobia* or *agoraphobia* or anything else that isn't the truth. Because you don't want to admit how he affected you—that would be letting him win and you're stronger than that.

So you agree with your mom when she says she'll home school you. You take that online college course instead of enrolling in person. You choose a job where you never have to leave the house and you make friends with women on the internet you've never met. And all the time this thing grows inside you, out of sight, a solid heavy mass that weighs you down and keeps you indoors.

Until someone comes along and forces you out into the open.

I'd been going deeper and deeper into myself, further and further into my past. I'd seen, maybe for the first time, how the thing inside me had ruined my life. And now I was finally back at the event that had birthed it.

I pushed back against Alexei and he locked his arms even tighter around me. He felt very far away, way up at the mouth of the cave. But his warmth and strength still reached me.

"I was eight," I said.

I felt his chest move—a silent intake of breath. He

hadn't guessed that, hadn't guessed I'd been that young. His arms seemed to grow harder around me, his muscles tensing in anger.

The simple act of saying my age made my stomach lurch. It felt as though the rocks in the dark cave had grown suddenly slippery. Just thinking about this stuff was risking a fall into the past, a full on meltdown that would make me small and weak again. That was exactly what had always stopped me from doing this on my own. But now, as long as I could feel that distant warmth from Alexei, I was okay.

"My mom had taken me to a shopping mall. Do you remember how big things feel, when you're small? Well, this place was vast, even for a grown up. And they'd only just opened it, so everything was shiny and new. I loved it—I was so excited. And then it got even better because my mom took me to the big department store inside the mall, and all the women there looked like princesses. I was running around the clothing displays, trying on hats. It was great."

I stopped for a moment. I could feel it taking shape around me: the smooth marble tiles beneath my little sneakers, the soft piped music...it was like viewing the past through a protective veil as thin and fragile as saran wrap. I could still feel Alexei behind me, warming my back, but my front had started to feel cold, so cold....

My mouth had suddenly gone dry. I wet my lips. "And then I turned around," I said, "and my mom wasn't there."

I felt Alexei grow tense behind me.

"At first, I thought she was playing a game. I ran around and tried to find her, but I couldn't. And the clothes around me weren't familiar—I'd been in coats and hats and now I was in shoes..." On the last word, my voice shifted and changed, becoming smaller. Younger.

"I looked around and I realized I was all alone. I was in this huge, echoing place within *another* huge place and I didn't know how to find my mom. What if she'd forgotten me and gone home without me? I didn't know my way home!" The fragile barrier between me and the past was melting away, now, the saran wrap becoming just a few insubstantial cobwebs. My voice was thick with fear. "I asked, out loud, if anyone had seen my mom, but no one heard. It was a brand new store and all the staff were too busy running around, restocking things. No one was listening to me."

I felt Alexei half-relax on the seat behind me. He'd heard the fear in my voice. He thought that he'd been wrong, that the trauma was just being lost in a store. He *wanted* that to be the case. And it killed me that I couldn't make it so. Part of me wanted to lie to him, but I owed him more than that.

"And then *he* appeared. Stan. He was plain-clothes security in the store and he said he'd help me find my mom. I was so relieved. I took his hand and he walked me right through the store"—I swallowed—"to the exit. He said he thought he'd seen my mom leave, up ahead, and I believed him."

I felt myself sliding in the darkness. There was no more barrier between the past and me. I fell right into it, immersed in it, as real as it had been then.

"He took me into another store, one that hadn't opened yet. And I thought we shouldn't be in there because there were big signs saying Do Not Enter and there was construction stuff inside and wires hanging from the ceiling. But he said it was all okay and my mom was just through here and that it was a short cut." My voice was running on automatic, now. My body went limp in Alexei's arms and he tensed as he felt the change. My eyes stared straight ahead. "There was an office in the back and—"

I was narrating the past. And then I was narrating the present.

"He...there's a table and I'm—"

"Gabriella," Alexei's voice was a faint echo from far, far above.

I looked around the empty office, frantic. Stan had sat me down on the edge of the table and my little legs were kicking nervously in the air. I could feel a warmth behind me, as if someone was there, but that made no sense because Stan was in front of me, unbuttoning—

"Why is he doing that? I'm scared—"

"Gabriella!"

"No," I told Stan, "don't. *I want to find my mommy!*"

"*Gabriella!*"

I was being shaken. I blinked two times. Three times. And then I was looking into blue eyes shot through with the coldest, most brutal anger I've ever seen.

"I will find him," Alexei said thickly. "And I will kill him."

I realized I was facing him. He'd turned me around and he'd been shaking me, too, desperately trying to bring me back. It felt like he'd only just succeeded. I wondered how close I'd come to being lost down there in the darkness forever, catatonic in a hospital ward.

I took a few breaths. It felt as if I was back up

above ground, now, looking at that dark cave mouth from a safe distance while Alexei held me.

"Some construction workers found me," I said. "Hours later. I'd crawled off the table where he'd left me and squeezed into an air conditioning duct—the smallest, safest place I could find. They never caught the guy, or even identified him. He didn't work for the store." I swallowed. "My mom had been maybe ten feet away, the whole time I was looking for her—she was on the other side of a display."

I pressed myself to him but, however, hard I tried, I couldn't seem to get warm. "My folks sent me for therapy, of course. And we all thought it worked, me included. By the time I realized it hadn't, my whole life had changed."

"And you were scared to go out," he said.

"In case I got lost again. In case there was no one there to help me."

His arms tightened around me and, at last, I started to feel his warmth seep into my fear-chilled body. "Gabriella," he said, "from now on, I promise there will always be someone there."

I wanted it to be true. I pressed my face to his chest and stayed there, with him holding me tight, until I *knew* it was true. And only then did the tears come, big hot floods of them soaking through his shirt.

It was a full hour before we moved from that position. But when we did, I felt stronger than I had in years. The thing inside me—the Dread—hadn't disappeared or even shrunk. But I felt as if I had a handle on what it was, at least. It was the first time I'd ever talked to anyone about it since my original, failed therapy.

When we got out of the old junker, the rain had

Kissing My Killer

stopped and the clouds had cleared. Alexei slipped his arm around my waist and pulled me close as we walked back to our car. It felt as if everything was new again and that gave me hope, despite our situation.

I spent the journey back casting little sidelong glances at Alexei, trying to get my head around the idea of this gorgeous, muscled beast of a man wanted *me*...and that he hadn't run a mile when he discovered the depths of my fucked-upness, and the reason for it.

But where did we go from here? We were still on the run, we still had a very dangerous man to find...when were we supposed to fit in *us?*

I figured we should start by talking. I'd sit down with him, back at the motel, and we'd spend some time actually getting to know each other. I knew almost nothing about him aside from his distrust of technology and his ruthless efficiency when it came to things like food. I didn't know what he did for fun. Did he even *have* fun?

That started a faint, twisting unease in my stomach. I started to think about how different we were. He was still planning to go back to the Bratva and take up his old job again if we got this whole mess straightened out. He believed that killing was all he was good for, that he couldn't change.

I had to convince him that he could.

One thing at a time. We'd go back to the motel and we'd talk. That'd be a start. And just to ensure it went well, I'd put the red sweater he liked back on. Even if the talking went nowhere, the sweater was sure to keep things positive. I remembered how he'd looked at me in it that morning, as if he'd wanted to leap right across the breakfast table and ravish me. And now that there was nothing holding him back...I gripped the edge of my seat and pressed my thighs together.

***

Back in our motel room, I checked the time and saw that we'd need to grab some lunch soon. But there was time for a talk first...and time for Alexei to pounce on me. Cheeks flushed in anticipation, I found the red sweater and held it up in the air in front of me, checking to see if it was too crumpled to wear.

A hole appeared in the sweater. A neat, circular hole right in the center. I felt my hair move as something shot past my head.

I lowered the sweater and saw the hole in the window, then turned and saw the hole in the wall behind me. And then Alexei was diving on me and knocking me to the floor as more bullets ripped through the room.

FIFTY

Alexei

IN THE ARMY, they drill you on things a thousand times over...and then they do it all again. It's not just sadism or breaking you down; it's to ensure that, when something happens for real, the reaction is so ingrained that you do it without even thinking about it. I'd come under fire, real and simulated, so many times that the feeling of my chest hitting the ground had come to feel like an echo of the shot. I should have just dived for cover.

But when that first shot rang out, I just stood there and stared at Gabriella. She looked back at me, holding her sweater with the hole in it. Lifting it up had probably saved her life—the gunman had had to guess where her head had been. I knew that and I knew he'd fire again, but still I didn't move. I was like a machine with jammed gears—all my army reflexes were clashing with my need to protect her.

I'd never had to worry about someone else, before. Not like *this*. Everything was different, since the junkyard. She wasn't a fellow soldier and she wasn't just a VIP, like when I'd sometimes been one of Luka's bodyguards. I'd fallen for her completely and it was only now that I realized how vulnerable that made both of us.

I finally unfroze and dived on her, knocking her to the floor behind the bed, just as a second shot rang out. I pressed her to the floor, patting her body to check for wounds.

"I'm okay," she said breathlessly.

But I kept checking her. Sometimes people are in shock, they don't know they've been hit and then they bleed out—

"I'm *okay*," she said again. I stared at her, still hunkered down over her. I'd never felt such pounding, all-consuming fear. I'd never felt so connected to anyone before. She was a part of me, now, and one I had to protect.

More shots slammed into the wall above us...and then they stopped. The gunman was probably across the street with a rifle, sights locked on the bed. He'd stopped firing in the hope we'd come out. As soon as one of us put our heads out—

"Stay down," I told Gabriella.

She nodded, her eyes huge with fear. "What do we do?"

Normally, it would be smart to wait it out. As long as we stayed behind the bed, we were safe. Someone had probably already called the cops and we could have just waited for them to arrive. But in our case, the cops would pull me in for questioning, maybe even implicate me or both of us in Lev's death. I couldn't protect Gabriella in jail.

"We have to get out of here," I told her. I looked

around. The foot of the bed was beyond the window—if we stayed low until we reached it, the gunman wouldn't be able to see us.

Hopefully.

I rolled off of her and lay on my belly, then motioned for her to do the same. "We're going to crawl out, okay? Belly-crawl, like this." I demonstrated. "Don't get up. Don't go any higher."

She nodded. She'd gone deathly pale.

I couldn't be sure I was right about how much of the room the gunman could see. If I was wrong, would he shoot me the second I crawled out from behind the bed? Or was he a professional—would he wait for me to report the coast was clear, then shoot Gabriella as she followed and finally shoot me too?

That's what I would have done, if it had been me. I felt sick at the thought. So much had changed!

I took a deep breath...and crawled out, bracing myself for the impact. None came. I took a second to look around the room. Everything was still and quiet. A few feathers were drifting around—one of the shots must have clipped a pillow.

I glanced at the door and realized it was on the same wall as the window. We'd be dead the instant we went out that way. The only other door led to the tiny bathroom and I knew the window in there was too small to climb through. But it was better than staying in the bedroom.

I belly-crawled across the carpet and then beckoned for Gabriella. She crawled across exactly as I'd shown her and I helped her to her feet in the bathroom, slamming the door behind us. The room was so small that the two of us took up most of the floor space. Both of us looked at the window: I'd been right: much too small.

The cops would be on their way. Three minutes at most and we'd be under arrest.

"Who is it?" asked Gabriella. "The Bratva?"

I shook my head, still looking around the room. "He's using a rifle and he almost got you with the first shot. I think it's Seventeen."

"How the hell did he find us?!"

"Think about it later. We have to get out of here."

I turned in a full circle. The window was too small to get through. One wall lead back into our room and the other was solid cinder-block. But the fourth wall, the one with the sink and the mirror...I frowned and tried to picture the layout of the room, and how the next room must join to it. I realized the bathrooms touched, back-to-back.

"The next room's bathroom is behind here," I said. I rapped on the wall—just a thin, cheap partition. I could hear sirens in the distance. *Shit!*

"Great, but how do we—"

My eyes searched the room for something to use as a hammer, but there was nothing. *We're going to get caught.* I had a vision of me dragged off in handcuffs and Gabriella left alone as cars full of Bratva thugs pulled up—

Fuck that.

I jumped up onto the toilet and slammed my foot down on the sink as hard as I could. One kick and it drooped. Two and it hung limply from the wall, water spraying from a broken pipe. I jumped down, wrapped my arms around it and *heaved*. The thing came loose, a hunk of porcelain and metal that weighed twenty pounds.

"Move back," I said.

Gabriella flattened herself against the door.

I smashed the sink against the partition wall. Water, plaster and dust filled the air and the plasterboard caved inward. I pulled back and slammed the sink into the wall again, almost throwing it. This time, I smashed a hole right through. A third hit and the hole was big enough to climb through. I tossed the sink down, grabbed Gabriella's hand and helped her through the hole, then climbed through after her.

The sirens were getting closer. We ran through the room—thankfully unoccupied—and over to the door. I stood against it, panting. If the gunman still had his rifle's scope zoomed in, watching our window, he wouldn't see us leave. If he'd guessed what we'd done and had pulled his view back, he'd shoot us as soon as we opened the door.

"Walk," I said. "Don't run."

She nodded and squeezed my hand.

I took a deep breath and opened the door, tensing in anticipation of the shot. I forced myself to walk into the open air and Gabriella followed right behind me. One step. Two steps.

No shots rang out.

We walked to the corner of the building and then, as soon as we were out of sight, ran for our car. By the time we were in it, the cops were pulling up at the front of the motel. We made it out of the street maybe three seconds before they shut it down.

I drove a couple of blocks away and then turned into the parking lot of a Dunkin' Donuts. We both slumped in our seats and stared at each other, hearts pounding. Then we grabbed each other and hugged tight.

Gabriella checked the clock on her phone and then showed me. It was 1:36pm. "I checked the time just before I held up that sweater," she told me. "It was exactly 1:30."

It had been less than six minutes since the first shot.

We did an inventory. The bags with our clothes in them were still in the motel room and so lost for good. Luckily, Gabriella had left her laptop bag in the car after the junkyard, so we had that. And she had her phone and some cash in her jeans. I had the two handguns I'd taken to the junkyard but was running low on ammunition.

"How did he find us?" Gabriella asked. This time, we had time to think about it.

"Did you go online?" I asked.

She shrugged. "Sure. I talked to some friends."

"But you didn't tell them where we were?"

"No! Of course not. And anyway, I trust those two."

"Did you hack Nikolai again? Could he have traced you that way?"

"No. I didn't go near his computer." And then she frowned at her laptop.

"What?"

"I just had a horrible thought."

FIFTY-ONE

Gabriella

I PRAYED I was wrong. But I got Alexei to drive us to the nearest electrical store and there I bought a new laptop, which took a good chunk of our remaining cash. We found a coffee shop that had WiFi and set up in a quiet corner: a hazelnut latte for me, a black Americano for Alexei, a couple of sandwiches and the new laptop, all crammed onto a table. I got online and opened up the private chatroom the Sisters of Invidia used.

lilywhite> What happened to you?

yolanda> Everything okay? What happened with your Russian?

diamondjack> I just got shot at but I'm okay. We're together+had sex. Listen, they tracked us down to that motel even though I didn't go near Nikolai's computer again.

lilywhite> Impossible

diamondjack> I've been offline for days. I only went online this morning...and suddenly Seventeen shows up. What if my laptop's infected? What if they sneaked malware onto it and it's reporting back to them?

lilywhite> Did you open files from Nikolai's computer?

diamondjack> Yup. But no virus/malware alerts. At least, nothing the normal virus checkers could detect. Yolanda, can you scan it?

yolanda> Yup.

I opened up my old laptop and connected it to the WiFi, too, then gave Yolanda remote access. I could see her running all sorts of specialized search programs. No one knew malware like Yolanda—if there was something there, she'd find it.

Alexei was sitting next to me, looking bemused. "Be ready to go," I told him. "If I'm right about this, they'll be tracking us down right now." He nodded and we ate quickly while Yolanda worked. It took less than ten minutes.

yolanda> SHIT

diamondjack> What?

yolanda> There was something there, hiding in

your hard drive's firmware. Squawking your position back to someone in Russia. Undetectable to all the normal virus checkers, real military-grade stuff. Which means it's the FSB.

lilywhite> Shit.

I turned to Alexei. "Who are—"
"Russian Federal security service," said Alexei. "Like your FBI."
I felt my chest close up. "Why would Nikolai be working with *them?!*" My voice was a scared little whisper.
"I have no idea. Some Bratva do deals with the FSB, but Luka stays away. Their help always comes at a price. If Nikolai is working with them, he must have offered them something big."

yolanda> You're in over your heads

It took a moment for me to type a reply. My hands were shaking.

diamondjack> Yeah, we just figured that out.

lilywhite> GO.

I shut down the old laptop and closed it. "She's right. They'll have our location now. Come on."
We got out of there. While Alexei drove, I pulled everything I needed off the old laptop. Then he pulled over at the next dumpster we saw and I hauled back the lid and—
I stood there, unable to let go. I'd had that laptop

for *years*. I'd done some of my best hacks on it. But we couldn't assume we'd found every bit of malware. Like my apartment, it was unsafe, now.

I threw it in and heard the plastic crack as it bounced off the bottom. Another piece of my old life, gone.

Back in the car, we drove in brooding silence, following the freeway until we figured out where to go. We'd scored one small victory in escaping their tracking, but our situation was much, much worse than we'd thought. We'd thought we were running from gangsters but this was a whole different level. The FSB had resources the Bratva couldn't dream of. Hell, what if they contacted the FBI and asked for some co-operation? They could tell the US government that Alexei was a wanted criminal or even a terrorist, and that I was his accomplice.

It got worse. Alexei attempted to call Luka to tell him what was going on, but few in the Bratva would even answer the phone to him and those who did warned him he was a marked man and hung up. I could see him getting more and more worked up—not just with frustration but at the fact he'd been so completely cut off by the people he thought of as his family. Eventually, he hurled his phone across the car. Any other phone would have smashed, but his brick-like Nokia chipped the window instead.

"We'd better ditch your phone, too," I told him. "Mine's okay—Nikolai doesn't know my number, but he knows yours." I threw his phone out of the window as we drove along.

We were completely on our own, with both the Russian mafia and a security agency looking for us. I felt an overwhelming sense of tiredness sweep over me—I just wanted to crawl into a dark, warm nest with Alexei, curl up and go to sleep.

Alexei glanced across at me, saw my expression and stroked his fingers through my hair. I pushed my head towards him, rubbing my cheek against that huge hand. "We still need to find out what Seventeen is planning so we can stop him," he said. "We might be the only ones who can. We're the only ones who know something's going on."

"But we can't find him. We know he's here in New York, but we don't have any leads. He's hunting us better than we're hunting him!"

"We need help," said Alexei. "But we can't go to the police, or they'll arrest us. My own people won't talk to us."

"So that leaves no one," I said miserably.

"Maybe one person. Konstantin Gulyev. The boss of Petrov, who in turn was the boss of Seventeen."

I stared at him. "I don't get it. I thought he was Luka's rival. Isn't he sort of the enemy?"

"Yes. But I've been thinking about it. Why did Nikolai pay Seventeen all that money to get him to quietly switch sides in the first place? Why use a hitman from a rival family when you've got plenty of your own?"

"Because he wants to do something off the books, something that can't be traced back to him?"

"Yes. And?"

Light finally dawned. "Because he can blame the whole thing on Konstantin?"

"That's what I think. Which means Konstantin will be a victim in all this, too. Which means maybe we can get him on our side."

"Can you even get to talk to him?"

"He's here in New York. He throws a party at his place outside the city every Friday night. All the super-rich Russians come. It's cocktails for the women, poker for the men."

"How do you know so much about him?"

He glanced at me, then looked away guiltily and finally stared fixedly at the road. "Konstantin has been Luka's rival for many years," he said.

My jaw dropped. "You were planning to kill him?!"

"I had to be ready to. I had to have a plan in place, in case Luka ever asked me to."

I suddenly felt cold. I hadn't really thought about what his life must have been like before I met him. Now I did and it wasn't comforting. A whole life spent watching people, learning their movements, planning their deaths. No wonder he was so cold, so ruthlessly efficient. "Jesus." I thought for a moment. "Did you plan to kill *me?*"

"Don't think about that," he said, his voice strained.

"I can't *not* think about it!"

"Gabriella—"

"Did you plan to kill me?" My voice was rising. "Did you plan it all out?"

Alexei suddenly swerved across two lanes, making horns blare behind us, and pulled up at the side of the freeway. "Get you to open the door, four steps to the office, two shots to the chest, walk out," he snapped.

We stared at each other, both breathless. He was fuming and I was staring back at him disbelievingly. The only sound was the cars whipping past beside us.

"It wasn't you!" he said. Then his voice softened a little. "It was meant to be some guy, some hacker!"

"I *am* some hacker. If I'd been someone else, you

would have done it—right?"

He was silent for a few seconds. I could tell he didn't want to say it. "Yes."

I turned away, staring out at the road through the windshield. *What the hell am I doing?* I'd fallen for this man...*hard*. But was I completely crazy? He'd killed. He'd been going to kill *me*.

I snapped my head around, staring right at him. His eyes had changed around...where once they'd been that icy gray with just a flicker of blue, now I swore they were the other way around.

He was capable of change. Sparing me was proof of that. I just had to be patient with him.

"Okay," I said.

"Okay what?" He was still tense, gripping the steering wheel like he wanted to rip it off.

"Okay I'm not going to think about it." I let out a long breath, trying to calm myself. And remembered what we'd been going to do in the motel room, before Seventeen started shooting. "There's something else, though. We need to talk."

"Talk?" He said it as suspiciously as most people would say *"Cyanide?"*

"About us." Then, defensively, "Look, a lot's happened today!"

And then I blinked, leaned my head back against the seat and slowly started to laugh.

Alexei frowned at me. "It's...*funny?*"

I shook my head, then nodded. "It's kind of funny." We'd been shot at, we were on the run from the authorities and I was still trying to find time for a *where is this going* conversation. I sighed. "Look, forget it. We'll figure it out."

He looked suddenly uncomfortable. "No. You need

to talk—we talk." And he switched off the engine.

I blinked.

He looked embarrassed. "I talked to Luka once. He said, American women are always needing to talk. If you don't talk to them, they get angry." He sighed with frustration but shook his head. "I don't want you angry. So talk."

I blinked at him again. My heart was swelling in my chest. He was so obviously way outside his comfort zone...and he was doing it for me.

"*Talk!*" he insisted.

"It's okay," I said. "I think you just answered every question I had."

He looked at me suspiciously, checking to see if it was a trick. Then he nodded uncertainly and restarted the engine. "Wasn't as bad as I thought," he muttered to himself.

Before he could take off the handbrake, I grabbed him, turned his face to mine and kissed him. He returned it and it wasn't like the kisses we'd shared before, with their undercurrent of raw sexual need. This was slow and gentle and it ended with us pressing our foreheads together, eyes closed. It was exactly the reassurance I needed.

When we leaned back, I said, "So your plan is: we go to some cocktail party thrown by your employer's rival...and hope he doesn't kill you on sight, and then hope he'll listen to us and help us?"

Alexei nodded.

"Aren't you going to try to persuade me not to come?" I asked.

He shook his head. "We need to get close to Konstantin before anyone realizes who I am. We'll be less conspicuous as a couple." He looked down at himself. "I'll need a tuxedo." Then his voice took on a dark hint of lust and his eyes ran down my body. "And you'll need a dress."

FIFTY-TWO

Gabriella

FOUR HOURS LATER, I was crouching behind a bush in a cocktail dress. Or what Alexei insisted was a cocktail dress. It had certainly been expensive, but it wasn't...subtle. It was cobalt-blue and made of a shiny, wet-look fabric that hugged every inch of me. It was basically a tube that went all the way down my body, almost to my ankles, and was tight enough that every curve of my ass and hips was outlined. Walking was possible, but only because the fabric was stretchy. Underwear wasn't an option.

All of which I could have lived with. Except—

"Don't you think it's a bit...low?" I'd asked weakly, when I'd seen myself in the boutique's mirror.

Alexei had come up behind me and put his arms around my waist. "It's perfect," he'd growled.

The dress covered me...*just*. If I so much as sneezed, my boobs were going to escape. It was an outfit designed to get attention, especially once I'd added a pair of towering heels. That made it the polar opposite of the jeans and sweatshirt I normally wore.

"Trust me," he'd said. "It's what all the other women will be wearing."

I'd relented, even though buying the dress and a tuxedo for Alexei took all of our remaining cash. But now, crouched behind a bush, I felt ridiculous. Alexei, on the other hand, looked fantastic, as if James Bond had turned to the dark side. The white shirt and flawless black jacket looked even better on him than his usual suit.

About ten feet beyond the bush was a wire mesh fence topped with razor wire. And patrolling the fence, on the other side, was a guard with a German Shepherd. I tensed when I saw the dog.

"It's okay," said Alexei. "We're downwind of it."

I cannot be doing this. I cannot be crouching in a bush in a party dress trying to sneak past a guard dog.

I held my breath as the guard walked past. I couldn't help noticing that he wasn't some aging, overweight guy in a cheap uniform, but a muscled, six-foot-plus Russian thug with a bulge under his suit jacket. There was a very real chance of getting shot, if this went wrong.

As soon as he'd passed, Alexei ran to the fence and cut a flap just large enough to squeeze through. The storm that morning had made the ground muddy and I had no idea how I was going to crawl through without getting filthy, but then Alexei unfolded a tarpaulin and placed it beneath the hole. I crawled through and he followed. He bent the flap of fence back down, folded up the tarp and shoved it under a bush and there was no sign anyone had entered.

"You're good at this," I whispered.

He looked guilty, then grim. "I've had a lot of practice."

He took my hand and ran with me towards the mansion—a huge old place built of stone, with warm light spilling out of every window. There were plenty of people already inside but more were still arriving: a non-stop procession of limos crept past the entrance, disgorging their passengers before making way for the next. Meanwhile, a stream of Lamborghinis, Ferraris and Aston Martins swept past us, heading for the parking at the rear of the mansion. Alexei had been right about the wealth on show...and everyone did seem to be in a couple.

We crept along the house to a side door—it was ajar, but I could see a guard just beyond it, standing with his back to the door to prevent any guests going through it.

Alexei flattened me against the wall. "It's time," he said. "Ready?"

I shook my head.

He smoothed my hair and then ran his hands down my body. Despite my fear, a rush of heat blazed out from everywhere he touched. "It's just acting," he said. "That's all it is."

I glanced sideways at the door, my breathing starting to speed up. I'd never been much good at acting.

He put a finger under my chin and gently turned my head so that I was looking at him. "I'm some Bratva gangster," he said, "and you're my American girlfriend." And then he leaned in and kissed me, a kiss that started slow but quickly turned heated and urgent. His tongue plunged into me, finding mine, while his hands slid down over my bare shoulders. I squirmed against him. *I'm his American girlfriend.* I could do that.

He started to move, backing towards the door while he kissed me. He kissed my jaw and then my throat, his hands sliding down to my ass. He pulled me hard against him just as he opened the door. I had my eyes closed, lost in what he was doing to me. He took my lower lip between his teeth and bit gently, drawing a groan from me. Then I felt one big hand slide all the way down between my thighs, cupping my groin through the tight fabric of the dress—*Oh my God! What's he doing?!*

"Hey!" An angry voice with a heavy Russian accent. Alexei must have backed right into the guard, pretending that he didn't even realize he was there.

I kept my eyes closed. My breath was hitching faster and faster, both from fear and from what Alexei was doing to me.

"What?" snapped Alexei. I imagined him glaring at the guard with that sub-zero gaze I knew so well. He had the palm of his hand hard up against my groin, the heel grinding against my clit while the fingers rubbed at my folds. Since I wasn't wearing panties, the silky material of the dress rubbed right against my naked flesh. My legs weakened and I began to pant, my hips moving helplessly in response to Alexei's touch. I knew that the guard was right there behind my closed eyelids, close enough to touch, staring right at me—

The guard's voice faltered a little. "You're not supposed to be out there!"

Alexei didn't apologize or attempt to explain. He kept backing up, pushing past the man and into the house. "I'm taking her upstairs," he said.

"The other floors are closed off!" the guard said quickly. Through the haze of pleasure, I realized what Alexei had done—he'd given the man a new problem to think about, jumping ahead before he had time to ask what we'd been doing outside.

"Then we'll find a bathroom!" Alexei snapped. And he led me away, one hand still massaging my groin, the other now cupping my breast. My whole body was throbbing with adrenaline. The fear and the excitement had twisted together and become something else, now, the pleasure thrashing and whipping inside me, dangerously hot. My cheeks were flushed and I was glad my eyes were closed. I didn't know how many people were watching us but, from the murmured conversations around us, it was a lot.

Alexei walked me out of the room and into a hallway and it was only then, when we were leaning against a wall, that he released me. "There," he said with satisfaction and a hint of lust. "Not so difficult."

I opened my eyes and stared at him for a second, then grabbed his face between my hands and kissed him hard, venting all of the tension as violent, scalding lust. He returned the kiss just as hard, then looked at me with hooded eyes. "Let's find Konstantin..." he said, his voice thick with need. He left the rest of the sentence unsaid: *...and then I'll take you home and...*

I nodded quickly.

We joined the flow of people passing through the hallway so that it didn't look as if we were skulking around. I grabbed a couple of champagne flutes from a passing waiter and handed one to Alexei. We moved into the next room and I caught my breath.

The room must have been eighty feet long but the vaulted ceiling and the huge expanse of polished wooden floor made it seem even bigger. It was full of people dancing and talking: men in tuxedos and women in—

Alexei had been right about the dress. Mine was tame compared to some of what I saw. I heard some of the women chattering away in Russian while some had American accents, but all of them wore similar things—lots of leg, lots of cleavage or both. Clearly, rich Russian men had very specific ideas when it came to how they wanted their women dressed. And yet, at the same time, the huge room and the waiters with their trays of champagne gave the party a classy feel. Some of the couples were even dancing to music from a string quartet.

Alexei nudged me and pointed to the quartet. "Konstantin got the idea from Luka. They're always trying to outdo each other."

"So they're enemies? Or just rivals?"

He thought about it for a second. "Just rivals. The families aren't at war with each other. Konstantin keeps mostly to St. Petersburg and Luka keeps mostly to Moscow. But..."

"What?"

"This is the Bratva. *Just rivals* still means you have plans in place to kill each other. Should the need arise."

I gave a little shudder. "Jesus."

He jerked his head. "Come on. Let's find Konstantin's poker game."

We threaded our way through the crowd, passing an elaborate ice sculpture and a cocktail bar. I was still trying to get used to the sheer amount of money that was evident. From what I could overhear of the conversations—at least, those few that were in English—there were CEOs and even politicians at the party. Anyone who could help Konstantin out with a favor, back home in St. Petersburg or here in New York.

We were heading towards a doorway. I could see a hallway beyond and, at the end, a door that led into a smaller, dimly-lit room. I glimpsed the circular green baize of a poker table, but most of the doorway was blocked by two guards. And these ones didn't have their guns hidden under their jackets like the one we'd seen outside: the both had sub-machine guns across their chests.

"We need to get in there," muttered Alexei. And he took a step towards the doorway.

"Are you *nuts?*" I squeaked. I grabbed his arm and steered him to the side. "They'll recognize you—correct?"

"Probably," he growled.

"And shoot you before you're halfway down the hallway!"

He scowled at me, but nodded. I succeeded in towing him away from the doorway and over to a quiet corner where we were hidden by the crowd.

"Okay," I said. "What was your plan when you were going to assassinate him?"

"Sniper rifle, from the bushes."

I winced. "Not all that useful if we want to talk to him. Did you have a backup plan?"

He sounded almost offended. "Of course. Sneak in like this, with a woman—"

"Wait. What woman?"

He flushed. "A prostitute. I was going to hire one

for the night."

"Oh." Now *I* flushed. And felt oddly, irrationally jealous. I didn't want to think of him with someone else, even if it was just for show.

"Konstantin would leave the poker table to take a break and mingle. But the woman would meet him and tell him she was a gift, sent by Vadim. She'd tell him she was his, for the night."

"Vadim does that? Sends call girls as...gifts?"

"Many men do. It's well known that Konstantin has certain...tastes." He looked embarrassed, as if those tastes weren't suitable for my ears. "He only accepts a few of these women, though—he only wants the best. The others, he just sends away."

"Arrogant bastard!"

"So I was going to hire the best call girl I could find and have her throw herself at him. If he liked her, he'd take her downstairs—"

"*Down*stairs?" Who had their bedroom in the basement?

"Yes. Downstairs, he has a—" Alexei wouldn't meet my eyes again. "Anyway, upstairs is heavily patrolled by the guards but it's easier to get downstairs. I'd sneak down there ahead of them and be waiting when they walked in. And then..."

I nodded quickly. I didn't want to think too hard about what he'd planned to do then.

"Neither plan is any use tonight," Alexei said. He looked towards the poker room. "Maybe rushing them is the best option."

I felt my chest tighten. "There's got to be a better way. We have all evening."

Alexei looked around and I could see the worry on his face.

Kissing My Killer

"Will the guests recognize you?" I asked.

"Probably not. The guards, yes, but not the guests. But if we start talking to them..."

I could see what he meant. Most of the guests seemed to know each other—everyone was kissing each other's cheeks and swapping gossip. They were going to spot us as outsiders in about three seconds if we tried to mingle. The only people *not* talking were the ones—

"We have to dance," I said.

Alexei went through a number of expressions very quickly. Bewilderment. Realization. Horror. "I don't—" he started.

"I don't either." I put our champagne flutes down on a table and grabbed his arm. "But it's better than nothing." *Better than him just storming into the poker room and getting shot.* Maybe it would give us time to come up with a new plan.

I had to almost drag him onto the dance floor. That at least meant that I didn't have time to get nervous. It was only when we reached the edge of the big, open space and everyone looked round at us that I stumbled to a stop. *I have no idea what to do!*

Everyone else was dancing as if they did this every day, twirling around the floor in couples. It seemed to involve a lot of sliding your feet around without stepping on each other's toes. I had a suspicion it might be a waltz.

"This is not a good idea," muttered Alexei.

"Just do it," I whispered. "It's not possible for you to be any worse than I am!" And I pulled him into a gap and—

Uh oh.

I'd massively underestimated how fast everything

was moving. We were meant to be spinning around in a couple while also moving in a big circle, keeping pace with everyone else. That alone was difficult enough, never mind trying to actually do the footwork or fit it all to the music. I grabbed his hands and tried just spinning around and around, but that just looked stupid. Then I tripped over my own feet and would have fallen if he hadn't grabbed me.

"I told you," he growled. His whole body was tense with embarrassment—this was way, way outside his comfort zone.

He was right. It had been a terrible idea. Now everyone was looking at us, which was exactly what we didn't want. "Umm..." I said, worried, and looked up at him.

And something happened. For some reason, me saying *umm* seemed to have an effect on him. His face softened.

He grabbed my hand, put his other hand on my back and started to—

I blinked and then gaped as he started to haul me into the right steps. "You can *dance?!*"

His cheeks reddened. "My grandmother made me learn," he said. "When I was a child."

I still had no idea what I was doing, but he was big enough and strong enough that he carried me through it. With a lot of looking down at my feet, I eventually managed to figure out the footwork, and soon I was only stepping on his toes every other beat.

We meshed with the pace of the other dancers...and disappeared into the dance. The people who'd been looking at us turned away and we both relaxed.

The feel of it changed. I knew we were still in

danger, knew we were just doing this to stay concealed, but...*I was with Alexei.* Dancing the waltz at a lavish party. It was the most romantic thing we'd done together and I was blown away by how *right* it felt. I'd missed all this, hiding in my apartment. I'd nearly missed *him.*

"You look...very beautiful, when you dance," growled Alexei.

I flushed and smiled. I seemed to get lighter on my feet, the music carrying me. Soon, I was barely treading on his toes at all.

The music ended and the couples gently slowed to a halt. I was grinning and surprisingly out of breath—I hadn't realized how tiring dancing was. I panted up at him and then, suddenly, he was kissing me. A soft, tender kiss on the lips that made me want to rise up on my tiptoes, it felt so good. We held the contact for a long time before finally breaking apart. And as we did, I caught Alexei smiling. Only for a second, before he remembered himself. But it happened.

He was changing. And he was doing it for me.

I really had fallen for this man. It felt so good it almost hurt. No way was I letting him run straight into that poker room and risk getting killed. No way.

"Let me find a bathroom," I told him, "And then we can think again. Promise me you won't do anything stupid until I come back?"

Alexei nodded reluctantly. I hurried out of the main room and through the ground floor, searching for a bathroom. When I eventually found one, there were smudges of white powder on the marble countertop. As I was washing my hands, my foot nudged something that had been left on the floor just beneath the counter—a black g-string. Alexei's comment earlier about finding a bathroom had been dead-on: this was how these people partied.

I walked out of the bathroom and headed back to the party. I was just nearing the door when a group of guards appeared, two in front of their charge and two behind him.

I stumbled to a stop.

The man they were guarding was as big as Alexei, but his opposite in a thousand subtle ways. Where Alexei's gorgeous looks came from brutish, brooding peasant stock, this man looked like a Roman emperor, with an elegant nose and soft, curling black hair. Where Alexei's body was all about brute strength, this man's was all about lean, coiled power. And where Alexei's magnetism was in that combination of cold, remorseless purpose and the burning fire that lay beneath, this guy was all about leadership. You could almost see it emanating from him like an aura—people fell aside to make room for him and every head turned as he passed.

He was hot as all hell. I was already Alexei's—that wasn't even a question. But if I'd been any other woman...wow.

I suddenly realized I'd been standing there staring for way too long and the group had almost reached me. I stepped left, but the guard on that side was still heading for me. I stepped right and now I was in the way of *that* guard. And then it was too late, because the whole group stopped just a few feet from me.

The guy they were guarding tilted his head infinitesimally to one side, judging me. It wasn't like the brutish stares the men had given me in the strip club, or on the ship. This was more like a connoisseur judging a fine wine. It was subtle at first, almost romantic, a look that took in my hair, my eyes, my mouth. And then, abruptly, it was so scorchingly sexual that it felt as though my dress had vanished. I swear his eyes never flicked down below my neck, but it felt as if he'd seen every part of me.

And approved.

I swallowed and actually swayed a little in my heels, a wave of heat washing down my body and ending in an ache between my thighs. I was horrified to feel I was getting wet, just from that look. *That did not happen,* I told myself firmly.

"Who are you?" His Russian accent was as strong as Alexei's, but very different. Instead of steel and rock, this reminded me of a flashing, lightning-fast knife carving the syllables into shape. The edges could be satin-smooth...or dangerously sharp.

"Jessica." Using my real name seemed like a bad idea and *Jessica* was the first thing I thought of.

He moved an inch closer. The air seemed to compress between us, growing thicker and hotter, until I could feel every inch of exposed skin throbbing. "Well, Jessica," he said. "I am Konstantin Gulyev. And while it's lovely to meet you..."—this time his eyes *did* skim down my body in a way that sent a fresh wave of heat rocketing down to my groin—"you should probably get back to your date."

I realized I'd known who he was, on some level, before he even said it. With his presence, he couldn't have been anyone else.

Out of the corner of my eye, I saw Alexei in the main party room, watching me with an expression between dread and fury. He was making *get out of there* gestures.

I thought of him storming into the poker room,

when Konstantin came back. Of him being shot by the guards before he even got a chance to tell our story.

I swallowed.

"I don't have a date," I said. "Vadim Andreyev sent me."

FIFTY-THREE

Gabriella

FOR A SECOND, I thought he didn't believe me. But then a strange smile touched his lips and he said, "Interesting." He only had to glance at the four men around him and they dispersed instantly. I evidently presented no threat.

My heart started to thump against my ribcage as he walked closer. I could still see Alexei out of the corner of my eye, looking horrified, but I tried not to look in that direction because I didn't want Konstantin to notice him.

Konstantin drew close enough to touch me. He reached out and took hold of the fabric of my dress, close to my hip, rubbing it between his finger and thumb as if testing its quality. "And what instructions did Vadim give you?" he asked. His voice had dropped to a low growl, almost a purr.

I tried to think of how a call girl at the classy end of the scale would phrase it. "That I was to do whatever it took to please you," I said. I went for *confident* but my voice didn't obey, coming out as a strained, tight whisper.

That didn't seem to bother him. Maybe he liked it, which scared me even more.

"Will you?" he asked, his voice teasing. He bent down and put his mouth right to my ear. "Will you do *anything* I ask?"

There was something about the way he said it that made a chill go through me—but the fear was mixed with unexpected excitement, heat rising to flush my face and sinking to pool in my groin. I shifted my feet, my heels clacking against the hallway's tiles. And nodded.

"Well," Konstantin said. "I was about to take a break anyway." He opened his jacket and showed me a bulging wad of cash—his poker winnings. "I think I need to give the other players a chance to recover. Why don't we go downstairs?"

Downstairs. Why *did* he have a bedroom downstairs? Just so that he could take a woman to bed without bothering to walk upstairs? Was it really any quicker? The thought of what would happen down there sent cold currents of fear spiraling up from the pit of my stomach. What would he expect me to do?

I forced myself to stay calm. What he expected was irrelevant. Alexei would be down there waiting for us, so nothing would happen. All I had to do was walk slowly and—

And then it all went wrong.

Konstantin nodded to a door at the end of the hall—not as grand as any of the huge oak doors that led to the main rooms. The door to a set of stairs.

We were already closer to it than Alexei. We were going to get there first.

I suddenly realized that I'd missed a crucial part of Alexei's plan—the woman had to intercept Konstantin well away from that door, so that Alexei had time to beat them to it.

Konstantin put a hand on the small of my back and turned me, gently but firmly, towards the door. He started walking and I found myself pushed along—it wasn't that he was forcing me, but I couldn't resist without making a scene.

Maybe I should make a scene. Maybe it was better to tell the truth now.

But the four guards, while they seemed happy to let us go downstairs on our own, were still hanging around in the hallway. If Alexei tried to get to Konstantin now, he'd likely get shot.

I'd just have to go down there with Konstantin and then stall until Alexei got there. *I can do that. I can get him talking. It's just...feminine wiles.*

Except I don't *have* any feminine wiles.

We were at the door, now. Konstantin pulled it open, revealing a set of steps.

Not the polished wooden steps I'd envisaged. Cold stone ones. *That's just because it's an old house. He's just keeping it authentic.* But I was starting to get a bad feeling.

I risked a glance over my shoulder as I stepped through the doorway. I could just see Alexei, still in the main party room, blocked from approaching by the four guards. He still looked angry at me, but the anger was subsumed by the fear, now.

Alexei was frightened for me.

Konstantin closed the door behind us and I was alone with him. He led me down the stone steps and I saw that they were lit not by electric lights but by candles on the walls. We seemed to descend forever.

At the bottom of the stairs were several doors, all ajar. These were as grand as the ones upstairs, but in a different way—dark oak banded with iron. They were built for strength. He opened one and gestured me inside.

The breath died in my chest.

It wasn't a bedroom.

FIFTY-FOUR

Gabriella

MY MIND REBELLED against the word, because places like that didn't really exist. But it was the only word that fitted.

Dungeon. I was in a dungeon.

The floor was formed by ancient gray flagstones. The walls were bare rock, the whole room hewn from the bones of the earth. I remembered how long we'd taken to descend, and looked up at the bare stone ceiling.

"We are twenty feet beneath the mansion," Konstantin said. "Rock is a very, *very* good soundproofer."

There was a creak and I turned to see him closing the door. I could see now how thick it was, almost a foot of wood and steel. It slammed shut and the whisper of noise from the party above was instantly cut off.

Alexei is coming, I told myself. *Alexei is coming.*

I turned back to the room. I recognized some

things: the bed—an ancient wooden four-poster in the center of the room, complete with scarlet drapes. A wood-burning stove for warmth, crackling and throwing out an amber glow. Even an old wooden dresser with drawers and a mirror. Those parts almost *did* make it look like a bedroom.

But there, the similarities ended.

There were oak beams overhead, ancient and black, with gleaming steel rings onto which things could be attached. There were a lot of those rings all over the room: some screwed into the walls, some bolted into the floor. Even, I noticed some attached to the bed and lacquered black to better match the wood.

Dangling from a beam a little above head height were things I recognized: black strips of padded leather with buckles. Manacles.

There were padded benches of different heights and angles and something that almost resembled...they couldn't really be stocks, could they? There was a polished wooden rack, of the sort some rich hunter would use to display his prize shotguns. But displayed here were paddles and crops, canes and—my insides turned to liquid—whips.

I spun around, but Konstantin had walked silently up behind me, so close that now we were almost touching. I stared up into his eyes, panting with fear.

He suddenly hooked an arm around my waist and spun me around so that I was facing the dungeon again and pulled me back against him, my ass to his crotch. I could see us in the dresser mirror: the powerful, handsome man in the suit, towering over the woman in the—God, I'd forgotten how low-cut the dress was! With the gilt edge around the mirror, it could have been some painting of a king and the maid he planned to ravish.

Alexei will be here soon, I told myself. *Soon.*

Konstantin grinned at our reflection—the slow, patient grin of the cat who has the mouse firmly trapped by the tail. I swallowed. I could feel his cock hard against my ass.

"Welcome to my world," he whispered in my ear.

FIFTY-FIVE

Alexei

I STOOD in the doorway of the main party room, one hand on the frame. I was squeezing it so hard I thought the wood might crack.

Everything had happened so fast. One minute we'd been dancing—*me, dancing!* And then suddenly she was with *him*.

Gabriella and Konstantin had been downstairs for several minutes, now, and the guards were still in the hallway. They'd started to chat, talking about some Russian soccer game they'd seen that afternoon.

I couldn't get past them—not without either getting shot or getting captured. Because we'd sneaked into the party, I had my guns with me, but shooting them wasn't an option. I couldn't turn this into a firefight while Konstantin had Gabriella or he'd use her as a hostage.

What the hell did she think she was doing?! But the hardest part was, I knew exactly what had been in her head: she'd wanted to stop me running into the poker room and getting shot. She'd been worried about me and she'd put herself at risk to save me. It was the first time anyone had given a shit about me since the army.

I groaned as the guards wandered towards the door Konstantin and Gabriella had disappeared through. They took up positions around it, one actually leaning against it.

Until I could think up a new plan, Gabriella was on her own.

FIFTY-SIX

Gabriella

He's coming. He'll be here any minute. The panic was rising in my throat, threatening to stifle my voice. I couldn't have that. I needed my voice. I had to stall him. I had to be like that woman in *Arabian Nights* and keep him talking for hours and—

"Why don't you start by taking off your dress?" asked Konstantin. It was phrased as a question, but it wasn't one.

"I—Maybe we could have a drink first?" *Perfect! Well done!*

"I didn't bring you down here to sip vodka and play chess," he said dryly. "I may give you some champagne later, but I'll have to feed it to you. By then, you won't be able to use your hands."

My knees weakened.

He leaned around me and brought his lips to mine.

I thought for a second he was going to kiss me, but he didn't—not quite. He whispered, his lips so close to mine that they brushed them with each syllable. "Can you guess how I'm going to feed it to you?"

I gulped. His lips were like silk over hot, throbbing steel. I thought of them forcing my mouth open, of bubbling champagne flowing inside, accompanied by his tongue.

And then his lips were gone. *He* was gone, and I had to whip around to find him. *Jesus,* he moved fast for such a big guy. He really was like a lion, all prowling, majestic strength one second and then speed and ferocity the next. I stared at him, unable to speak. Something was happening, something that had started upstairs and was progressing with every second I stayed in his presence. It wasn't that soul-deep *wrench* I got when I saw Alexei. It was something simpler and baser, like the shudder when you see a spider or the *aww* when you see a kitten. Not a feeling but a *reaction*.

The closest I can get to it is the way a medieval king used to ride through a village and all the serfs used to bow their heads. Alexei made me feel like a princess, ravished by some rough, muscled conqueror; Konstantin made me feel like a peasant, ravished by the king.

"Take off your dress," said Konstantin, leaning against the bed. This time, he didn't even phrase it as a question.

I had no choice. I'd already probably acted too scared, too hesitant. If I delayed any more, he was going to guess I wasn't a call girl sent by Vadim. And then both Alexei and I would be in danger.

I can do this. I'd already been fully naked in the

steam bath with Vadim looking on.

Except...Vadim might have appreciated me, but he hadn't been looking to have sex with me. He wasn't expecting to tie me up and spank me and whip me and God knows what, throw me on the bed and—

Breathe. Just breathe.

I reached back and fiddled with the zipper. Konstantin stopped leaning on the bed and straightened up, his eyes raking up and down my body. With every pass, it was as though I was being heated up by a laser.

Where the hell is Alexei? Stall! Stall!

I swallowed. "Um...I think the zipper's stuck," I said. "Could you...?"

Now he'd walk over to me and I could maybe accidentally turn the wrong way, moving the zipper away from him. I could do that a few times, and then I could fidget and make it difficult to get the zipper down and—

He covered the distance to me in two large paces. One big hand caught in the neck of the dress and then there was a ripping sound so loud it seemed to tear the air itself. The dress went loose around me and fell around my waist. "There," he said in a voice like silver-coated iron. "Now it's unstuck."

I tried to gather the tops of the dress around me but the shreds were already hanging down over my hips. I crossed my arms in a protective "X" over my breasts, my chest heaving in fear. And yet, as his eyes burned into mine, I felt that unbidden ache in my groin.

My nipples were hardening. I told myself it was the sudden shock of the air.

"Take off the rest," he said. "Or would you like me

to rip that off you, too?"

With shaking hands, I pushed the dress off my hips. It slithered to the floor and then I was naked except for my heels. I stood there panting, staring at him, and he stared back at me. The heat in the room seemed to steadily rise and rise. Then he gripped my wrist and led me over to something that almost looked like a bench you'd find in a gym...but much, much older. The frame was made of iron, the pads from soft, dark red leather.

Konstantin pointed to it. "Get on."

I gulped, the blood rushing in my ears. The thing was shaped like a stool, but it was too high—the seat was waist height. And there were two long pads extending from it, a little like chair arms...but instead of being up above the seat, they were down low.

It was for kneeling on, I realized. The victim knelt with their lower legs on the pads and their torso flat on the "seat." There were black leather straps along both parts. Once in, I could be completely restrained. He'd be able to do anything he wanted to me.

I swallowed. "Umm...."

"You did say, did you not, that you'd do whatever it took to please me?" he asked. I didn't miss the little caress his accent gave to *please*.

Alexei will be here. Just hang on a few more seconds. He'll be here.

I climbed onto the bench.

FIFTY-SEVEN

Alexei

I STOOD THERE fuming in the doorway as the seconds ticked past, my mind running wild. I knew about Konstantin's tastes, but Gabriella had gone down there with no conception of what he was into. Right now, he might have her on her back...or on her knees. Or—

I did something I hadn't done since the coffee shop: I lost my temper.

The hell with the four guards. Four hundred wouldn't be enough to stop me.

I stalked into the party room, found the table with the ice sculpture and kicked a table leg hard enough to snap it off. The table fell sideways and the sculpture went crashing to the floor with a sound like the end of the world, accompanied by screams and yelps from the people around it.

I got back to the doorway just as one of the guards ran in. I swung my arm into his throat as he passed, knocking him to the ground.

That was one.

I marched down the hallway towards the remaining guards. Another one was running towards me, eyes wide at the sight of his comrade on the ground. I side-stepped him, grabbed his jacket and hurled him towards a huge ornamental vase and then walked on. Behind me, I heard the crash as he slammed into it and the groan as he fell to the floor.

That was two.

The remaining two were trying to get their guns out, but fear was making them clumsy and slow. I didn't blame them. I'd be scared of me, too.

I reached them just as one of them finally got his gun out. I banged their heads together hard and stepped past their crumpling bodies to haul the door open.

I was halfway down the stairs when I heard a gun being cocked behind me. *"Stop there!"*

I froze. The voice was hoarse and I could see the guy's shadow on the wall next to me: he was rubbing his neck. It was the guy I'd hit in the throat. *I should have hit him harder.*

I glanced down the stairs. One door was shut—that would be the room they were in. I was *so close*. The need to just storm on down the stairs and save her was dragging my limbs forward. But the guy behind me had the drop on me. If I took another step, he was going to put two bullets in my back and I'd never get to Gabriella.

Gritting my teeth, I raised my hands.

FIFTY-EIGHT

Gabriella

Where is Alexei? It felt like it had been hours since Konstantin took me downstairs. What if something had happened to him?

I lowered my chest onto the padded leather surface. My head projected off the end, my hair hanging down. I shifted uneasily, my knees pressing into their pads. The position of the pads meant that my legs had to be slightly parted. My naked ass seemed to throb as the air brushed against it. I'd never felt so...*displayed*.

Then he started to buckle me in. First a wide strap across my back, holding me down to the leather. Then smaller straps just below my knees and across my ankles. I thought he was going to leave my arms free, but then he drew them gently up behind me and folded them back on themselves so that my forearms were together, and wrapped some sort of leather sleeve around them to hold them in place. Now I was kneeling, a few feet off the ground...and I couldn't move at all.

And then he was beside me, brushing aside my hair so that he could put his mouth to my ear. I knew he was going to tell me whatever depraved thing he planned to do to me and I braced myself.

"I can tell you are not one of Vadim's girls," he told me. "Now, you will tell me who you are."

FIFTY-NINE

Alexei

I WAITED until the guy came right up behind me and reached around me to take my gun from its holster. Then I snapped my head back into his nose and felt it break. As he dropped his gun, I grabbed him and *pulled,* and we went rolling down the stairs together, landing in a heap. I got to my feet, threw open the door and—

Gabriella was naked and kneeling. Konstantin had her strapped to a bench and was just raising his hand to deliver a hard slap across her ass.

I thought I'd been angry before. Now, I completely lost control. I ran at Konstantin, head low and arms out, and slammed him to the ground. We rolled, trading punches.

"Stop!" yelled a voice behind me. The guard was staggering in, gun raised, blood pouring from his nose.

I slugged Konstantin across the face. He landed a

good hit on my jaw and I reeled, but shook it off.

"*Stop!*" yelled Gabriella

The guard put his gun right to my temple. I growled, but I had no choice. I went limp.

Konstantin climbed off of me, adjusting his clothes. "Alexei Borinskov," he spat. He looked at my dinner jacket, then turned to the guard. "You didn't recognize him? You let him walk right into my party?"

The guard started to stammer an apology. Konstantin ignored him and turned to Gabriella. "And *you*...he hired you to get me down here? A call girl, just not from Vadim?"

I stood up, scowling at Konstantin. "She's not a call girl," I spat.

He blinked at me, then looked at Gabriella. He brushed the hair back from her face so that we could see her expression. She was pale with fear, but there was a defiant look in her eyes.

"I see," said Konstantin. To my surprise, he began to unfasten the buckles holding Gabriella down. "The last thing I heard," he said, "the notorious Alexei Borinskov had turned on his employers...because he'd fallen for some girl." He undid the last buckle. Gabriella quickly got up off the bench, trying to cover her nakedness with her hands. "This, I take it, is the girl."

I looked at Gabriella...and my heart swelled in my chest. I nodded.

Konstantin sighed. Then he surprised me again by slipping off his jacket and putting it around Gabriella's shoulders, covering most of her. He left his hands on her shoulders when it was done. "You sent her right into my arms, just to get me alone? You'd use her like that?" His voice was cold with disgust.

Kissing My Killer

Protective of her.

"No!" said Gabriella quickly. She hung her head. "Alexei would never do that. It was my idea."

Konstantin stared at me. Then one final surprise: he gave Gabriella a light push, sending her into my arms. She clung to me, her near-naked warmth throbbing through my shirt.

"Did he hurt you?" I asked, stroking her hair.

She shook her head, her face flushed.

"What was the plan?" asked Konstantin. "To kill me?"

I took a deep breath before answering, trying to reign in my anger. Now that Gabriella was safe, now that I knew he hadn't...*done* anything to her, I was a little calmer. But just the fact he'd seen her naked made me want to kill him. "I needed to talk to you," I said.

Konstantin threw out his arms to indicate the scene. "This is how you talk to me?"

"I knew you'd shoot me as soon as you recognized me."

"Very astute. Nikolai called me. He's *very* anxious to get hold of you. Dead or alive. Preferably dead."

"Nikolai hired a man called Slava Federoff," I told him. "People call him 'Seventeen.' He works for one of your men - Petrov Denakin. Nikolai's planning something and it's big, because he's got the FSB helping him. Whatever it is, he wants you to get the blame."

I watched Konstantin closely to see his reaction. After a long moment, he said, "That is an interesting story. A conspiracy, with Nikolai trying to frame me." He paused. "I will..."—he glanced at Gabriella—"how do you Americans say it? I will *take it under advisement."*

Shit.

"But Nikolai wants you dead and he works for Luka. I'm not risking a war with Luka." He sighed with regret and then looked at Gabriella. His voice softened a little. "You, I will allow to walk out of here." He nodded towards the door, then looked at Alexei. "But you..." He nodded to the guard. "Kill him."

SIXTY

Gabriella

It felt as if my heart stopped. "No!" I screamed. "Wait!"

Alexei looked down into my eyes. He swallowed. "Go," he told me.

I flattened myself against his body. "No! I won't let them!"

"*Go!*" His voice was low but firm.

I turned to Konstantin. "Please! He's not your enemy! Nikolai is!"

Konstantin shook his head sadly. "Gabriella...you are very beautiful. And loyal. But you don't understand how the Bratva operates. Go."

Both he and Konstantin were staring down at me with very similar expressions. That was what made it so frustrating, that they both seemed to believe it was inevitable, that the Bratva rules of loyalty and discipline ran so deep that this was going to happen, even though neither of them wanted it to. Alexei had sealed his fate as soon as he'd refused to shoot me, and everything since then had just been stalling for time.

"No," I said in a small voice.

The guard was getting nervous. He was a young guy and jumpy, and he'd already been reprimanded by Konstantin once. Any second, he was going to just go ahead and pull the trigger, whether I was there or not.

"You need to go," said Alexei

I could feel tears brimming in my eyes. *It can't end like this. It can't!*

"*Go!*" Alexei told me.

They were going to take my man away from me. This whole stupid, macho organization, bound by tradition and rules, they were going to take him away when all he'd done was to do the right thing, to protect me. The tears were spilling down my cheeks, now. They were going to take him away from me....

Well, I wasn't going to let them.

I flung myself at Alexei, grabbing him around the waist and hugging him tight. I fell to my knees and let myself slide down his legs, my face pressed hard against him. I heard Konstantin give a low sigh of regret and step forward to pull me off of him.

I pulled Alexei's pant cuff up and clawed the spare gun from his ankle holster. I whipped around, clicked the safety catch off, and pointed it right at Konstantin.

"Don't you fucking dare," I panted through my tears.

The room went absolutely silent.

Very slowly, I got to my feet. I tried not to think about the fact I was basically naked, Konstantin's jacket flapping around me. I tried not to think about the guard's gun, pointed at Alexei, or what would happen if the guy panicked.

My eyes never left Konstantin and his never left mine. I edged towards the door, grabbing Alexei's arm as I passed him and pulling him with me. It seemed to take a thousand tiny, careful steps to get there. If I stumbled, if my gun wavered from Konstantin's chest for a split-second....

We reached the door. Alexei bent and picked up his gun from the bottom of the stairs. He pointed it at the guard and the guard finally, reluctantly, lowered his own weapon.

I looked up the stairs, ready to ascend, but Alexei shook his head. "No. They're waiting for us up there."

"Where, then?"

He walked over to another door, much smaller than the one that led to the dungeon. This one was made of iron and secured with thick metal bolts. He slid them back and threw it open to reveal a tunnel.

"Konstantin's escape route," he said. "All the Bratva bosses have them."

"How did *you* know about it?"

"I found the architect." He looked momentarily guilty. "And broke his arm." He pushed me into the tunnel.

"Gabriella?" Konstantin's voice rang out from the dungeon. It was tight with anger, but there was just a touch of amusement and an edge of lust there, too. "I really hope we get the chance to meet again someday."

I flushed, remembering how he'd made me feel, and said nothing.

"And Alexei?" Konstantin asked, "I hope you realize what a woman you've got there."

Alexei glanced at me for a second and the look he gave me made my heart lift and soar.

He took my hand and we ran.

SIXTY-ONE

Gabriella

THE ONLY LIGHT came from some flickering overhead bulbs, barely enough to see by. The passage was lined with slabs of stone, rough under my fingertips as I skimmed them along it. Running in my heels was impossible, so I had to haul Alexei to a stop and pull them off my feet, then run with them dangling from my hand. From behind us, we could hear shouts—with their boss safe, the guards had given chase.

The tunnel seemed to come to a dead end. But then Alexei pointed to the rungs of a ladder, leading up into the darkness. He pushed me over to it and I discarded my shoes completely and started climbing. The iron rungs were like ice against my bare feet and hands.

We climbed for what felt like forever. There were no bulbs towards the top and we were in total darkness. Just as I thought I couldn't haul myself up another rung, my knuckles scraped the ceiling. "There's no way out!" I yelled down, panicked.

Then Alexei was with me, climbing up around me so that his chest was pressed to my back. Just the warmth of him against my chilled body made me feel better. "There's a manhole cover," he told me.

Footsteps below us. A torch probed the darkness, lighting us up.

Alexei reached up and heaved. There was a scrape of metal and a circle of starlit sky appeared. "Up!" he growled in my ear.

I climbed up and crawled out onto the ground. The Dread came back, that feeling of being all alone, so small in a huge, unfamiliar place....

I steeled myself, digging my fingernails into my palms. We were in the gardens of the mansion, hidden from the house itself by trees. A muddy path led through a hole in a hedge and at the end of the path I could see a car. *Escape. Focus on that.*

Alexei climbed out behind me and immediately I felt better. I could see torch beams stabbing up out of the hole, Konstantin's guards were climbing the ladder and they were nearly at the top—

Alexei slid the manhole cover back over the hole, thought for a moment and then stood on it. Seconds later, the cover rocked as the guards tried to lift it.

"Get the car started!" said Alexei.

I ran down the path. But the heavy rain that morning had turned it into a quagmire and I was in bare feet, the mud oozing up between my toes. The further I went, the deeper I sank. Soon, I was gasping and panting, up to my knees in it.

"Hurry!" yelled Alexei. I looked back. The manhole cover was rocking violently—two or three guards must have been trying to lift his weight.

I gritted my teeth and waded on, every step

exhausting. At the end of the path, I clawed my way up the grassy bank that led to the car. It wasn't the sort of escape vehicle I'd pictured Konstantin having. It wasn't an armored limo or a flashy sports car, just a nondescript Toyota. Maybe that was the point.

I stumbled up to it, my legs close to giving way. I grabbed the door handle. Locked. *Shit!*

"There'll be a key somewhere," Alexei yelled. "Look underneath!" The manhole cover was tipping crazily—he looked like a surfer trying to stay on his board.

I was almost sobbing with panic, now. I knelt down next to the car, the grass sticking to my muddy knees, and searched with both hands. Nothing, nothing, nothing...*there!* A metal box, fixed with a magnet. I ripped it off, tipped the key fob into my hand and hit the button. The car's lights flashed as it unlocked.

I looked back to see Alexei jump off the manhole cover and run towards me. I scrambled in and got the engine started as guards poured out of the tunnel behind him. By the time he reached the car, there were at least six in pursuit.

"Go!" yelled Alexei as he threw himself in next to me. I hit the gas and we shot forward. At the end of the short access road we crashed through some bushes...and then we were on the main road and picking up speed.

I drove us back into the city, eventually pulling up on a busy street. I turned off the engine and slumped back in my seat, exhausted.

I tried to assess the situation. We were now on the run from Konstantin's people as well as Nikolai's. We'd failed to gain his help or get any more information about Seventeen. I was cold, nearly naked, covered in mud and utterly dejected.

"We should find a motel," Alexei said. It came out almost as a groan of resignation.

I'd had enough.

"The hell with a motel," I snapped. And I was out of the car before he could stop me, marching across the street. Tourists stopped to stare at the crazy woman wearing only a suit jacket, but I kept my eyes on the prize. Alexei caught up with me just as I walked up to the reception desk of the luxury hotel.

"I'd like a room," I said. "No, a suite. The best you have."

The clerk looked me up and down, trying to come up with a reply.

I pulled the thick stack of bills from the pocket of Konstantin's jacket and slapped them down on the desk. "Now," I said firmly.

Neither of us saw the car cruise slowly past outside—the same one that had been following us ever since we'd left Konstantin's mansion. It pulled up across the street....and waited.

SIXTY-TWO

Alexei

AFTER A FULL half-hour in the shower, Gabriella strolled back into the bedroom wearing a satisfied smirk and a white, fluffy hotel robe.

And, from what I could tell, nothing else. I felt my cock harden as she walked towards me.

"I was right about this place," she told me proudly. "Go try the shower."

I sighed. "We shouldn't stay. This place is too public. Too many people saw our faces, on the way in."

"Go. And try. The shower. *Then* tell me you want to leave."

I could feel myself weakening and that in itself made me angry. I'd never bent to anyone's will before but with Gabriella I found myself wanting to make her happy. I was also learning that, once she'd made up her mind about something, she was about as easy to move as a tank, despite her small size.

Maybe it would be okay to stay, just for a little while. She deserved a little luxury.

"Fine," I said. "I'll get clean, you sleep a little, and then we'll go." I grabbed a towel.

Gabriella jumped onto the bed and rolled onto her back. When I was halfway to the shower, she called after me. "Don't be *too* long."

I glanced back over my shoulder...and stumbled. She was lying back against the pillows and the neck of the robe had fallen open a little to reveal those smooth, soft breasts I loved so much. She had her hips twisted to one side and her legs pressed together so that she didn't flash me, but the robe had ridden up enough to reveal tempting glimpses of upper thigh. Then she met my eyes, looking up at me from beneath her lids, and that was a thousand times sexier than any amount of skin.

I regained my footing and shut myself in the bathroom, then let out a long breath and slammed my hand against the tiles, frustrated by my own weakness. That woman damn well owned me. If I wasn't worrying about her being in danger, I was wanting her. If I wasn't wanting her, I was dreaming of some impossible future together.

Was it impossible? I sighed, my eyes closed and my head bowed. At the junkyard I'd told her how I felt. Since then, we'd barely had time to talk and, when we had, I kept thinking I was going to say the wrong thing and scare her away. My only experience of women had been one night stands: no last names, just clothes strewn on the floor and roughly fucking her until dawn. I had no idea how to do *dating* or *romance*.

I was in love with her. I knew that much. But

where the hell did we go from here? Right now, things seemed to be going okay...but that was while we were running for our lives. If we came through this—and that would take a small miracle—and things calmed down and she had time to think about who I really was, *what* I was...would she hate me? Start to fear me again, like she did when we first met? She kept saying that it was okay, that I could change, but could I?

I straightened up and headed into the shower, determined not to enjoy it. I'd never understood the fascination women have with baths and showers. In the army, we used to have two minutes of icy water, no more, and nothing at all once we were out in the field. Days or weeks crawling through mud, and it never did us any—

Ahh.

The water didn't splutter and drip like the shower head in my apartment: it crashed down like rain in a typhoon, soaking me instantly. And it wasn't just barely warm, like the one at home—it was almost scalding hot, reaching deep down into my bones and banishing the chill there.

Just as I thought it couldn't get any better, four more jets switched on, pummeling my body from the sides. The water didn't feel like water anymore, more like I was being wrapped in a hot, healing blanket.

Maybe it wouldn't hurt to stay in for a few minutes. Just so that I could say I'd tried it.

I stayed in for a lot longer. Twenty minutes, thirty—maybe longer than Gabriella had. Luxury felt *good*. I drifted off into a warm haze—a paradise where we weren't being hunted, where I could be with Gabriella forever. I knew I was weakening, losing my edge. But the feeling of being relaxed and happy was just too seductive. I pushed all our problems away—they could wait until morning. For once, the most difficult decision I faced was whether to stay in the shower or go back to the bedroom where a gorgeous woman was waiting for me.

And that was no decision at all.

I cranked off the shower, toweled myself halfway dry and walked naked into the bedroom. It was all so alien to me, a world of softness and luxury I'd only ever glimpsed before—Luka's limo, when I was a bodyguard, or the hotel room of a target, when I broke in to kill him.

The bedroom was as big as my apartment and this was just one room—the suite had a living area, too. There was an ice bucket with a complimentary bottle of champagne, three sorts of coffee and room service menus offering any conceivable type of food. Everything was polished until it gleamed, from the dark iron of the bed to the piano-black big-screen TV. Even the floor shone like glass. The bed was big enough for three or four and covered in white sheets and a silky purple comforter, together with a small mountain of bolster pillows and throw cushions. It was all too much...and yet, with Gabriella sitting in the middle, it looked just right: exactly what a woman of her beauty deserved.

She sat up a little, eyes widening in expectation. Then her gaze fell to my hardening cock. I said nothing, just stood there and gazed at her as she gazed at me, a feedback loop that made me harder and harder, hornier and hornier. I wanted her. I *needed* her.

I stepped closer. She looked so small on the bed, so vulnerable. So *soft*. And yet the last few hours had proven her to be anything but. Beneath that beautiful soft skin lay a core of pure steel.

"Thank you," I said. I could hear the low growl in my voice. I just wanted to dive on her, but I needed to say this first.

"For what?"

"You saved me." I winced as I thought of the danger she'd put herself in.

She looked up into my eyes. "You saved me first."

I stepped even closer and she swung herself around on the bed and knelt up so that she was closer to my height. The movement made her breasts bob and sway under the robe. I swallowed. "You shouldn't have done that—gone down to the basement with him."

I thought she'd just nod, but she was unrepentant. "You told me he took call girls down there. You didn't say it was a dungeon."

"It was dangerous!" I started to get frustrated with her. "Dungeon, bedroom, it doesn't matter." Just the thought of some other man touching her sent white-hot rage through my veins. "Once you were alone with him, he could have done *anything* to you!"

Her eyes widened in fear...but then she squared her shoulders. "Better than you getting shot, trying to fight your way to Konstantin."

I stared at her. This fragile little thing would do anything for me, I realized. She thought I was worth saving. She seemed so *sure*.

For the first time, I allowed myself to believe that she might be right. Maybe I could be more than just a killer. My anger collapsed.

"Just...don't do it again," I managed.

"Okay," she whispered, eyes huge. And then I was

kissing her, falling towards those eyes and that body like a parched man diving into the sea. I devoured her, both hands sliding across her cheeks to hold her in place while my tongue met hers. We both groaned as we moved with it. Every instant that our lips were in contact, it was as if an electrical circuit had been completed, the current throbbing through my body. I could feel my cock standing up against my stomach like a rock. My fingers tangled in her hair, so soft against my skin, and all I could think about was that creamy, satiny body under the robe—

And then I was pushing her back on the bed and climbing onto it atop her. I hunkered down over her, kissing down her neck, hating the robe for being in the way and yet loving it because now I'd get to slowly unwrap her. I pressed her down into the bed with my body—

She let out a little yelp. Not pain, exactly, but a warning.

I lifted up—and realized that her legs were awkwardly bent under her. I'd pressed her back onto the bed when she was kneeling and she hadn't had room to straighten them. "Sorry," I grunted guiltily, and lifted off her so that she could untangle herself.

She smiled up at me and unfolded her legs: a symphony of long, pale thighs and shapely calves that took my breath away.

I glanced down at us: her, so small and fragile; me, the big ape. "I didn't mean to hurt you," I blurted. Then, "You need to tell me, if I hurt you."

"You didn't," she said quickly. "And I will."

I lowered myself again, this time easing myself between her thighs. I didn't want to go slow. I wanted to do things to her that would make one of Vadim's hookers blush, but I was suddenly scared—Russian men can be rough in bed and I'd always been one of the roughest. And Gabriella was so...*innocent.* Back in the junkyard, we'd both lost control and I hadn't thought about it. But now....

I battled with it, going back and forth. I could feel her soft body against mine, the heat of her throbbing against my cock through the robe. Every time I moved, her breasts rolled and squashed between us. All I wanted to do was to rip the top of it open and bare her...but, at the same time, all I could think about was that bastard Konstantin, tying her up so that he could have his twisted pleasure with her. Was I really any better?

"What?" she asked, looking up at me. "Alexei, what?"

I wasn't good at this—talking about sex. I loved sex, but Russians don't talk about it the way Americans do, with their endless magazine articles about thirty-six reasons to do this and seventeen ways to do that. We just *do it.* "You're sure he didn't hurt you?" I muttered.

She nodded firmly. "You got there before he had a chance to."

"But you must have been scared." I gently brushed her hair away from her face. "He had you tied up."

"I'm okay," she said softly. "I mean, it *was* scary, but it wasn't like he was doing it to scare me—he thought I was a call girl, doing it all willingly. I'm glad you came when you did. But...you know. Being tied up was okay. Not with him—I didn't even know him. But being tied up *itself* was okay."

And then she suddenly looked away and her cheeks flared red, as if she realized she'd said too much. I stared down at her, stunned.

"Being tied up was okay?" I said slowly.

She met my eyes for a second. "I don't mean I wanted Konstantin—you're the only one I want. But, you know, afterwards, when I'd had time to process it..." She looked away again, not meeting my eyes. "It sort of got me thinking that...maybe, umm...you know...being tied up by someone I trusted, someone I wanted to be with..." Her eyes went left, right...everywhere but at me. "Maybe that wouldn't necessarily be the worst thing in the world." She finally met my eyes, her expression asking whether that had answered my question.

I pressed my hands into the bed, lifting myself up. I saw her gulp a little as she realized the questioning wasn't over. "Not the worst thing in the world?" I echoed.

She swallowed and squirmed. "No. I mean, not the *worst* thing."

I blinked down at her, trying to work out if I was really hearing what I thought I was hearing.

She flushed red and looked determinedly towards the window. "I'm just telling you because you asked."

I felt myself nod. "Mm-hmm." My mind was still trying to catch up. I was thinking of all the things I'd wanted to do to her, ever since I'd first seen her. I was realizing that maybe "inexperienced," maybe even "sheltered," aren't the same as "innocent." I still hated Konstantin for seeing her naked, but he'd revealed a new side to her, one I'd had no idea existed.

She turned her head and looked up at me. An understanding passed between us. I could hear the blood rushing in my ears. We stayed like that for a few seconds, making our minds up, breathing faster and faster with each passing second.

"We should have a safe word, she said suddenly. "Like, *Stormcloud*."

"What's a safe word?"

"If I *really* want you to stop."

"But otherwise...I should keep going?" I asked.

She squirmed under me, rolling her hips. "You should keep going," she said, her voice high and shaky with excitement.

My hands were still pressed into the bed. I looked down at them—at my arms, my chest, the tattoos that marked me as Bratva for life. I traced her cheek with one finger, my hand huge against her face. I felt as if the room was spinning. She wanted my hands on her—all over her. She wanted me to fuck her and she didn't want me to stop. "Stormcloud," I muttered, nodding.

And then I began to strip her naked.

SIXTY-THREE

Gabriella

What. The hell. Did I just do?

I was shocked at how brazen I'd been about it. Well, brazen *for me*.

Did I really just tell him not to stop? Do I really have to say a freaking safeword or he'll—

Just.

Keep.

Going.

I looked up at him, at those broad pecs and the solid, heavy swells of his shoulders, following them down past his thick biceps to the veined, hard mass of his forearms. So much strength, so much powerful, tanned *man*...and the fact he was naked as he hulked over me made it even more intense, as if all of that power was concentrated into the throbbing, weighty shaft that pressed against my stomach.

His tattoos were a reminder of what he was and they still brought the same hard edge of fear. He was so utterly unlike me, from a world where life itself could be bought and sold, snuffed out at a moment's notice. That life had owned him...and yet he'd turned away from it for me. That's why I trusted him, why I knew he'd never hurt me.

His hand slid up my leg to the robe's belt and hooked underneath it. With a savage jerk, he pulled the belt through the loops and then opened the robe wide.

I gasped, suddenly naked. My body was still warm and damp from the shower and the cool air of the room made every inch of skin throb. In the steam bath and the junkyard, there had been shadows to hide in. Here, I was completely exposed to him. I put my arm over my breasts and my hand over my groin, out of instinct as much as anything. It was exactly what I'd done with Konstantin.

Alexei shook his head. "No," he growled, as if he could read my mind. "He doesn't get to see you. I do." And he grabbed my wrist and pulled my arm away, pressing it down to the bed. His fingers were like iron—not painful but utterly inescapable. The feeling sent an unexpected tremor through me.

I watched as he lowered his head and stared at my breasts. It was obvious to me, now, that he really loved them. I'd never had that before, never had a part of my body exert that much power over a man. It felt fantastic.

With his free hand, he began to explore them, stroking each one with his fingertips. I gritted my teeth at the slow, building pleasure, arching my back, and that only thrust them more wantonly into his hands. He teased me, touching only the edges of my breasts, staying clear of their centers. He stroked me over and over, until my breasts ached and throbbed for firmer contact and my nipples stood up hard.

Then he was engulfing me with his lips, sucking the whole center of one breast into his mouth, and I tried to arch and twist, to release the pleasure that crackled through me. But his hand pinned my arm down to the bed and suddenly his other hand was on my shoulder, holding me motionless. I sucked in a long, shuddering breath, forced to lie there and take it as his tongue flicked over my nipple and his lips sucked.

I'd assumed that, given opportunity, he'd be fast—brutal. I thought that he'd concentrate on his own pleasure. I never expected him to go slow, to use the power he had over me to tease me. But he was almost leisurely, exploring every part of my breast from the crinkled skin around my nipple to the soft flesh right at the bottom. The pleasure built and built, circling and twisting until I was exquisitely sensitized, rolling my head from side to side on the pillow every time his tongue lashed and flicked. Just as it was becoming too much, he stopped and stared down at my flushed, wide-eyed face. We stared at one another: him in complete control, me totally beyond it.

Then he switched to my other breast, leaving the first one shining wetly, and took me on the same journey again, and this time it was twice as good. He had me pinned down so I couldn't buck and thrash—I had to settle for gasping and circling my ass against the bed as I stared down at the sight of my creamy flesh being licked and sucked. He made it last for long, agonizing minutes and by the end I was a sweating, panting wreck.

He looked at the hand I still had over my groin, then jerked his head to the side to indicate that I should move it.

I kept it where it was. I could feel his eyes boring straight through it and my groin twinged in helpless response behind my fingers.

"Gabriella," he said warningly. "Move your hand."

I didn't. I wasn't disobeying to taunt him—at least, I don't think I was. I was just shell-shocked from what he'd just done to my breasts, and I was trying to figure out if I could handle him doing the same thing down there.

Then he took the choice away from me. He grabbed my wrist and pulled my hand away from my groin, then pinned it down to the bed beside my hip. He brought my other arm down, too, and pinned that hand next to my other hip. He shoved his knee between mine and started to slowly lever them apart even as I tried to keep them together. I'm not even sure *why* I tried to keep them together: I wanted his mouth on me more than anything.

It didn't make any difference. His nakedness meant that I could see the moment his powerful hips flexed and my legs helplessly spread, my bare heels skittering across the comforter as they fought for grip. I felt myself open for him, the cool air of the room on my most sensitive places. *God*, the soft breeze from the ceiling fan hit me and I tensed and gasped as I felt how wet I was.

His hands kept mine pressed to the bed as he moved lower. He used those massive shoulders to keep me spread wide for him. Then his head dipped and—

I threw back my head, crying out as his tongue made the first delicious contact, gliding over my outer lips. I'd forgotten how good he was at this—and this time, he had me pinned down and helpless: he could make it last as long as he wanted. His tongue drew elegant lines and swirls, teasing me open and then plunging in to sample me. I writhed against him, feeling my smoothness caress him.

It was gentle, but the pleasure was a darker shade than in the junkyard, threads of oily black instead of silver. It was something about being unable to move, having to lie there and take whatever he did to me. The black threads swirled upward, spreading out like ink in water, making my thighs tense and my groin hump off the bed towards him. I tightened all the way up to my shoulders and, as he started an insistent rhythm right on my clit, I started to press my upper body to the bed in time with him. I was inching steadily towards my climax but I needed more: harder, faster, *now!* "God," I panted, "please!"

He released my hands. Immediately, I shot one hand down between my thighs—I needed to rub myself, as he licked. That would send me over the edge—

But my hand was captured again. He pulled it roughly back to the bed and held it there, glaring at me. Then he let it go again.

I grabbed for my groin again. This time, I didn't even get close. He grabbed both wrists and dragged them up over my head, pinning them to the bed and moving up my body all in one movement. His face loomed close to mine and I shrank instinctively back. No one *loomed* like Alexei.

His voice was raspy with need. "If you can't play nice," he said, the *nice* reminding me of cold steel on stone, "I'll have to tie you."

"No," I panted. Something was happening—I felt

almost drunk and we hadn't even touched the free champagne. "Don't tie me up."

He yanked the belt of the robe completely free.

"Please don't tie me up!" My voice was hoarse with need.

He ignored me. He pulled the robe the rest of the way off, leaving me completely naked. Then he took my wrists and crossed them in an "X" and started to wrap the robe's belt around the point where they joined.

I tried to sit up. He straddled me, applying maybe a tenth of his weight, and I was pinned. The tying continued. "Don't," I said, feeling the soft cloth tighten around my wrists. "Please don't!"

Every time I said *don't* and he ignored me, I got a strange twinge in my groin. He finished with my wrists and I saw his eyes go to the iron bedstead. My eyes bugged out as he dragged my bound wrists towards them. "God, don't tie me to the bed!"

I was dimly aware that I probably wasn't a very good actress. And also that that didn't matter at all.

The bedstead was made up of several thick vertical iron bars and Alexei tied my wrists to the very center one. He did it quickly and expertly, leaving me almost no slack. I panted as I tested my bondage and found that I really couldn't move at all.

Then he moved slowly down my body, making it very clear where he was going.

It's a shocking feeling, to have your hands tied high above your head. They're so completely useless, so far away from where they could do any good at all. My whole body felt vulnerable in a way it hadn't when my hands were just pinned by my sides. I really was defenseless: his plaything.

His head dipped between my thighs again but this time he was able to use his hands, too. He started with this thumb, drawing it along the line of my lips while he circled my clit with his tongue. Then, as I opened to him again, he started to roughly fuck me with one, two, *Jesus,* three fingers, building the pace until the black heat had travelled all the way up my body and was thundering in my ears. My knees were bent, feet scrunching at the comforter as I panted and thrashed.

My arms jerked and twisted on the belt, hard enough that some half-hearted bondage by a normal boyfriend might have come loose. Alexei's bonds didn't move at all. That was the scariest—and the hottest—part: when this guy tied you to the bed, he really *tied you to the bed.*

Just like before, he drew me upward towards a shattering climax but refused to quite let me peak. The pleasure built and built until I thought I'd explode. Then he lifted his head and looked up at me. With one thumb, he drew circles on my clit. With the other hand, he continued to finger-fuck me. "Gabriella," he growled. "My *krasivaya malen'kaya shlyukha.*"

I didn't know what that meant in English, but I was pretty sure it was both complimentary and filthy. The words seemed to scorch my skin. I felt them throbbing against my breasts, lashing at my spread thighs as I lay there bound. Whatever a *shlyukha* was, I felt like one. "Please," I said, flushing at how desperate my voice sounded.

He didn't quicken his movements. My hips made desperate little humping motions towards him.

"Please what?" he asked. The *what* was drawn out, like the slow hiss of a sword easing from a scabbard.

"Please let me—" I flushed.

He shook his head and the movement made his fingers twist just a little inside me, making me gasp. "I want to hear you say it," he said.

What? Why? Why did he want to hear *me* say something like that? It wasn't as if I had a sexy accent or anything. I swallowed. "Please let me...come," I panted.

He grinned a slow grin of satisfaction. Then his fingers sped up and his hand rocked in just the right way, the heel grinding against my clit, and—

I heaved so hard on the belt that my shoulders actually lifted off the bed for a second, all my weight on my wrists and ass. My thighs squeezed against his shoulders as the pleasure pumped through me, shudder after shudder of exquisite black heat. It filled my lungs, my mind—I saw an image of us, me pale and bound to the bed, the hulking, tanned Russian on top of me, and I arched my back and spasmed again, grinding and grinding against him. It must have been close to a minute before I lay still in a twitching, panting mess.

If he moves, I thought, *if he even breathes on me....* I was so sensitized, even a touch would have been unbearable. But to my relief, he let me recover for a moment. My breathing gradually slowed, evidenced by how my breasts stopped *heaving,* and went back to just moving. I didn't miss how Alexei's eyes were locked on them. I got the impression he'd enjoyed the heaving.

I realized I was glistening with sweat—Alexei, too, the result of keeping my legs spread open and my body pressed down on the bed throughout all of my thrashing and arching. *This should count as a workout,* I thought. *The Ravished by a Russian Workout.*

Eventually, I was calm. Alexei drew his fingers from me, which made me aware of just how soaking wet I was. Then his muscled hips were pressing between my thighs, spreading me even wider than before. I looked up just in time to see him rolling the condom down his thick, erect cock.

I tugged at the fabric belt that bound my wrists, but I was utterly trapped. It's difficult to explain how that made it better, but it did—a thousand-fold. Being tied up *by him* made me feel somehow safe, rooted in the moment. The opposite of the dreaded slide into darkness I got when I panicked. Tied to the bed, I was *his* and nothing could change that—not even me.

In the junkyard it had all happened so fast. Now, he seemed to relish every second: the slow slide of his body against mine as he moved down; the kiss of his cock against my slickened lips. God, he was so...*big*: just looking at the size of him, poised for entry like that, made my heart flutter. And the solid heft of his body, the tight ass and the hard thighs—the power to drive into me for hours. I was more turned on than I'd ever been and yet, as he prepared to do it, I tugged again and again on the belt, testing my bonds, because their solid grip on me made it feel even better.

This time, I didn't bother with the *don'ts* and the *pleases*. My acting wasn't up to pretending I didn't want it. I just stared up at him, my breath quickening, as he lowered himself atop me, putting his face so close to mine that our lips almost touched. I realized he wanted to look into my eyes while he did it.

"I wanted you," he told me, "from the first moment I saw you." Then his voice changed, an edge of lust creeping in. His eyes went from icy blue to frozen gray—the old Alexei, his dark side. "And now I'm going to make you mine, my gorgeous *shlyukha printsessa.*"

He gave a thrust of his hips and I cried out in shock as he sank into me. My head rocked back, my eyes fluttering closed for a second at the stretching, solid heat of him—steel wrapped in silk. My mind swam with how good it felt, little sparks of silver flaring everywhere his cock touched me. Another thrust and I cried out again at the sensation of being filled. My legs went limp for a second against his thighs and then drew up, my knees bending and the soles of my feet sliding along the bed. I couldn't even pretend to resist anymore, it felt so good. He drew back a little, nudged my legs wider and then—

I gave a high little cry as he filled me completely, the base of him snugged up tight against my folds. I panted with the feel of it, the hot length of him *so deep,* my whole body seeming to wrap around him and squeeze, sparks of pleasure bursting free all over....

"*Tebe nravitsya eto?*" he grunted. I looked into his eyes and went weak at what I saw there. I'd never seen him like this—so completely fired up. It hit me for the first time that he'd always been tightly under control, even at the junkyard. With me, he trusted himself enough to let go.

"*Tebe nravitsya eto?*" he asked again, twisting his hips in a way that made the pleasure bloom and flare. I realized he was asking in Russian if I liked it. I nodded.

He pulled back and I groaned at the slick, perfect drag of him against me, every millimeter of my flesh

Kissing My Killer

alive with pleasure. The need built immediately. It was an ache inside me, a creature that demanded to be fed. I wanted him back inside me, *now*.

He thrust into me again, harder, this time, and I felt the brush of his balls against me. The sensation of having him inside me was incredible—I could scarcely breathe, scarcely think, my whole focus on that slick, hot tightness.

And then I saw us. There was a mirror over the dresser with angled panels and one had caught us from the side. I could see every detail—my pale, bound wrists, my legs shamelessly open and spread for him, my toes clutching at the comforter in ecstasy...and between my thighs, the huge, tanned Russian, his hulking body making mine look tiny. His muscled ass looked magnificent from that three-quarters view, and then he thrust into me again and the view got even better. My eyes opened wide as I took in the sight of his ass cheeks flexing and the unmistakable forward lunge of his hips...and my own answering cry of pleasure. It was the hottest thing I'd ever seen.

Alexei leaned on his elbows and slid his hands over my breasts. My nipples were still achingly hard, stroking like damp pebbles against his palms. He squeezed gently. "*Sovershennyye grudi*," he told me. Something about my breasts, I guessed. The unfamiliar shapes of the words didn't matter—what mattered was the lust I could hear in them. "*Ya khochu, chtoby lizat' ikh chasami.*" He kept thrusting as he said it. Something about what he wanted to *do* to my breasts? "*Izat' ikh, a zatem trakhnut' ikh,*" he told me, his eyes gleaming. Yes, definitely something he wanted to do to my breasts.

I nodded wildly.

He sped up and the pleasure started to thrash and slam around inside me like a living thing, desperate for release. I wanted to grab him, to claw at his shoulders and urge him to go even faster, but all I could do was jerk my wrists uselessly against the belt. I had to take things at his speed and that loss of control, weirdly, felt incredible. It felt *right,* in some indefinable way, like something I'd been missing in my life.

He was pressed tight against me now. With each thrust, the whole length of his sweat-slick body slid against mine, caressing every part of me from my knees to my chest. My breasts were lifted and exquisitely stroked by the solid slabs of his pecs, the nipples scraping along them, then pushed down again as he moved out of me. The hard muscle at the base of his cock was grinding on my clit each time he filled me. I was trembling, close to my peak. Sex had never been like this before. *Nothing* had ever been like this before. I felt so close to him, even though we were playing this twisted game, even though he had me tied up...maybe *because* he had me tied up.

Maybe I'd needed someone to take control and maybe he'd needed to lose it, for once.

He sped up again and I went crazy, wrapping my legs around him and pressing my cheek hard against his—the closest I could get to folding him into my arms, since my wrists were tied. I could tell he was getting close, that gorgeous face set hard as he strained to hold back—

And then suddenly he pulled himself from me, grabbed me by the waist and turned me over onto my stomach. The belt that tied my wrists to the bedstead twisted, giving me even less slack. I landed panting, my breasts squashed under me, and craned around to see what he was doing.

He was grabbing one of the cylindrical bolster pillows from the head of the bed. A second later, he shoved it under my hips, raising them up. My ass thrust up towards him, my back arched.

His knees knocked my legs apart. He bent low over me, his mouth to my ear. Everything had happened so fast, I was reeling. "*Ya sobirayus' k poshel na khuy, kak eto,*" he told me. He brushed a lock of hair away from my ear and the rawness of the lust in his voice sent a tremor through me. "*Szadi.*"

I didn't need to understand to know that he was telling me what he was about to do. I nodded, frantic with need. Then gasped as he started to enter me.

"God, I love the feel of you," he hissed in my ear. "You're so—"

"S—*Say it in Russian!*" I blurted. Then I reddened. "I—I like it when you say it in Russian."

I glanced in the mirror and saw him smile.

"Vy tak krepko i goryachaya," he told me as he sank into me. It was so much better in Russian—the knowledge that it was darkly filthy but with the mystery of exactly what he was saying. The unfamiliar words, together with *that* accent, were like glowing chunks of molten rock dropping into my soul, heating me up from within. The pillow he'd put my hips on was firm, almost hard, and I started to grind myself against it.

He gasped and went deeper. God, it felt different like this—he could go deeper and yet I felt even tighter around him. I checked the mirror again and the sight of him sliding into me from behind burned itself into my mind forever. I couldn't look away.

His body came to rest against mine, his balls nestled close to my clit. He covered me completely, his hands stroking my bound arms, his legs bracing mine apart and his torso pressed up against me all the way from ass to shoulder. "You are mine," he whispered in my ear, and again there was that ferocious edge of lust, the parts of himself he'd been holding back all this time. "You are my *printsessa* and my *shlyukha*, my *boginya* and my *igrushka*."

I squirmed under him. I had no idea what those things were—although one of them had sounded like *princess*—but I wanted to be all of them.

He started to thrust and, immediately, I felt myself rocketing towards my climax. The tight friction of it, the feel of his hard-as-rock body against mine—it was just too much for me to hold on for very long. Then he shoved his hands beneath me and cupped my breasts, rubbing my nipples with his thumbs, and the pleasure lashed at my brain. "Yes!" I called out.

His thrusts grew faster, harder, hammering into me, and I twisted and writhed under him, jerking on the belt that bound my wrists, utterly his, soaring upward and upward until—

I shook and pushed back against him, wanting every part of him inside me, and felt myself clench and tremble around him. My head went back, eyes searching the heavens, and then he was leaning over me and his mouth was coming down on mine, kissing me as I felt the sudden bloom of heat through the condom that told me he was coming, too. I could feel every contraction of his muscled ass as he pumped into me. At the same time, his tongue was sliding into my mouth, taking possession of me there, too, as I pressed my body to his and panted my way through my climax.

When we finished, he climbed off me with exaggerated care and turned me onto my back. His eyes were full of concern as he untied my wrists, the brutal lust gone...for now. "Did I hurt you?" he asked.

I shook my head. "Did I shock you?" I asked in a small voice.

He blinked at me.

"Wanting to be tied up. And the talking. I mean, I liked it when you called me those names."

"Did you know what they meant?"

"No."

"Would you like to?"

I squirmed. "Maybe. I sort of like the mystery. And I think I got the sentiment. And I liked it."

He shook his head. "Why would I be shocked?" Then he frowned. "Most American women aren't into that?"

"No." Then I thought about it. I didn't have many close friends I could talk to about sex. "Actually, I'm not sure." Lilywhite *had* said some stuff about her cowboy and ropes....

Alexei shook his head. "I know one other American woman who's with a Russian man. Luka's Arianna. And *she* likes it rough."

I gaped at him, horrified. "You can't—don't tell me that! I shouldn't know that!"

He shook his head sadly. "It's not like you'll ever meet her, now. Or any of those people."

I felt a pang of regret—God, I really had taken his whole life away from him. "How do you even know what she likes in bed? Did Luka say something?" I couldn't imagine a Bratva boss discussing his sex life with anyone.

Alexei shook his head. "I've been one of Luka's bodyguards a few times, when he's visited the US and brought her with him. Sometimes, I have the room next to theirs." He grinned. "I have a great story. Once, I heard them—"

I held up my hand. "Stop! Even if I never meet them. That's private."

He sighed good-naturedly. "As you wish." Then he sobered up and rubbed my wrist. "So I didn't hurt you?"

"No. And I didn't shock you?"

"No." He took my face between his hands. "Gabriella, you're exactly what I dreamed you'd be. And all the things I didn't dare to dream you'd be."

A hot throb went through me and I reached for him. "Maybe you could tell me a *little* of that story," I murmured.

He rolled over onto his back, pulling me on top of him, and we didn't get to sleep until dawn. For those handful of hours, everything was perfect.

Neither of us even remotely suspected what the morning would bring.

SIXTY-FOUR

Gabriella

WE SLEPT IN and took a long, luxurious shower together before we even thought about getting dressed. But eventually, reluctantly, we decided it was time.

To my delight, I discovered that a hotel will move mountains to make you happy when you're spending over a thousand dollars a night on a suite. When I asked if they could send someone to buy me some clothes, the response wasn't a shocked, "*What?!*" but a courteous, "What sort of thing did you have in mind and will you require shoes?"

Yes, I told them, clutching Konstantin's poker winnings. Yes, I would definitely require shoes.

We ordered a room service breakfast and fed each other bites of pancakes, maple syrup and strawberries while we waited. It was Alexei's first experience of pancakes and it was a little like watching a bear taste honey. Before long, he dispensed with me feeding him and devoured the whole plateful, and we had to order more.

The concierge sent up a selection of clothes for me to pick from. I went with a pair of black jeans—that fit me so perfectly I wanted to know where they'd been all my life— and a red angora sweater that was high-necked, but clingy enough that Alexei immediately declared I had to keep it. They sent up a couple of pairs of heels, but I ignored them as soon as I saw the black calfskin knee boots.

When I was all shopped out, we flopped down on the bed to think. Our situation was worse than ever: now Konstantin's people were after us as well as Nikolai's, and we knew that Nikolai had the Russian security forces on his side. Clearly, he was planning something big, but we had no idea what and no clue how to find his hired killer, the mysterious Seventeen.

"I'm going upstairs," said Alexei eventually. "There's a roof terrace."

I thought of all that open space and my stomach twisted. The Dread had receded a lot since the junkyard, but the idea of the whole city laid out around me like a toy town was too much. "Go ahead," I told him weakly. "I'll stay here."

When he'd gone, I put on the jeans, sweater and knee boots. The boots, in particular, made me feel better—for all their soft leather and expensive price tag, they looked like badass boots: boots you could kick ass in. If only I had some idea of *how* to kick ass.

I sighed. I needed to do something to help. I didn't want to be dead weight. Maybe I could figure out what Nikolai was planning. I still had the new laptop and my phone—I could do some careful hacking, maybe talk to Lilywhite and Yolanda...and maybe it was time for some baby steps, now that the Dread was less of a problem. I might not be able to handle the roof terrace with Alexei, but the hotel had a coffee shop in the lobby, not so very different to the one back at my old apartment block. With the help of the kick-ass boots, I figured I could just about brave that.

I shoved my phone into the back pocket of my jeans and was just looking for something to write a note to Alexei on when there was a knock at the door.

Shit.

I'd learned enough, by now, not to open it. I flattened myself against the wall and closed my eyes, waiting for bullets to tear through the wood—

But nothing happened.

I gingerly checked the spyhole. One of the hotel's waiters, standing behind an empty room service trolley. I let out my breath and unlocked the door. My time with Alexei had left me a paranoid wreck.

The waiter quietly closed the door behind him and began to collect the breakfast plates, while I dug in my purse for some bills to tip him with. "Thank you," I said, as he passed behind me. "Hey, do you have a pen? I need to write a note."

"Yes, of course."

His accent took me by surprise. Russian. I spun around just in time to see him take something from his pocket. Something cylindrical, but not a pen.

"We'll talk soon," said Seventeen. And pushed the needle into my neck.

SIXTY-FIVE

Alexei

I WANTED to worry. I wanted to be angry. I even wanted to be afraid, and fear is usually a killer's enemy.

I wanted to feel any of those things, because I understood them. I didn't understand this.

I'd thought that, when I woke up, all of our problems would be back and everything we'd done the night before would seem like a mistake—that one of us would have regrets and that there'd be a fight or another attempt by one of us to push the other away. But it hadn't happened. I'd woken having slept better than I ever had in my life and then there'd been another of those fantastic, luxurious showers, elevated to pure heaven by having Gabriella's naked body rubbing up against me. And pancakes. And the sight of Gabriella, happy as a child on Christmas morning, trying on her new clothes, and *that* sweater—

I was....*happy.*

And it felt too good to let anyone take it away from me, ever.

Could I really have this life? Gabriella had started to make me believe I could be something more than a killer. I wanted it to be true....

But it didn't change our situation. I sighed, my breath coming out as long wisps of white vapor in the freezing air. All around me, New York was laid out like a map. Somewhere down here, Konstantin's people and Nikolai's people were hunting us, drawing quietly closer....

And then another solution swam into my head, dark and seductive.

Maybe we didn't have to figure out what Nikolai was up to. I'd thought all along that that was our only chance, that unless we could catch him in the act and restore my reputation, we'd never get out alive. But I hadn't known how smart and resourceful Gabriella was. She'd saved my life. Working together, maybe we *could* disappear. South America, maybe, somewhere like Colombia or Venezuela.

But doing that would mean turning my back on everything I'd ever known—Luka, the Bratva, even Russia itself. I'd never be able to go back there, nor even back to New York.

But it would be worth it. For her.

I marched back inside and down the stairs, heading for our room. We'd leave today. By that evening, we could be somewhere far away. We'd change our names and hunker down in some jungle hideaway where no one would ever find us—

I unlocked the door and pushed it open, already excitedly saying her name.

But Gabriella was gone.

SIXTY-SIX

Gabriella

I WAS SITTING on something hard and smooth and I was hunched up tight: my knees were drawn up to my chest, my arms were wrapped around them and my head had been pushed down. Something was in my mouth and my head throbbed and spun from whatever drug he'd given me.

I tried to uncurl myself but immediately there was pain, biting into my wrists. I'd been bound with something hard and it was cutting into me.

Voices. A couple discussing which restaurant to eat at for lunch. Then the sickening sensation of the floor dropping out from under me. I was in an elevator. I wanted to call out for help but my tongue wouldn't move and I didn't seem to have even the strength to move air in my lungs.

The *ding* of the elevator as it reached a new floor. More voices, all around me, as people got on. Everyone sounded happy, relaxed. It made no sense. *Why don't they help me?* I was sitting right next to

them, bound and gagged. *Can't they see me?*
But no one could.

SIXTY-SEVEN

Alexei

I MOVED slowly at first, saying her name again. Was it a joke? Was she hiding in the bathroom, waiting to pounce on me? Then, when I found the room was empty, the panic slowly grew.

Could she have gone out? She'd have left a note...and then I saw her laptop on the counter and I knew she'd been taken. Gabriella would never go anywhere without her laptop.

All of those things I'd been wishing I could feel up on the roof came back. Worry. Anger. *Fear.* They had her. God knows what they'd do to her.

Think! I'd been up on the roof terrace for no more than ten minutes. Whoever took her might still be in the hotel. I could catch them, if I moved fast.

I felt my old army training take over. They'd taught us to track enemies, to look for clues. What did I see? What did I *not* see?

The door was intact. Either he'd had a key, or she'd let him in. Either way, he must be disguised as someone who worked at the hotel.

The breakfast plates were missing. *A room service waiter!* I'd seen them wheeling their trolleys around on my way up to the roof. The trolleys had a lower section covered by a white cloth—just big enough to conceal a person, if that person was tied up small.

Jesus, he was wheeling her right through the fucking hotel!

I ran for the stairs and sprinted all the way down to the ground floor. He'd need to get her outside, to transfer her to a car or van. I hit the buttons for all the elevators and stood there panting as I waited for them to arrive. Too late, I realized I hadn't brought a gun. Well, fuck it. The mood I was in, I'd tear the guy's head clean off.

The first door opened. Tourists.

The second. Two women, chatting.

The third. A whole group of tourists and, at the back, a room service waiter with his trolley. Breakfast plates on top, a white cloth covering the bottom. He started to wheel it past me, eyes down—

I grabbed him by the collar of his starched white shirt and hurled him against the wall. A woman screamed. I ripped the white cloth off the trolley—

More dirty dishes.

Shit! I whirled around. A few of the elevators were still on their way down. I could wait for them...or maybe I'd already missed her. Where would the guy take her? Out the front?

No. The back. Through the kitchens and the service entrance.

I raced into the kitchen, ignoring the angry shouts of the chefs. *Shit!* There were at least six waiters wheeling trolleys around and they all looked the same.

And I couldn't pick out the guy who'd taken her—I had no idea what he looked like. I tried to narrow it down by the breakfast plates on top, looking for ours, but I couldn't see them. Eggs—we hadn't had eggs. Waffles—we hadn't had waffles. *Where was she?!*

I searched and searched, eventually resorting to tipping over every trolley I could find. But I already knew I'd made a mistake. I could feel her slipping away.

I missed something. We must have been followed, when we left Konstantin's mansion. Or word had gotten out about a half-naked woman showing up at the hotel. I should never have let Gabriella talk me into this place; we shouldn't have stayed there so long....

This is all my fault. I was meant to be protecting her but I'd lost my edge. I'd gotten lost in a dream where I could have some sort of life with her. And now I'd lost her, probably forever.

I stood there in numb shock, ignoring the chef and the hotel manager who were yelling for an explanation. If I'd been able to see past them and out into the lobby, I'd have seen the final elevator arrive. I'd have seen a room service waiter push his trolley, its plates sticky with maple syrup and strawberries, out through a side door to the parking lot and into a waiting van.

SIXTY-EIGHT

Gabriella

I WAS STANDING...no, I was *dangling*. Slumped over, my knees slack and my head lolling down. Why hadn't I fallen over? It would feel so good...a split-second of pain as my head hit the floor and then blessed sleep. Concrete would feel like a feather mattress, I was so tired—

Water hit me in the face and I woke up fast, spluttering and coughing. I discovered that I hadn't fallen over because my hands were tied above my head, my arms already aching from bearing my weight. I managed to get my feet under me and straighten my legs. Where was I? Back in Konstantin's dungeon? I remembered the manacles hanging from the ceiling. I blinked the water out of my eyes and looked down to see if I was naked. No, fully dressed. And this wasn't Konstantin's dungeon.

This was much, much worse.

It seemed to be a sawmill, but one that had closed many years before. There was still a faint tang of sawdust in the air and some lengths of lumber, but all of the tools hanging from the ceiling alongside me were brown with rust. It didn't make them look any less dangerous, though. There were hand saws with tarnished metal blades and circular saws as big as my head with huge, jagged teeth. There were drills, some as slender as a pencil and some thicker than my finger. There were chisels and awls, tools for slicing and chopping and—

I looked away, trying not to go into full-on panic mode. But the Dread was back, creeping up inside me. I was alone with a strange man, I had no idea where I was...and no one was coming to save me. Alexei would have no way to find me.

Seventeen stepped forward, screwing the cap back onto a bottle of water. It was the first time I'd gotten a good look at him. He was a year or two younger than Alexei and a little smaller—still heavily muscled but in a less balanced, more pumped-up way. And he didn't have Alexei's presence, that way of holding himself that told other men he feared nothing. Konstantin had had that, too, but Seventeen didn't.

He made up for it by being simply, utterly terrifying.

There are some things that are just *wrong*. Disturbing. You can't explain why they are, they just are. If someone asks you why you don't like spiders, you can talk about them having too many legs or the way they scuttle too fast or the thought of them running across your face in the night, but you can't really define it. You just get a sick fear when you see one. It's a survival instinct, a primal urge to run.

That's what it was like with Seventeen. He didn't have scary tattoos or horrible scars. He wasn't holding a gun or even a knife. He even smiled. But I've never, ever felt such an overwhelming desire to flee.

"You're Gabriella," he said. "I am Slava."

The voice was wrong. Subtly, yet hugely wrong. The intonation was too flat. It was as if he'd read a book on how to talk to people, but hadn't understood it...or didn't care.

He had sandy-blond hair, but he'd either started to go bald very young or something had happened to him to make him lose it because his hairline went way, way back. What hair was left was cropped very short, little more than blond, patchy fuzz. His eyes were a faded blue, like a copy of a copy of a real person's.

I knew the question I was meant to ask was, *what do you want with me?* But I was terrified of hearing the answer. I glanced around me at the tools designed to cut and shred and I prayed I was wrong about why he'd brought me there, but I knew deep down that I wasn't.

"I don't know anything," I croaked.

Seventeen nodded understandingly. And then he lifted down a rusty circular saw blade the size of a dinner plate and I began to scream.

Helena Newbury

SIXTY-NINE

Alexei

I stood in the center of our hotel suite and stared. Somewhere, *somewhere,* there must be a clue.

I'd come back upstairs on instinct—my first thought had been to grab my guns. But now that I had them, I realized how useless they were. This wasn't a problem I could solve with violence. She was gone and I had to use my head if I wanted to get her back.

Think! There has to be some clue!

Except there didn't have to be. Whoever had taken her—and my guess was Seventeen, given how slick the whole thing had been—knew better than to leave clues. What was I expecting, a fucking matchbook with an address on it? I wouldn't make a mistake like that and neither would he.

Gabriella could be anywhere in a thirty mile radius, by now, and that circle was expanding with every second.

Think! What did I see? What *didn't* I see?

Her purse. Her purse was gone. And her phone,

that thin lozenge of metal she was so proud of—

Wait. Her phone. *I can track it down, if it's stolen,* she'd said.

And her laptop was right there.

I clawed open the screen and watched as it lit up. Immediately, I groaned. She had about fifty different windows open—web browsers and conversations and pages of what I assumed were computer code. I might as well have been trying to operate a nuclear reactor.

She's going to die. She's going to die unless I can figure this out.

I took a deep breath and put my finger on the touchpad. The thing felt like a child's toy under my big, cumbersome hands. I started to search through menus and icons, looking for anything to do with phones. Eventually, I got the idea to just Google for it and laboriously typed in *Find my phone.*

And there it was, a dot on a map of New York. She was less than five miles away.

I grabbed the laptop and ran for the door.

SEVENTY

Gabriella

SEVENTEEN brought the saw blade right up to my face and my screams died abruptly. I could feel one of the blade's teeth pushing against the soft skin of my cheek, indenting it but not breaking the surface....yet. If I so much as exhaled, it was going to cut me.

Seventeen brushed my hair back from my forehead. His touch made me want to vomit—clammy and cold, utterly alien.

"He must really like you," said Seventeen. "For him to betray the Bratva."

He glanced down at my body and I tensed, waiting for some question about whether I was good in bed, some stinging, sexist jibe. But there was nothing. I realized something was missing: that unspoken edge of male lust. It had been ugly and brutal with Petrov, aboard the ship. With Konstantin it had been subtle and refined. It had even been there with Vadim, in the steam bath, despite his age. But with Seventeen, there was nothing, no hint that he thought of me in that way at all. The total absence of it was almost more disturbing. It was as if we were different species.

Seventeen looked into my eyes again and pressed the saw blade inwards, rolling it as he did so. The teeth pressed harder and harder, threatening to break my skin, and I went rigid, not daring to shy away from him, taking tiny breaths through my nose. The blade slid between my lips and clacked against my teeth, pushing and rolling. I had to open my mouth or it would have started to scratch away at them. It slipped into position between my jaws, just as he'd intended, with its teeth pricking at the corners of my mouth...and stopped.

I took slow, shuddering breaths, tasting steel and feeling the rough texture of rust against my tongue. I couldn't speak, couldn't move at all or I'd slice myself open.

"Close your teeth," said Seventeen.

I gingerly closed my teeth on the blade. It was heavy and, when he let go, the weight of it made it tip alarmingly, but I managed to hold it by tipping my head very slightly back. I tried not to think of what would happen if it slid any further in.

"Now," said Seventeen. "Nikolai wants me to ask you some questions. You will answer by nodding or shaking your head. And if I think you're lying, even once...I will use *this*."

He picked up a hammer...and mimed knocking the saw blade into my mouth as hard as he possibly could.

I had to stop myself throwing up from fear. With the blade in my mouth I didn't dare even do that. Instead, silent tears started to trickle down my cheeks. I wanted to be strong, like Alexei had taught me, but all I felt was tiny and insignificant. The Dread had me now, as powerful as it had ever been. I was all alone in this place, and no one was ever going to find me.

"Now," said Seventeen again. "Who—"

His phone rang. Without anger or frustration, he laid the hammer neatly down on a table and pulled the phone from his back pocket. I could only hear his side of the conversation that followed. I knew it might be important and I fought my fear and tried to listen, but it was all in Russian. The only part I got was a name: Lizaveta. He said the phrase twice, as if confirming an order: "*Dazhe Lizaveta.*"

Then he pocketed the phone and turned back to me. He gave me a smile and even that was *wrong*: plastic and cold, as if he'd copied it from a picture. That whole side of his personality, the part that tells us how to deal with people...it wasn't just broken, it was *missing*.

Jesus Christ, I was so scared.

"Who else knows about Nikolai and me?" he asked. "Have you told any hacker friends?"

No way was I leading him to Lilywhite and Yolanda. Very slowly and carefully, I shook my head. I was crying so hard that I could only see him as a hazy shadow through the tears.

He tilted his head to the side. "I think, perhaps, you're lying."

And he picked up the hammer.

SEVENTY-ONE

Gabriella

THE END WALL of the sawmill exploded into blinding daylight and shards of glass and metal as a car crashed through it. I glimpsed Alexei hunched over the wheel, grimly determined.

Seventeen drew his gun and got off a single shot before he had to dodge and roll out of the way. I saw him scramble towards a back room as the car slewed to a halt just in front of me.

Alexei climbed out, his face like thunder. He looked towards the doorway Seventeen had disappeared through, then looked at me. I wanted to tell him to go after Seventeen, that I'd be okay for a moment. I didn't want him to risk turning his back on that door. But I was going to go insane if I had that saw blade in my mouth another second.

Alexei must have been able to see it in my eyes because he reached gently in, grasped the blade between thumb and forefingers and eased it all the way out, then tossed it aside. I kept my lips as wide apart as possible as he did it, shaking the whole time. Then it was out and I wanted to weep in relief.

He glanced up at what was holding my arms, checked the door again and then grabbed a chisel and used it on something between my wrists. I heard plastic snap and then I was falling into his arms, burying my face in his chest. He eased me down to the floor, sitting me with my back against the leg of the table, and silently pressed my shoulders to tell me that I should stay there. Then he ran towards the back room. He hadn't even reached the outer door, though, when we heard a car start up. Seconds later, we saw it blast past the windows. Alexei swore and kicked the wall.

He walked back to me and lifted me up, hugging me close. "What did that bastard do to you?" he asked.

I shook my head. "Nothing. Just this." I touched my mouth. There was pain at the corners, but not too bad. I wondered what I looked like.

Alexei put his arms around me and squeezed me again, then led me to the car. Luckily the sawmill was only built from cheap corrugated iron sheets and panes of glass, so going through the wall hadn't totaled it. There was a gunshot hole in the windshield, though—we'd have to change cars as soon as possible.

Alexei backed us out of the sawmill with a grind and scream of tortured metal and we got out of there before someone called the cops. A few streets away, he pulled into an alley. I flipped down the sunshade so that I could have a look at myself in the mirror.

I looked like a different person. Mascara rivers ran all the way down both cheeks below red, swollen eyes. The corners of my mouth had been cut by the sawblade's teeth—not so deeply that I'd need stitches, but there were trickles of blood going down to my chin. I wiped them angrily away and they immediately reformed. I wiped them again. Again—

Alexei grabbed my hand. "Stop," he said urgently.

I'd thought that I was okay, but I wasn't. Seeing myself had made the whole thing real. I realized I was shaking...and I couldn't stop.

"I'll take you somewhere safe," said Alexei.

"Where?" I hugged my arms around myself but I couldn't seem to get warm.

"Somewhere I've never taken anyone."

SEVENTY-TWO

Gabriella

HE DROVE watching the rear view mirror, turning down side street after side street to check we weren't being followed. When we were still a block away, he left the car entirely and led me on foot, cutting through back alleys. We eventually came to an aging apartment block and he led me inside and up the stairs. *A safe house?* But wouldn't the rest of the Bratva know about it? *A friend?* But then why hadn't we come here from the start?

On the fourth floor, Alexei knocked on a green-painted door. A moment later, the door was swung wide.

The woman was no more than half his height and must have been at least eighty. Her skin was the same shade as Alexei's, but transformed by wrinkles into a million tanned peaks and valleys. When she saw him and ran forward to embrace him, her eyes crinkled up so much they almost disappeared. *"Alexei!"* she gasped.

Alexei hugged her back, flushing. "My grandmother," he said.

***

We sat down and there was a long conversation between Alexei and his grandmother, entirely in Russian. There was lots of nodding and smiling in my direction. I hoped that was positive. I took the opportunity to look around the room. There were faded photos of people who I guessed were Alexei's other relatives. A radio played Russian folk songs and I could smell vegetables cooking. The couch I was sitting on was old and a little threadbare, but it was also really comfortable, in that way that only furniture that's been worn in for decades can be.

"Sorry," said Alexei, when they'd finished. "She doesn't speak any English. She's only been over here a few years. I brought her over when my parents died." He winced. "I have to keep her a secret."

I nodded, dumbfounded. "No one knows she's here?"

He shook his head. "Someone could use her against me." He hesitated, glancing at her. "She likes you."

The old lady nodded at me approvingly and said something in Russian.

"What was that?" I asked.

He flushed. "Nothing."

His grandmother bustled off into the kitchen and I heard water splash into a kettle. Alexei took my hand. "How are you feeling?"

I realized I was slowly calming down. I'd stopped shaking and I was starting to warm up. His tactic of bringing me here had worked. It was something about the normality of it, the permanence. Motels and even luxury hotels can be comfortable but they're not comfort*ing*. This place was. I let out a long breath, starting to feel better.

There was another aspect to me coming here. It meant that Alexei trusted me more than anyone else he knew...and he was *introducing me to his family*. That was huge.

Alexei leaned towards me. "She has no idea what I do," he said.

I nodded quickly. "I won't tell her."

His grandmother returned with cups of tea and strange Russian pastries, with the promise of soup as soon as it was cooked. Then she gave Alexei a string of instructions in Russian, pointing at the kitchen.

"Sorry," he said. "She wants me to unblock the sink."

As soon as he'd left us alone, Alexei's grandmother leaned forward and put her hand on mine. Despite her age, her grip was warm and strong.

"You are good for him," she said quietly. "Russian girls too moody."

I blinked at her in astonishment. "You speak English," I said stupidly.

She shrugged. "I don't tell him. Makes him feel needed. Otherwise he never visit."

I grinned and squeezed her hand.

She leaned even closer. "You have to get him away from Bratva. Away from killing."

I blinked at her again. *She knew*. She stared right back at me. Eighty years old but she was still sharp as a knife. I wasn't alone in my quest to save Alexei, and that strengthened my resolve.

"I'll try," I told her.

My shakiness faded the longer we stayed there. When Alexei came back and sat beside me on the couch, I felt even better and by the time Alexei's grandmother had fed us soup and bread, it had gone almost completely. I finally felt strong enough to go to the bathroom and look at myself in the mirror—the very thing that had started me off in the first place. The blood at the corners of my mouth had finally dried. I looked a mess but, this time, it didn't start a panic. I washed my face and then clung onto the edge of the sink. I was realizing I had a decision to make.

I'd heard something, while I was with Seventeen. Something potentially important. I could tell Alexei....

...or I could just keep it to myself. Without any more clues to follow, we could just quietly disappear. I could get him out of the Bratva for good, just like I wanted.

But that would mean lying to him.

I stood in the bathroom for a long time before I walked back to Alexei. I nodded towards the hallway. "We need to talk," I told him.

SEVENTY-THREE

Gabriella

"*Lizaveta?*" he said. "You're sure that's what he said?"

I nodded. "*Dazhe Lizaveta.*" I did my best with the pronunciation.

The change that came across Alexei was astonishing, almost frightening. I'd seen him angry and I'd seen him sad, but I'd never seen him shocked. He was so used to this world of violence that I'd thought nothing could faze him. This did. He actually went pale. "*Even Lizaveta,*" he translated.

"Who's Lizaveta?"

He ignored my question and ran back into the living room. He hugged his grandmother, telling her we had to go. She and I exchanged worried glances. Then he was towing me out of the apartment and down the stairs.

"*Who's Lizaveta?*" I repeated.

He slowly shook his head viciously. "I'm a *fucking* idiot. I had it all wrong."

I had to almost run to keep up with him. "Who is she?"

"This whole time, I thought Nikolai was doing some deal, something he didn't want Luka to find out about—trafficking women, maybe. But we underestimated him. We were thinking too small. He's going to kill them. He's going to kill the whole Malakov family: Luka, his girlfriend, his dad, his cousins—he's going to kill them all and then take over himself. We thought this was a deal, but it's not. It's a coup."

It hurt to speak—moving my mouth opened up the cuts at the corners. "That makes no sense. The Bratva's all about loyalty—that's why they're after us. If Nikolai kills your boss, the rest of the Bratva will hunt him down and kill him."

Alexei shook his head. "That's why he needs Seventeen. That psycho will do all the killing...and everyone will pin it on Konstantin, because Seventeen works for him."

I drew in my breath. "There'll be a gang war."

Alexei nodded as we burst out onto the street. "And Nikolai will be there to step in and take over." He started to lead me back toward where we'd parked the car, a direct route, this time. "He'll be the hero of the hour, leading what's left of our people against Konstantin. It's the perfect way to do it. And then, once he's in charge, he can get rid of all the rules Luka has against trafficking women. Remember how all this started? You found Nikolai because he was talking to that trafficking bastard, Carl. You were right all along. He's planning his trafficking business, for when he takes over."

"So who's Lizaveta?" I croaked. I knew the answer

wasn't going to be good.

"That's how I know it's going to be all of the Malakovs," said Alexei. "Luka has two cousins. Irina, the older one, and Lizaveta, the younger one." He swallowed. "*Even Lizaveta*. Lizaveta is eight years old."

"Oh Jesus."

"I even know where he'll do it. The Malakovs go on holiday every year. They have a holiday home, deep in the forest outside Moscow. The cousins always come too. Seventeen will do it then."

"When?"

"Same time every year. They go away on Unity Day—the fourth of November."

The last few days had been so crazy, I had to check my phone to be sure. It was the third of November. The massacre was going to happen *tomorrow*.

"You have to warn them," I said.

"I can't. Who are they going to listen to—a disgraced killer who can't follow orders, or a man who's been loyal to them for twenty years?" We'd just reached the car and he thumped his fist on its roof. "*Durak dolboeb!* I should have seen this!"

We got into the car, my heart racing and my stomach in a tight, hard knot. I could see how this was tearing him apart inside. I hadn't fully understood until that moment just how much the Bratva meant to him. He'd thought he was going to lose it forever, thanks to me, and that had been nearly unbearable. But now the family he served—*loved*—were going to be wiped out. That was *unthinkable*.

And Jesus, I nearly didn't tell him. He would have never forgiven me, if he'd heard of the massacre on the news.

Alexei threw the car into gear and pulled away, heading into the city.

"Where are we going?" I asked. I looked at the bullet hole in the windshield. "Shouldn't we change cars?"

But he wouldn't answer. He just shook his head and kept on driving.

I'd done the right thing...but I was terrified of the course I'd set him on.

SEVENTY-FOUR

Gabriella

WHEN WE PULLED UP outside Penn Station, I thought we were just changing cars. But Alexei pressed my purse and laptop into my arms and hustled me inside, stopping only once at a ticket machine. He dragged me to a platform where a train was already waiting. The screens said it left in four minutes.

"Washington?" I asked. "We're going to Washington?"

He pushed me onto the train. "Big city," he said. "You can change trains there, go anywhere."

I grabbed his arm. "*You?*" My voice broke. "What do you mean, *you?*"

We stared at each other.

"No," I said. "No, no, *no!*"

He pressed the ticket into my hand. "I have to go to Russia, to try to save the Malakovs."

"But they won't listen to you! They think you're a traitor! They'll shoot you on sight!"

"I have to try."

"Take me with you! I can help!"

"I need to know you're safe."

This is not happening. I felt that *wrench* again, the same one I'd felt when I first saw him, except this was a thousand times worse. This was like my heart being ripped out. "Alexei, *no!*"

Last-minute passengers scrambled aboard, pushing me away from the door. They couldn't understand why I kicked and struggled, trying to get past them. "*No!*" I yelled. "Let me through!" Then I heard the warning beep as the doors prepared to close. I shoved people out of the way and got back to the door just too late. I slammed my hand against the window, my eyes filling up with tears.

Alexei put his hand to the other side of the glass. "I love you," he said. "I'll never forget you."

He turned away. His eyes were shining.

The train started to move.

"Alexei!" I sobbed. "*Alexei!*"

SEVENTY-FIVE

Alexei

I TURNED AWAY from the train, trying to shut out the sound of her sobs behind me. *Don't think. Don't feel.* I had to pretend I was back in the army. Think only of the job at hand. Steal a new car. Get to the airport. Get to Russia and save the Malakovs.

I knew I was never going to see her again. I was going up against Seventeen and Nikolai *and* all of my own people. I'd likely be shot before I even got close to Luka. But I had to try.

If I hadn't been concentrating so fiercely on being cold and efficient, on shutting out the pain in my heart, I would have missed him. He could have been any other commuter, in his smart suit. But I glimpsed the knife he was holding down by his waist, half-hidden by his coat. And I recognized his face. He was one of the men who'd shot up the motel. One of Nikolai's men.

I remembered the car, with its gunshot hole and its

ruined front end. Konstantin's escape vehicle—it had been with us far too long, ever since the night before. I hadn't had time to change it, even though I'd known the police would be looking for it. And Nikolai no doubt had some friends in the NYPD, feeding him tips...

I darted forward and grabbed the guy's arm. It was exactly the sort of thing I'd been trained to do, exactly what I was good at...except now, for the first time, I was worried about the people around me. I couldn't get into a knife fight in the middle of a crowd. I imagined the blade slicing into the stomach of some woman, some child...

I heaved the guy around and slammed him into the side of a bagel stand. The knife went clattering to the ground. One good punch across the jaw and the guy sagged to his knees.

I pushed quickly through the crowd, looking for the others. There would be four or five at least: one would be waiting by the car, in case we came back. I could see one over by the exit and another by the ticket office, but where were the other two?

Unless...

Unless they'd seen us come in and....

Oh no. Oh, *shit,* no.

Gabriella's train was still pulling out of the station. For now, it was moving slowly enough that I could outrun it if I ran, but I knew that wouldn't last long. I sprinted down the platform, checking each carriage as I passed. Commuters. Tourists. The train was picking up speed—I could barely stay ahead. Commuters. More commuters—

The train pulled ahead of me, going faster than I could run. That was when I saw them. Two more of

Nikolai's men, making their way slowly through the carriages, checking faces.

They were on the train.

SEVENTY-SIX

Gabriella

THE OTHER passengers couldn't understand what was wrong with me. At first, they—especially the women—thought it was just a normal break up. They patted my back, helped me to a seat and told me there were plenty of other men out there.

I told them viciously to *fuck the fuck off*.

I stumbled to the bathroom and shut myself in. Tears were streaming down my face—this time, there wasn't any mascara to run. And this time, the fear was worse than even what I'd felt with Seventeen.

I'd lost him. I'd really lost him. The greatest man who'd ever entered my life, the man who'd become my protector, my safe place, was gone. I was on a train filled with strangers, heading to a city I'd never been to before, to start a new life I didn't want. The Dread welled up inside me, worse than ever. I'd never felt so utterly alone.

There wasn't much space in the tiny room, but I

bent my knees and slid down until I was sitting on the floor, hunched up against the door.

He was going to die. At Seventeen's hands or, even worse, at the hands of the people he was trying to save. Bratva violence was going to claim him and there was nothing I could do about it. And this was all my fault. If I hadn't hacked Nikolai's computer in the first place, no one would have known about his plan. Alexei would still be in the same old life, doing his master's bidding.

I began to sob—huge, wracking sobs that hurt my chest, my wet eyes pressed against the knees of my jeans. I cried for what we'd had together and what we could have had.

And then someone knocked on the door of the bathroom.

SEVENTY-SEVEN

Alexei

I HAD TO beat the train. That was my only chance: beat the train to the next station and get on. I checked the screens. The train had left Penn Station at exactly 2pm. It stopped at Newark Penn Station at twelve minutes past.

I had less than twelve minutes to save her.

Nikolai's thug at the exit didn't even see me coming. I hit him like a truck, sending him sprawling across the tiles, and sprinted straight for the parking lot. As I'd thought, they had a guy watching the car. When he saw me, he reached for his gun. I grabbed him and slammed him into the hood. He was still sliding to the ground when I pulled away and sped off down the street.

I should never have left her! I'd just been trying to keep her safe, but the only safe place was at my side.

If I got her back, I was never letting her go again.

I sped over the Hudson River doing eighty and saw

the train up ahead. Then the road curved away from the train tracks, a route that would take me close to an hour.

I turned off the road and went in a straight line instead, ignoring a red light. Cars coming the other way slammed on their brakes, honking their horns. I didn't even look up. I just pressed the gas pedal to the floor, honking my own horn to get people out of the way, slewing onto the sidewalk when the traffic was too slow. I checked my watch. 2:08. My stomach lurched. I tried to deny what my brain was telling me.

By now, the men on the train would have found her.

Even if I caught the train, I was going to be too late.

SEVENTY-EIGHT

Gabriella

I IGNORED the knocking at the bathroom door for a while—they could damn well *wait!* But it was so persistent, I eventually relented. I opened the lock through blurry, tear-filled eyes and swung open the door. I tried to step past the person, not wanting them to see my tear-streaked face. But a hand on my stomach sent me staggering back into the bathroom.

I looked up to see a guy in a suit. I recognized the look immediately: the close-cropped, ex-military haircut, the big muscles stretching out the suit jacket. One of Nikolai's men. He stepped inside the bathroom and locked the door.

This is how I die. Beaten or strangled to death while the other passengers sat unaware, just outside. I knew I should scream, but the man's big hands were already extending towards me and I was frozen with fear.

I looked up into his face and saw the same cold

stare there that Alexei had once had. He was just doing his job. Just following orders. He was going to tie up the loose end I represented and then probably kill Alexei, too and Nikolai would be free to wipe out the Malakovs. He was assisting in the murder of a whole family and he didn't even know it. I wanted to sob at the stupidity of it. The world didn't need men like him; it needed men like Alexei.

His hands came down on my shoulders. That felt oddly familiar. The start of a pattern I'd learned over and over. I felt the instinctual need to pull away.

Alexei's voice in my head. *Grab him around the neck with both hands.*

I came back to life and my arms seemed to act on their own. My fingertips dug into the fleshy warmth of his neck and I pulled down, *hard,* stepping back as I did it. He let out a gasp, almost a laugh, as if he couldn't believe someone like me was trying to fight.

I brought my knee up into his chest. That took him completely by surprise and he folded, his head coming down. I felt the change in him as he started to take this seriously. He tried to rise, but I pulled his head hard against my breast. I was operating on autopilot, now, my body just doing what came next in the sequence. *Swing my arm up. Edge of my wrist against his windpipe.*

Push.

My stomach lurched as I felt his windpipe, gristly against my bone. He began to fight, panicking and slapping at me, but Alexei had taught me well. Even with my small body, I had the advantage in this position.

He thrashed, feet kicking at the door behind him. I pushed harder, closing my eyes to shut out the reality of what I was doing, wincing as his hands slapped and punched at me—

And then, suddenly, I felt him change. He went from being a fighting, kicking person to just a heavy load. I released his neck and he slithered to the floor, nearly bringing me down with him. I scrambled to check his pulse.

Still breathing. Just unconscious.

I heaved him up onto the toilet—it was the only way I could get the door open. Then I backed out of the door, closing it behind me—

And almost walked right into the second man. He was marching towards me with the same icy stare as the first, pushing people when they got out of his way.

I turned and ran.

I fled through the next passenger car and the dining car, trying to resist the urge to look over my shoulder. Every time I turned, he was closer. He was bigger than me, scarier than me—the same people who blocked me jumped out of his way. *Should I stop? Ask for help?* But then what? I remembered how these men had sprayed bullets into our motel room. They'd gladly kill a few bystanders, just to get to me.

I could feel the train slowing down. We must be nearing a station—could I get off? But the slowing only made things worse: without the train rocking around, it was easier to run...and he could run faster than me. By the time the train stopped, he was almost on me.

I dived for a door, but it was blocked by people swarming on. Then I felt a hand on my collar, dragging me back into the train. He pulled me across the carriage towards the far door, the one that was still locked because it led onto the tracks. Then he slammed me up against it, knocking the air out of me.

He was taller than me and his big body blocked mine from sight. Then his hand pressed over my mouth and I couldn't even scream for help. No one could see what he was doing, and everyone was too busy trying to get onto the train and find a seat—they ran right past us.

There was a metallic click and I looked down to see a flick knife pointing at my belly. On instinct, I grabbed his wrist with both of mine, straining to hold it away from me. But I was exhausted and sobbing and no match for his strength. The shining blade started to ease closer and closer.

SEVENTY-NINE

Alexei

I screeched to a stop in front of the main entrance of Newark Penn Station, leaving the car in the street with the engine still running. The clock outside said 2:12. All the way across town, the rage had been building and building inside me—now, as I ran into the station, it solidified into diamond-hard intent. I'd come to hate what I was, to want to be better than a cold-blooded killer. But at that moment, the killer in me was back. I was going to get to her and the hell with anyone who got in my way.

I sprinted through the building, yelling the same thing at anyone I saw: *"Washington train! Which platform?"*

A man in a uniform said, "Three," his hands up to try to calm me. All around me, people were backing away, wide-eyed and afraid.

I found a sign that pointed to platform three and ran, jumping the ticket barriers. I saw the train! It was sitting right there—there was still time!

A whistle blew.

I ran faster than I ever thought I could. Lungs burning, muscles on fire, I drew alongside the train...just as it began to move.

I hit the button to open the nearest door. Nothing happened. A guard on the platform up ahead shouted for me *stand clear*.

I ignored him and ran on, passing carriage after carriage. The guard who'd shouted put his arms out, trying to block me. I shoved him aside.

Then I saw her. She was directly across from me, almost hidden by one of Nikolai's men. He had a knife to her stomach and was trying to drive it in. I slammed my fist against the glass but they didn't even hear me.

The train gained speed, pulling away from me. I felt her slipping away...and with her, every good thing in my entire life. Everything she'd made me, everything she'd changed about me. If I lost her, I might still be able to save Luka's family...but I'd no longer care.

I snarled, drew my gun and fired through the window. My first shot shattered the glass and made the thug spin around. My second caught him right between the eyes.

I lunged at the door and put my hand through the window, searching for an emergency button to stop the train, but then I heard the brakes hiss on—the driver must have heard the shots. I found the door release and jumped aboard before the train had stopped moving. Gabriella was hunched in the far doorway, her hands to her face, shying away from the body. I grabbed her and pulled up her sweater, checking her stomach.

Smooth, creamy skin. No wound.

I pulled her into my arms and hugged her closer than ever before.

I could hear panicked shouts and the hiss and crackle of radios—armed guards would be coming and the cops, too. We had to move...but I couldn't let her go, yet. My whole body was locked up tight with fear, my heart crushed as if by a fist. *I almost lost her!*

I brought my lips down on hers and it was like coming home. That softness, that strawberry scent in her hair. My arms tightened around her waist, locking her in tight. Anyone who wanted her was going to have to tear her from my arms. Both of us let out a choked moan of relief.

I lifted her and carried her off the train in my arms. Station guards were running towards us, but they backed off when they saw the expression on my face. I marched straight to the nearest exit and then into the streets, plunging into the back alleys to lose anyone following us. Only when I was sure we were safe did I put her down.

Or try to. She wouldn't let go. She clung to me and put her mouth to my ear. *"Tell me it's over!"* she begged. "Tell me you won't go to Russia, now. Tell me you'll stay with me!"

I opened my mouth to tell her *yes*—

But I couldn't do it.

She'd known that would be the answer. Her body went tense against mine, her arms clutching me even harder. *"Please!"*

I shook my head in despair. I didn't want to ever let go of her again. But....

I explained it the only way I could. "Lizaveta is

eight years old."

She sniffed and I felt that her cheeks were wet with tears. I felt my heart tearing in two....

But then she nodded and drew back so that she could look at me.

"Okay then," she said, her voice husky. "Okay. Then we do it. We try to save them. *Together.*"

I stared at her. This incredible woman had amazed me yet again.

"But you promise me," she said. "You *fucking promise me*: if we save them, you leave. You're out. Forever."

I looked at her for a long time. The Bratva ran through my veins....

But she owned my soul.

I nodded. "I promise," I said, my voice thick with emotion.

She clutched me close again. "Then let's go to Russia."

EIGHTY

Gabriella

WE KNEW the FSB was looking for us. No way could we get through Russian immigration with our real passports. It seemed impossible.

Then I remembered Lilywhite.

I dispensed with the normal chatroom and just called her and explained what we'd found out. "Is there any way that—"

"Two fake passports?" she asked. "Russian for him, American for you? New identities and all hooked up in the immigration databases in Russia *and* America?"

"Yes," I squeaked, realizing what a ridiculous request it was.

"Piece of cake." I heard her rub her hands together. "It'll be just like old times."

I realized there was a lot I didn't know about Lilywhite.

"Give me a headshot of each of you," she said.

I got my phone out and took the photos. Moments

later, they were sliding out of her printer.

"Well, damn," I heard her mutter. "Now I see why you fell for him."

I blushed...but, despite everything, I smiled. "We have to get a flight to Moscow this evening," I said, "Luka and his family start their vacation tomorrow."

"It'll be too late for a courier," Lilywhite said.

My heart sank.

"So I'll fly out and meet you at the airport."

My jaw dropped. "You'd...do that?" None of the Sisters of Invidia had ever met. Until she'd seen my photo just now, none of us had even known what the other ones looked like. Anonymity was part of our security.

"For you? You're damn right I would. You're the closest thing I have to a friend."

I got an unexpected lump in my throat. "Thank you, um...Lilywhite."

"Lily," she said quietly. "Just Lily. I'll see you soon." Just as she hung up the phone, I heard her yell, *"Bull! Pack a bag!"*

Bull? Must be a nickname.

***

We had to go shopping, keeping a watchful eye out for Nikolai's men. This time, we didn't make the mistake of keeping the same car too long, boosting one from a long-stay parking lot where it wouldn't be missed for a while.

I expected the shopping mall to trigger me. But I found that, as long as I pressed close to Alexei, I didn't slide into the past. Something had changed, that morning. We'd been together...but now we were inseparable. If we came through this, we were together forever—I knew it like I knew my own name.

He never left my side, which was exactly what I needed. He even came into the changing room with me, despite the shocked protests of the sales clerks, and stood watching me undress and then dress again in the tiny space. I didn't complain—after everything I'd been through, the closeness felt wonderful.

We bought travelling clothes for both of us. I wanted to go with another pair of jeans, but Alexei shook his head. "Skirt," he told me. "Short skirt."

"In November?"

"Skirt," he said firmly, and refused to explain further. Well, fine. It was a small sacrifice—we were going to be on a plane anyway so it shouldn't be crazy-cold. I found a loose, short black skirt and bought a pair of thick nylons—Alexei threw an extra pair in, as well, which confused me. I added a bottle-green ribbed sweater and new underwear, then a bag to put it all in.

Next, Alexei took me to an outdoors store to buy what he called "practical" clothes—boots and warm, waterproof layers. I looked down at myself, dressed all in black. The clothes were the closest to combat fatigues that Alexei could find. It brought home to me that we really were going into action.

The last thing Alexei did, just before we arrived at the airport, was to dump his guns. We had no way to get them past the metal detectors so it was the only way, but I could see the worry on his face as he did it. We'd be going in completely defenseless. We'd just have to hope that we could get close to Luka and warn him before Seventeen showed up.

Minutes before check-in for our flight closed, a

gorgeous woman with long dark hair ran up to me. She looked vaguely Italian, and not at all how I'd pictured Lilywhite. "*Lily?*" I asked in astonishment.

She thrust two passports into my hands. "You're all set."

A man jogged up behind her. A *huge* man. Alexei-big, but with a very different look—All-American, with soft brown hair and the big brown eyes to match...and a cowboy hat on his head.

"Thank you," I said. "I mean, I don't know how—"

"What are friends for?" Lily squeezed my shoulder.

"Yeah, but—We've never even *met*. I didn't think that—"

Lily glanced over her shoulder at Bull. "It's been brought home to me that maybe life online ain't all that," she said. "You get home safe and we'll have a proper meet up. You, me and Yolanda."

I nodded. "I'd like that."

She gripped my shoulder. "Listen...you see Luka, you tell him I said hi, okay?"

I blinked. "You *know* Luka?"

She nodded at the passports. "He was a client, back when...well, back when I used to do more of these. I wanted to call him, to plead your case, but I don't have a way to contact him—everything was always one way, him to me, for security."

I nodded. "You've done more than enough." I looked over her shoulder to where Bull was standing. He and Alexei were eying each other as if unsure of what to say. They settled for a respectful nod. Then Alexei turned and looked at me and I drew in my breath—even now, that smoldering, ice-fire look was enough to make me weak.

Lily saw it. "You're in as deep as I was," she

muttered. She gave me a squeeze and then slapped me on the ass, pushing me towards the check-in desk.

***

It was an overnight flight and most people slept. An hour into the flight, with most of the cabin gently dozing around us, Alexei nudged me and jerked his head towards the back of the plane. *He must want to discuss the plan,* I thought. I unbuckled my seatbelt and followed him all the way to the back.

To my surprise, he checked around for cabin crew and then opened the door to one of the toilets and nodded me inside. Did we have to be *that* careful? Couldn't we just whisper? But I slipped inside and waited until he'd joined me and closed the door.

"What?" I asked. "Did something happen? Do you think Seventeen knows we're coming? Could he—"

I was silenced by Alexei pushing me back against the wall and kissing me hard. His lips possessed mine, hard and hungry, his mouth forcing my head back and my mouth open, his tongue pressing my lips apart. My breasts crushed against his chest and the feel of him, the hardness of him, set up an immediate response in my body, a low throbbing that went straight down to my groin.

"Oh," I managed when we came up for air.

Lust made his accent even stronger. "We've had no time, since I got you back from that bastard." His hand slid up under my sweater, his palm caressing my bare skin. "I need you."

And then I realized why I was wearing a skirt.

He lifted me under the arms and perched me on the sink. He swept my new green sweater up my body, bunching it under my arms, and then flipped up the cups of my bra. I groaned as he pushed between my legs and took a breast in his mouth, tongue lapping at the nipple. I buried my fingers in his hair, twisting them into his dark locks, and tried not to think about what might be going on outside. I'd never done anything remotely like this. *Did someone see us go in here? Did one of the cabin crew see?*

His hands worked their way down my naked back and over my ass. Then he jerked my legs apart. *Is someone about to knock on the door?*

I wasn't sure how he was going to manage the nylons. Then he simply pushed his thumb through the thin material at my groin, making a hole. I remembered him throwing in a second pair when we'd been shopping. My man was nothing if not practical.

An instant later, he had my panties pushed to the side. I stiffened as his fingers entered me, finding me warm and wet. He opened his pants and rolled a condom onto his cock—God, he was already hard, he'd been thinking about this for hours. He positioned himself for entry and I glanced once more at the door. *Wait—did he lock it?*

And then he slid into me and I stopped caring about getting caught...or anything else. I let out a long, low cry, much louder than I'd intended to, as he pushed all the way up into me. Immediately, his palm pressed over my mouth. I looked up into his eyes and he was smirking at me.

He started to thrust and I rocked against him, wedged between his huge body and the wall. The movement was slow and silky smooth—perfection. The heat of him throbbed inside me, adding to my own rising lust, and my legs came up to wrap around him. My hands grabbed for his ass, then slid up his back to cling to his shoulders. His thrusts got harder and the pleasure expanded, a liquid-hot core wrapped around silver and satin, so good I was glad of the hand over my mouth because I wanted to scream. We were so tightly wedged that there was almost no noise—just our quiet breathing and the sound of his hardness pumping into me.

I felt myself ratcheting higher and higher, my groin twisting and jerking towards him as I climbed. He shoved one hand between us and palmed my spit-wet breast and that made it even better, a slow circling that joined to the main spiral of pleasure. Alexei's thrusts were getting faster and faster, hammering into me, and as we both reached our peak he leaned in to whisper in my ear. *"Kogda eto budet sdelano , i vy zhivete so mnoy, ya sobirayus' yebat' vas kazhdyy moment, my poluchayem."*

I had no idea what it meant, but the lust in his voice was all I needed to hear. I wrapped my arms around him and pulled him in close as I shuddered and rocked through a silent climax, and heard him groan low in his throat as he did the same.

When we emerged, the cabin was still in semi-darkness—I'd had visions of everyone wide awake and turning around to applaud. Back at our seats, I whispered to him, "What did you say to me?"

He put a finger on my cheek and turned my head so that I was looking into his eyes. "When this is done and you live with me," he said, "I'm going to fuck you every moment we get."

I felt myself flush, but I cuddled in to his chest. It might not have been the most romantic speech ever, but it sounded really, really good.

EIGHTY-ONE

Alexei

WE HIRED a car at the airport, making sure to get something with four wheel drive. It looked dry outside but bitterly cold and we changed into our hiking gear in the airport toilets. God, Gabriella looked fantastic even in the unisex baggy pants and jacket.

We bought road snacks and coffee to keep us going, with me helping Gabriella with the unfamiliar Russian candy labels. Thanks to the time difference, it was mid-afternoon. It would take two hours to get to Luka's holiday home. As we drove along the highway, I saw Gabriella staring out of the window. "I never thought I'd see this," she said after a while.

"Moscow? Russia?"

"Another country," she said in a small voice.

"You okay?" I asked, running my fingers through her hair.

She turned to me, took a deep breath and nodded. "As long as I'm with you." She turned back to the window.

As we drove out of Moscow, heading north-east, the city gave way to towns and then villages and then finally just trees. The roads changed from asphalt to dirt and soon become little more than logging tracks, pitted with tire marks and potholes.

Luckily, I'd been to the Malakov holiday home once before, when I'd stood in as one of Luka's bodyguards, and I remembered the route, and that they usually arrived late afternoon. I just hoped that we would get there before them.

For the last hour, we barely saw anyone at all and the vehicles we did pass were logging trucks. The forest closed around us, a green canopy that almost shut out the sky.

At last, we came to the private road I remembered. We dumped the car out of sight and we went the rest of the way on foot, with me giving Gabriella a crash course in how to move quietly.

We found the checkpoint where Luka's car would wait for a moment before entering the compound. Beyond the gate, a winding road led up to the luxurious, chalet-style house complex, while smaller roads led to the guards' and servants' quarters. We crouched down in the trees to wait.

In some ways, it was just like being on a job. I'd been in this position many times, sitting waiting for a car to drive up before quickly taking out the driver and his passenger. But now everything was backwards: I was the one trying to stop the killing and it was my own people who'd be trying to shoot me. I glanced to my side. And the most important difference of all: I wasn't out there on my own, with only me to worry about. I had Gabriella and that was wonderful and terrifying all at the same time.

Within a few minutes, the SUV arrived. I recognized Yuri at the wheel, Luka's ever-reliable driver and head bodyguard. Luka himself and his girlfriend, Arianna, would be in the back, hidden behind tinted glass. I held my breath....

...and stepped out into view, hands above my head. *"Don't shoot!"* I yelled in Russian.

Yuri had his window down, talking to the two guards at the checkpoint. As soon as he saw movement out of the corner of his eye, he slammed the SUV into reverse and tore off backwards down the track, then swung it around in a one-eighty, ready to drive off. The two guards had sub-machine guns and both of them were suddenly pointed right at me.

I fell to my knees and put my hands behind my head. *"Don't shoot!"* I repeated.

The guards' radios blared—Yuri, asking what was happening. One of them told him that they had the situation under control. A little way down the track, the SUV stayed where it was...but Yuri kept the engine running.

"Tell him it's Alexei Borinskov," I said. The ground was frozen almost solid beneath my knees, the cold soaking through my clothes. "I just want to talk. Tell Yuri I have information—an attempt on Luka's life."

One of the guards must have called for backup, because more guards arrived, Soon, there were five of them, all pointing their guns at me. Some of them started cautiously hunting through the bushes, looking for my accomplices. Any second now, they'd find Gabriella. "Please," I said. "I just want to talk."

There was a moment of silence. Then the SUV slowly turned around and drove back up to the checkpoint. Yuri got out first, gun pointed at me the whole time. He opened the rear door and Luka climbed out.

It had been a while—I'd forgotten just how big Luka was, one of the few men who can look me right in the eye. Glossy black hair not so different to my own and his usual immaculate suit, together with a long gray overcoat to ward off the cold. Beside him, Arianna, his girlfriend—small and slight—attractive, in her way, but she didn't have Gabriella's incredible, soft femininity. Supposedly, she used to be CIA.

"Alexei," said Luka. And immediately, I knew this had been a mistake. His voice cut right to my soul like a whip soaked in ice water. He almost *spat* my name. "Nikolai has told me everything."

I shook my head, but he didn't give me a chance to speak.

"You betrayed him...and so you betrayed me. You betrayed our whole family, Alexei."

I swallowed. "No—"

"Nikolai says you've shot or injured several of our people. That you went to see Konstantin, to cut some sort of a deal with him, maybe selling our secrets—"

"No!"

Luka motioned to Yuri and Yuri passed him his handgun. Luka leveled it at my head. Then he glanced at Arianna. "Close the door," he told her in English. "Don't look."

She shook her head, looking between us. "Luka, don't," she said in a small voice.

"Close the door!" he said firmly.

Arianna shook her head in dismay, but closed the door of the SUV.

"He told you to kill one of our enemies, but you

refused," Luka told me. "He thinks you're conspiring, maybe with Konstantin. Maybe you have a plan to overthrow me. Maybe something else. It doesn't matter." He cocked the gun. "I cannot have traitors in our family."

I talked fast, my heart thumping in my chest. I was scared...but not with the fear of dying. It was the look on Luka's face that terrified me, the thought that I'd die with him thinking I'd betrayed him. "Do you know who it was, I was meant to kill?"

Luka shook his head. "I don't care."

And he pulled the trigger.

EIGHTY-TWO

Gabriella

I COULDN'T understand their words, but I understood the tone. I watched as the man who must be Luka pointed the gun at Alexei. I watched right up until the point that his finger tightened on the trigger and then I couldn't stand it anymore. I jumped up and burst out through the bushes, right in front of them. "*Wait!*" I yelled.

A shot rang out.

Everyone stared at me in shock.

At first, I wondered if maybe the bullet had hit me because Alexei seemed to be okay. But there was no pain, just a ringing in my ears. Then Alexei gingerly put his hand to his ear and it came away wet with blood. Luka's hand had jerked and the bullet had just grazed his earlobe.

Half of the guards pointed their guns at me. The rest kept them on Alexei. I put my hands in the air.

"It was her," said Alexei in English, panting with tension. "Nikolai told me to kill *her*."

Luka frowned at me. I could get a proper look at him, now. He was huge, as big as Alexei—did they put something in the water, in Russia? He had similar jet-black hair, but his features were different, brutally handsome, noble and even regal in a way that reminded me of Konstantin. You'd know which one was the leader in a heartbeat.

"Why?" asked Luka suspiciously. He kept his gun pointing at Alexei, but he'd switched to English, presumably for my benefit, and that had to be a good sign.

"Nikolai is the one who's betraying you," said Alexei. "Gabriella is a hacker. She found evidence on his computer—that's why he wanted her dead."

"Betray me?" Luka echoed. "Nikolai has been loyal for twenty years."

I shook my head. "He wants to move into trafficking women."

"I don't allow that," Luka said firmly.

"That's why he means to kill you," said Alexei. "You, your father, Arianna—your cousins, too."

For the first time, Luka lowered his gun a little. He turned to glance at the SUV. "Ridiculous," he said at last. But he sounded shaken.

"He's hired a guy they call Seventeen—he works for a guy who works for Konstantin," I said. "Seventeen's going to kill your whole family—*here, today*. Konstantin will get the blame and it'll start a gang war. Nikolai will step in as the new leader."

Luka stared at me. Then he turned and stared at the man who'd been driving the SUV, an older guy. *He must be Yuri, the head bodyguard.* Alexei had told me about him. Yuri considered for a long time and then gave a sideways nod of his head. "Nikolai *is* ambitious," he grunted.

Luka looked at me and then at Alexei. "If this is true," he said slowly, "then how did you find out about it? Why did you betray Nikolai in the first place? Why didn't you just kill her?"

It took Alexei a few seconds to form the words. "I fell in love with her," he said at last.

I thought Luka's eyes were going to bug out of his head. "*You?*"

The door of the SUV opened and Arianna slid out. "It's true," she said.

Everyone stared at her.

"I can see the way he looks at her," Arianna said. "I think he's telling the truth."

Luka sighed in frustration. I could tell part of him wanted to tell her to get back in the car, but that, equally, he knew he was way out of his depth. He cocked his head at Arianna as if to say, *are you sure?*

Arianna nodded and I nodded, too.

Luka very slowly lowered his gun. The guards did the same. I let out a long breath I hadn't realized I'd been holding. My whole body was shaky with tension.

"Where is everyone?" Alexei asked. "Where's your father and your cousins?"

"Already here," said Luka. "In the house. Nikolai's here, too."

"Then you need to get them out," said Alexei. "Seventeen could already be here."

"He's psychotic," I said. I looked at Arianna, remembering the sawmill. "You can't let him anywhere near your family."

Yuri shook his head irritably. "We have over twenty guards here. Well-trained men. Well-armed."

"Nikolai will have thought of that," said Alexei. He

looked at the handful of guards that were with us. "Where are the rest?"

"Guardhouse," Yuri replied, "being assigned their weapons." Then he glanced at Luka, his expression growing nauseous. He grabbed a radio off one of the guards and started to speak.

There was a sound like a giant's foot hitting the ground. The noise echoed through the trees, followed by a warm wind and the patter of things hitting the ground. A cloud of smoke started to rise in the distance and I could just make out the sound of people screaming. Yuri stared towards where the guardhouse had been, his face pale.

Luka turned to look at Alexei, his eyes wide with shock. Then he gave Yuri back his handgun and took one of the sub-machine guns from a guard. "Get Arianna to safety," he told Yuri. "I'm going to get the others."

Alexei stepped forward. "I can help,"

I almost prayed for Luka to turn him down, but he slowly nodded. Alexei took a handgun from one of the guards. The smoke from the explosion was billowing through the trees towards us, now, and I tried to shut out the screams of the injured. I stepped towards Alexei.

"No," Alexei told me. "You go with Arianna."

I shook my head, panicked. "Don't leave me again!" I grabbed at his shirt, pulling myself close to his chest.

"I don't want to...but I can't protect you in a firefight," he said gently. He took my hands in his much bigger ones. "Yuri is a great bodyguard and the SUV is armored. It's the best place for you."

I nodded reluctantly, but it felt wrong. Yuri herded

me towards the SUV and pushed me into the back alongside a white-faced Arianna. The last thing I saw was Luka throwing Alexei a radio and the two of them setting off into the forest towards the house.

My chest closed up as I realized that might be the last time I saw him.

Helena Newbury

EIGHTY-THREE

Gabriella

YURI TURNED the SUV around and we started to bounce over the rutted, pitted track. Inside, everything was cream leather and polished chrome. It felt as if we'd already been spirited away from the muddy forest. Alexei was right—we probably *were* safe in there.

But I couldn't get the idea that this was wrong out of my head. *I should be helping him, not running away.*

I looked at Yuri's reflection in the rear view mirror. He looked grim...and shaken. Like me, he was probably still trying to wrap his head around what had happened to the guards. How many had been killed in that explosion—all of them, save for the handful near the checkpoint? Fifteen men...more? All just to clear the way for more murder.... I closed my eyes, my head swimming with the brutality of it. *This is not my world.*

But it was Alexei's world. If I wanted to save him, I

couldn't retreat down into the warm safety that I knew.

I opened my eyes and looked across at Arianna. She was an American, too. She must have faced this same decision with Luka. She glanced at me and our eyes met.

"We can't just let them go in there alone," I blurted.

Yuri heard and shook his head. "Is better you stay here." He glanced outside. White smoke from the explosion was curling along the ground like mist. "Is no place for you two."

"You don't know Seventeen!" I snapped. "He's not just a hitman, he's crazy. Literally psychotic."

"Luka said to take care of you," said Yuri tersely. "I am taking care."

"He needs us," said Arianna quietly. "She's right, Yuri. We have to help. Irina and Lizaveta are in there. *And* Luka's dad. The men can't do it all on their own." She glanced at me and nodded and I felt a warm little glow of unity—our own minor revolution, right there on the back seat. I liked her already.

Yuri drove on in silence for a few seconds. But his shoulders were hunching as if he was trying to shut us out. We were getting to him. "There is nothing you can do," he said at last.

"Maybe there is," I said. "Does this place have a security station, where all the cameras route to? Somewhere not in the house?"

Yuri nodded reluctantly. "*Da.*"

"Take us to it. I can use the cameras, warn them of danger."

Yuri shook his head. "It is secure computer. Passwords and codes. Only the guards had access."

For the first time all day, I felt solid ground under my feet. "Trust me. I can get in."

"And I'll help," said Arianna. She shot a look at me. "Everything'll be in Russian."

I hadn't thought of that. "Okay. Yuri, let's go."

Yuri said nothing. He kept driving in sullen silence for another five seconds and then he muttered something in Russian and swung the SUV around so hard we bounced against the doors.

"What did he say?" I murmured to Arianna.

She leaned close. *"American women will be the death of me."*

EIGHTY-FOUR

Alexei

THE GUARDS from the checkpoint had run on ahead. As Luka and I approached the open area in front of the house, three shots rang out from the west and three of the guards fell, tumbling to the ground like rag dolls. Seventeen, using his sniper rifle again. The rest of us flattened ourselves against trees.

"My father will be in his office, on the far side of the house," said Luka. "My cousins will most likely be upstairs, in their room."

I nodded. "I'll get them. You get your father."

I'd been in dangerous situations plenty of times in the army. I'd felt fear before, but now it was different.

I'd thought that all I was good for was killing, and part of that life was knowing you could die at any time. Death from a bullet is usually quick and it hadn't scared me...because I'd never had anything to lose, until now.

I'd always thought of myself as strong and my

victims weak, because they were caught up in their lives and I was wholly focused on my work, without anything else to distract me. Now, it felt like it was the other way around. I didn't feel strong; I felt as though I'd wasted every day until I'd met her. I thought of the strawberry scent of Gabriella's hair and the little gasps she made when she came. I wanted more. More soft beds, more breakfasts, more *life*...but mainly, more of *her*.

The house was eerily still. The white smoke from the explosion hadn't penetrated in here and the place was still set up for guests: a white linen tablecloth and silver cutlery, magazines artfully fanned out on a coffee table. Hopefully the servants were safe, hiding in their quarters, and could stay there until this was all over. I crept upstairs.

Just as I reached the top, the door in front of me exploded, torn apart by a shotgun blast. I threw myself down on my face, half on the landing and half on the stairs. Chunks of wood pattered down onto my back. I looked up at the hole in the door: if I'd been even one step further, the blast would have taken my head off.

"*Stop right there!*" a female voice yelled in Russian. "*Or you can have the other barrel!*"

Irina. She must have heard the stairs creak. "Don't shoot!" I yelled back, still hugging the floor. "I'm here to help!"

"I don't recognize your voice!" she snapped back. "You're not one of the guards!"

"I work for Luka! You've never met me, but I've been his bodyguard a few times." Then I twisted round on the stairs to look behind me—had that been a noise, downstairs...or just my imagination? I was a sitting duck if anyone came up the stairs behind me. "Look, we have to go! Luka sent me to get you out of here!"

"He'd send someone we know!" Irina yelled.

Another noise from downstairs, and this time I was sure. I dropped my voice. "Irina, the guards are all dead. And the man who blew up the guardhouse is downstairs. We need to leave *right now.*"

"Don't come in here!" she snapped. "I swear I'll blow your head off."

I could feel the frustration and panic coiling together, pushing me to do something stupid. I was utterly trapped. Another few minutes and Seventeen would find me and shoot me in the back. If I moved forward, Irina would shoot me in the front. I couldn't solve this with force, or shouting. Nothing in the army or the years since had prepared me for this.

What would Gabriella do?

She'd be quiet and calm. She'd listen.

Against every instinct, I closed my eyes.

We. He'd send someone we know, Irina had said. I strained my ears and could just make out the sound of sobbing. Irina must have Lizaveta with her, the eight year-old. God, both of them must be terrified!

Talk. Gabriella would talk to her.

"Listen," I said. "My name is Alexei. Alexei Borinskov. Your name is Irina, yes? You're...how old, now—nineteen?"

"Twenty!" she said defensively.

"Twenty, okay. Listen...I know that you're scared. I know that you want to be with Luka—and Arianna. My—uh—girlfriend is American, too. Her name's Gabriella. She's in Luka's SUV with Arianna and Yuri right now, I can take you to them. But we're going to have to trust each other. So I'm going to stand up, very slowly, with my hands empty, and walk to the door...and you're not going to shoot me. Okay?"

Silence.

I could hear footsteps approaching downstairs. *Now or never.* I climbed gingerly to my feet, shoving the handgun into the back of my pants and raising my hands above my head. I stepped towards the door, bracing myself...but no shot came.

Through the hole in the door, I could see into the room. Irina, a slender girl with platinum-blonde hair, was crouched behind an armchair, the shotgun poking out over the top. Behind her, peeking nervously out of a closet, was the honey-haired, big-eyed Lizaveta.

"You *look* evil," said Irina. "But I don't think you are." She stood up.

At that moment, I heard the stairs creak as someone started up them. I glanced around quickly—the bedroom the girls had been hiding in had no other exit, so staying there wasn't an option. I waved them to me and Irina scooped up Lizaveta and followed. We hurried across the landing and made it through a heavy oak door just as Seventeen rounded the top of the stairs.

It was the first time I'd seen him since the sawmill. He'd abandoned his rifle and was brandishing a shotgun. When he saw me, the scariest thing was that there was none of the rage or hatred that any normal man would display. He raised the shotgun as emotionlessly as a man lifting a fly swatter to kill a bug.

I slammed the door shut and locked it. A shotgun blast tore into the wood from the other side, splintering it but not quite breaking through. Another few shots, though, and it would be shredded.

We were in a hallway, with three doors to choose from. Nikolai might well be lying in wait, especially if Seventeen had reported my position. I might lead the girls right into an ambush.

The shotgun fired again and the first holes appeared in the door.

EIGHTY-FIVE

Gabriella

YURI LED US down into the security station, his gun drawn. It was a concrete box that had been sunk into the ground, with only a few tiny windows high on the walls for light. Screens stood ready to show views from CCTV cameras...but they were all dark. A solitary computer screen glowed.

"As I told you, all locked up," said Yuri bitterly. "We would need *them* to unlock it."

That was the part I was trying hard not to look at. Sitting at the control desk were two guards. Both had been shot in the back—probably Seventeen's first move, when he'd arrived.

"Just...help me move them," I said, my stomach churning. Together, we heaved the bodies out of their chairs and laid them gently against the wall. *Shouldn't I say something, or something?* They were somebody's brothers, maybe somebody's fathers.... I settled for closing their eyes.

Back at the desk, Yuri and Arianna leaned over me

as I went to work. Arianna translated the Russian and I started to skirt my way around the security protocols. Yuri got bored after thirty seconds and went to guard the door, which left the two of us in the gloom. For long minutes, the only sound was her voice telling me what the machine was asking for and the skittering of my fingers on the keys.

I sidestepped the last layer of security and the screens suddenly came to life: hallways and reception rooms, garages and a swimming pool.

Then I saw Alexei. He was in a hallway, sheltering a young woman who in turn was carrying a child. The door next to them was slowly splintering from gunfire. My stomach shot up into my throat. *"Alexei!"* I yelled.

"He can't hear you," said Arianna. "Use this." She threw me a radio.

I tried the channels until I got him. "Alexei?"

I saw him pull the radio from his belt. *"Gabriella?!"*

"I can see you on the cameras. I'm going to guide you out." One screen showed a map. "Go right down to the end of the hallway and through the last door on your left."

"Do you see Nikolai anywhere?"

I scanned the screens. "No. You're clear. Go, I'll keep watch!"

He hauled the two girls along with him and ran. Behind him, I could see the door crack down the center and Seventeen's arm reach through, fumbling for the lock.

"Turn right!" I yelled to Alexei. "Onto the balcony!"

"That's a dead end!"

"There's a fire escape."

I watched as he burst out into the open air and

then hustled the girls down the fire escape. "No sign of Nikolai?"

I couldn't see anyone around the house but them. "None." Then I saw something on the far side of the house—Luka, together with a man in his fifties. "Luka's out, with his dad!" I heard Arianna give a groan of relief. "We're at the security station—come get us." There were cameras throughout the forest—I'd be able to watch his back the whole way.

I saw Alexei nod. Then he must have spotted the camera I was watching through, because he looked right into it. "Thank you," he said into his radio. "I love you."

My heart melted. Then the three of them were off and running and I slumped back in my chair in relief.

I heard the noise behind me just too late.

EIGHTY-SIX

Gabriella

THE BACK of my head exploded into pain, a cloud of red agony shot through with white spikes. I half-fell out of my chair, close to throwing up. When I managed to get my legs under me and turn around, I saw a man in his forties standing there, his suit disheveled and stained with mud. Behind him, through the doorway, I could see Yuri's crumpled body lying on the ground—dead or unconscious, it was impossible to tell.

The man was pointing a gun at Arianna and me. I realized that he must have slugged me with the barrel. And I realized there was only one person he could be.

"Nikolai." I croaked.

He might have been handsome, once, but bitterness had etched deep lines across his forehead and jaw, giving him a permanent scowl. In the gloom of the bunker, his eyes seemed to be the brightest part of him, two circles of dirty gray ice, without any of Alexei's hint of blue.

"Alexei is coming," I managed. Every word, every movement, made my head throb. "He'll be here any minute."

"No he won't," spat Nikolai. He grabbed the radio I'd been using and switched the channel. He kept the gun on us, but started glancing at the screens and speaking in Russian into the radio. I didn't need Arianna to translate what was going on. He was talking to Seventeen. He was using the cameras to lead him right to Alexei and the cousins.

EIGHTY-SEVEN

Alexei

PROGRESS WAS SLOW—Irina still had Lizaveta in her arms, and she was getting tired.

"I'll take her," I offered, holding out my arms for the child.

Lizaveta shook her head wildly, clinging desperately to Irina. "No!"

I sighed under my breath. *She knows,* a little voice in my head whispered. *Even a kid knows you're a killer.*

A bullet whipped past my ear. I spun around, firing blindly into the trees, but I couldn't see anyone. I hustled the girls on, choosing a different path through the forest, trying to be quick but quiet.

A moment later, another shot whistled past my shoulder. I fired again, but I still couldn't see anyone...and I was almost out of bullets. *How does he know where we are?*

A twig cracked in the trees behind us. I dived at the girls, pushing them out of the way, and the bullets missed us by inches. As we sprawled on the ground, Seventeen emerged from the trees, lazily reloading his handgun. I managed to get my gun pointed at him just in time to have him kick it out of my hands.

He turned towards the girls. As he raised his gun, Irina pushed Lizaveta behind her, spreading her arms defensively. Seventeen hesitated, cocking his head as if he found her self-sacrifice to be a curious, alien concept.

That hesitation was all I needed. With a guttural yell, I dived at Seventeen, wrapping my arms around his legs and slamming him to the ground. I was already punching him as we landed.

Seventeen tried to rise but I pinned him down, absorbing his punches on my face and chest and focusing on beating him into submission. I had the size advantage and I was powered by raw, desperate fear. *I will not let this happen! Not Irina! Not Lizaveta!*

It looked as if I'd win. He started to go limp. I drew my arm back to deliver the final blow....

But I'd never fought anyone like him before. All the people I'd fought had been sane—they had personalities, with all the doubts and insecurities that came with them. Faced with defeat, they went fearful and weak.

I didn't even see Seventeen reach down and pull the knife from his belt. He shoved it into my side with such expert, surgical precision that I barely felt it go in. I only felt it as a weakness, my arms losing their strength, my weight slumping sideways....

Seventeen rolled out from under me as I fell to the ground. My eyes were open so I could see things unfold, but I couldn't do a thing to stop them. My whole body was going numb.

Seventeen got to his feet, staggering a little, and looked around. He'd dropped his gun when he went down and it was lost amongst the leaves and twigs on the forest floor. He picked up my gun, instead.

I stared helplessly at Irina. She wasn't crying—brave until the end. Behind her, Lizaveta was sobbing and clinging to her leg.

I could barely feel my legs, now. I knew that I must be bleeding internally. On some level, I actually admired him for how perfectly he'd done it—the wound would take a long time to kill me, but it took me out of the fight completely. I had nothing left to give.

Seventeen didn't even bother to hurry as he retrieved my gun. He checked the clip, sighed, then cocked it. He walked over to the girls. Lizaveta immediately hid behind Irina.

"Show me your sister," Seventeen told Irina in that flat, emotionless tone.

Irina's eyes widened in astonishment. "*What?* No! Fuck you!" She spread her arms wide again. "You want her, you're going to have to come through me!"

Seventeen showed her the gun. "There's only one round left," he said calmly. "I can make it quick, but only for one of you."

Irina stared at him in horror and shook her head.

Seventeen tilted his head to the side, confused. I think he was making a genuine attempt to be humane, even if it was only based on what he'd heard was the right thing to do. "Don't you want it to be quick for her?"

Now Irina did start to cry. Seventeen just waited, as if he had all the time in the world. Lizaveta was howling, big heaving gasps, her face red with tears.

I could see the straining tension in Irina's body as she slowly pulled her younger sister in front of her. Lizaveta resisted and Irina had to use all her strength to drag her heels through the mud. "Shh," she said. "Shh, it'll be okay."

I'd failed them. Irina and Lizaveta, and then, shortly after, Luka, his dad, Arianna, and Gabriella. They were all going to die because I couldn't even do one thing right. I stared at the red-faced, screaming child and my eyes started to get hot, then wet. *You pathetic fuck, Alexei. Killing's all you're good for and you couldn't even do that.*

And then I saw it: Seventeen's gun, half-buried under the leaves. But it was three feet beyond my reach and my body wouldn't move at all.

Irina turned Lizaveta around. "Put your head on my chest," she told the girl, tears running down her cheeks. "And close your eyes."

It started as a smell—the strawberry scent of her hair. Then I could feel her under my fingers, that creamy, smooth skin and the warm press of her breasts against my chest. I heard her breath in my ear, the moist air tickling. *"Alexei."*

I knew I must be hallucinating from the pain and the shock. My heart must be barely pumping, by now, my blood pressure crashing. I was hallucinating...

...or maybe there was more to me than there used to be. Maybe I'd gained something, since that day in the coffee shop. I'd always been grimly proud of living on my own, in solitary pain, thinking that it made me strong. But maybe *this*, this thing I was feeling right now, made me stronger. And maybe it made me more than just a killer.

Irina stroked Lizaveta's hair, then put her hands over the child's ears. "Do it," she sobbed. "Do it, you bastard."

Seventeen put the muzzle of the gun against Lizaveta's temple. She screwed her eyes shut.

It wasn't anything logical or rational that powered me—there was none of that left. It was pure, stubborn rage, fury at the injustice of it all: that Seventeen was going to live, that these innocents were going to die, that Nikolai was going to come to power. Most of all, that Gabriella and I wouldn't be together.

All in one movement, I heaved myself up onto my knees, threw myself forward, and grabbed for the gun. I felt my strength plummeting and the world grew dark around the edges. But I could see Seventeen in front of me, turning in surprise. And I had just enough strength to pull the trigger.

EIGHTY-EIGHT

Alexei

I WAS LYING on my face, sliding rapidly into black warmth. Then someone was on top of me, grunting and—

Something deep inside me began to move. *Ow! No, don't do that! That—*

I yelled into the leaves and dirt as the knife slid out of me. A second later, something pressed into my side and the pain got even worse. My whole body was coated in sweat and I was shaking.

"Hold that in place," said a voice. "Press hard."

I pressed against the wadded fabric The pain doubled but the world got a little brighter. I blinked and rolled over on my side.

Irina was crouching next to me. Her dress was torn at the bottom and I realized that's where the fabric came from. Behind her, Seventeen's body lay on the ground. It looked as if my bullet had clipped the back of his skull. I wasn't sure if he was dead, but he wasn't going anywhere.

"Lie still," Irina said. "I can go and get help."

I shook my head. "Radio," I croaked. I'd figured out how Seventeen found us so easily...but I prayed I was wrong.

Irina pressed the radio into my hand. I called Gabriella again and again. Nothing.

He had them. That bastard Nikolai had Gabriella *and* Arianna.

Pressing on the wound was working, slowing the internal bleeding and letting my blood pressure come back up. I still needed a hospital, but I could survive like this for a little while. I picked up Seventeen's gun. Unlike mine, it still had a few rounds left in it. Standing took all my effort and I wavered, unsure if I was going to fall. Irina quickly put her shoulder under my arm.

"Security station," I said determinedly. *We must be only a few minutes away, by now.*

But just then, we heard the distant roar of a car engine starting up. Irina and I looked at each other. I knew how Nikolai's mind worked. If he'd just seen my fight with Seventeen on the cameras and knew he'd lost, he'd take hostages. He'd take Gabriella...and I'd never see her again.

"The road curves around," said Irina, pointing. "We can cut him off. Hurry!" And she scooped up Lizaveta again.

We ran. I was fueled purely on adrenaline now, close to collapse, one hand clasped to my side. Luckily, most of the route was downhill.

As we burst out onto the road, the SUV shot around the bend. I could see Nikolai at the wheel. I just had to hope Gabriella and Arianna were in the back seat, and not lying dead back at the security station.

I stepped out into the middle of the road and put three bullets into the front tires. The car swerved as it flashed past me and my guts tightened as I saw it head straight for Irina and Lizaveta. The sisters jumped out of the way, fleeing in different directions...and the car slammed into a tree.

EIGHTY-NINE

Gabriella

I SHOOK MY HEAD, trying to clear it. The pain from the blow to my head was still there and now the crash had thrown me around again...but at least Arianna and I had had our belts on. Nikolai, in the driver's seat, was slumped over the wheel, blood pouring from his forehead.

I turned to Arianna. She seemed unhurt, but she didn't seem to know I was there. She was staring straight ahead of her, at the seat in front. "Arianna?" I asked.

She still didn't look at me. "Mom?"

Shit. I heaved open my door and climbed out. My heart lifted when I saw Alexei running towards us...but then Nikolai started to wake up. I hurried around the car and hauled open Arianna's door. She finally turned to look at me, but her eyes were distant.

"Come on!" I said. "We have to go!"

She just stared at me. I had to lean in and unfasten her belt, then drag her from the car. I started backing away, pulling her with me. Alexei was close, now, but Nikolai's door was opening. He stumbled out, gun drawn. His forehead was dripping blood down his face and he was panting in fear and anger. All his plans had unraveled in just a few minutes.

Luka and his dad burst from the trees and started closing in on us from the other direction. I kept backing away from Nikolai. We were safe, now, too far away for him to grab. Then I saw Irina on the other side of the road. She was safe, too.

Too late, we all saw Lizaveta. She was standing on her own, tears streaming down her face, far too close to—

Nikolai ran forward and grabbed her, just as Alexei, Luka and his dad arrived. He put his arm around her neck. "Back away!" he yelled.

The men slowed to a stop, glancing fearfully at one another.

"I'm walking out of here!" Nikolai yelled. "Don't try and stop me!" He cinched his arm tighter under Lizaveta's chin, almost lifting her off her feet. "Be good," he snapped at her.

I learned two things about Russians that day. Firstly, they're stubborn creatures who never, ever do what you tell them.

Lizaveta grabbed Nikolai's arm with both hands and bit his bare wrist as hard as she could. Nikolai swore and flung her aside.

Secondly, don't mess with their families.

Alexei, Luka and his dad all raised their guns and fired until they were empty, their faces set into masks of cold fury. Nikolai fell to the ground.

Then Luka was running towards me, scooping Arianna from my arms and pulling her close. She mumbled incoherently into his neck. Irina and Luka's dad descended on Lizaveta, completely engulfing her in hugs. And then Alexei was picking me up and lifting me, pressing me so close to him that it was as if he wanted to melt right into me.

I knew the feeling. I wanted to melt right into him, too.

"Careful," said Irina. "He's hurt."

"Hurt?" I pushed Alexei back. That's when I saw the blood staining his shirt, the sticky pad that was pressed against his side. "Oh, Jesus!"

"I'll be okay," whispered Alexei, sagging a little against me. "Everything is going to be okay, now."

NINETY

Gabriella

THE POLICE arrived, closely followed by the ambulances. At first, guns were pointed at Luka and his dad—*Vasiliy,* I learned his name was. I thought the whole family were going to be arrested. Then, quite suddenly, all the guns went down and everyone was shaking hands. "What happened?" I whispered to Alexei.

"The right cops showed up," he told me. When I looked blank, he said, "The ones on Vasiliy's payroll."

Paramedics inspected Alexei's wound and told him he'd need surgery, and that I would need checking over for concussion, but that there were more critical cases they needed to get back to Moscow first. More guards had survived the explosion than we'd thought, though many of them were seriously injured.

The first person to be shuttled to hospital, though, was Seventeen. The police found him in the forest, close to death but still breathing. Luka argued with Vasiliy about it, making the case that they should quietly finish him off, but Vasiliy told him the whole investigation would be over sooner if someone could be sent to jail—and, this way, Seventeen could be blamed for the whole thing. None of the other families needed to know that Nikolai had betrayed his employer. Such a thing might be seen as a weakness.

While the other ambulances shuttled back and forth to the hospital, a few were left to serve as field hospitals. Alexei sat on the doorstep of one, his side swaddled in bandages, hooked up to a blood pressure monitor and an IV bag. I sat beside him. The forest seemed very still and calm...which made no sense at all, because the place was swarming with cops and paramedics. It took me a while to realize that the calm was coming from within me. The Dread was gone, at least for now. Now that we'd finally stopped running and with Alexei firmly by my side, the world didn't seem so big and scary anymore. In fact, it was kind of beautiful, now I could really look at it.

Lizaveta appeared, pushed from behind by Irina. She muttered something in Russian, looking mostly at her feet.

"In English," said Irina, poking her. "So Gabriella can understand."

"Um...thank you," Lizaveta said. "For saving us." Then, to everyone's surprise, she threw her arms around Alexei's neck. "Irina's right," she said. "You look evil. But I don't think you are."

Alexei and I looked at each other over her back. I nodded at him, blinking away tears.

Vasiliy walked up. "Next year," Irina asked, "Can we please holiday in New York instead?"

Vasiliy swore in Russian. "Always with the *New York*, with this one," he told us. "All she wants to do is go to this Tenthook Academy."

"*Fenbrook* Academy," said Irina through gritted teeth.

Vasiliy rolled his eyes as he led her away. "What is wrong with the Bolshoi?"

Luka and Arianna were next to stop by. Luka shook Alexei's hand...then pulled him into a bear hug that set all the medical monitors beeping. "You will always have a place in our family," he told Alexei. "Here, or in New York."

That was it. Exactly what he'd been wanting to hear, since this whole thing started. I held my breath.

Alexei nodded. Then he looked at me. "Thank you," he said. "But no." And he pulled me close.

When Luka had walked away, Arianna put a hand on my shoulder. "Sorry I freaked out," she said. She looked better, now—still shaken, but her color was back. "I was in a crash, once."

I pulled her into a hug. "When it comes to freakouts, I got you beat."

Yuri showed up at that point, a bandage tied around his head. He'd been unconscious the entire time, knocked out by Nikolai, and seemed to take the fact he'd missed everything as a personal affront. He quietly but firmly towed the family away towards a waiting car.

"Oh!" I said suddenly. "I nearly forgot! Lily says hi."

Luka turned to me, astonished. "You know Lily?!"

Arianna gave him a glare. "*The* Lily?"

Oops. "She's a friend," I said awkwardly. *Surely Lily and Luka couldn't have...*But Arianna didn't seem *that* annoyed. It must be something else. "She helped us get here," I blurted. "We couldn't have done it without her."

Arianna's face softened. Nope, definitely not an affair—no woman would relent that easily. "In that case," she told me, "you can tell Lily she's *just about forgiven for Paris*." And she slipped her arm around Luka's waist and led him away.

"Paris?" I asked. "What happened in Paris?" But she'd gone.

The paramedics announced that the next ambulance was ours and bundled Alexei and me into it. We sat facing each other, holding hands. "What now?" I asked.

He held his side. "I go to hospital. They patch me up. Then back to New York and we live together."

I blinked and scrambled for words. "We do? I mean, that sounds..." Actually, it sounded absolutely fantastic. I just hadn't been expecting him to say it like that. He sounded so *certain*. "And then what?"

"And then..." He smiled and leaned into me, his lips at my ear. "I already told you what happens, when we live together."

I drew in my breath, feeling the heat blossom inside me and throb straight down to my groin. And I kissed him.

EPILOGUE

One month later

Gabriella

"It doesn't work." Alexei's voice was grumpy...but it had lost the edge it used to have when he got frustrated. He was a lot less angry in general, these days.

I was luxuriating under the shower, but I'd left the bathroom door open because I'd known he might run into problems. "Type it in carefully," I said. I didn't have to force myself to sound calm and patient: this shower would make anyone placid. "Double-you, double-you, double-you, dot Netflix dot com."

One of the things I'd insisted on, when we moved to the new, bigger apartment, was a very serious shower, of the kind we'd experienced at the luxury hotel. Alexei made a show of saying it was ridiculous and decadent, but he only kept up the pretence for a day or two. He now spent more time in it than I did.

From the living area, there came the slow tapping of single-fingered typing. I was going to have to teach him to touch type at some point, but...*baby steps*. I grinned as the spray hit me from both sides and above, washing the strawberry soap from me.

"It still doesn't work." Alexei sounded as if he was losing his patience, so I finally cranked off the water—thirty minutes probably *was* enough—and wrapped a towel around me. Damp and half-naked, I padded through the apartment and walked up behind the couch he was sitting on.

"No," I said gently. "Netflix. With an 'X.'"

Alexei threw down the keyboard. "What was wrong with renting a movie from a store?"

I leaned over from behind and put my arms around his neck. "When was the last time you *had* a movie night, 1993? And also, that would involve going out."

"You *can* go out, now."

"Doesn't mean I always want to. This isn't fear—it's good, healthy laziness."

Water dripped from my hair onto his chest, which made him finally turn around and realize I was only wearing a towel. His eyes got *that* look and he twisted around, grabbed me and hauled me over the back of the sofa. I yelped, delighted, and landed in his lap. The towel came off.

"I am going to do *very bad things* to you," Alexei told me gravely.

And he did.

***

We wound up never getting to the movie, though we did stop for pizza sometime around midnight. We

Kissing My Killer

woke up with the dawn, because both of us had been too distracted to close the curtains.

"Did you think any more about what I asked you?" I said. I was lying on my stomach, watching the sunrise, my arm around his shoulders as he lay next to me. "Lily and Yolanda agree—we need someone to provide security for us, in case things ever get physical again."

He looked at me. "I would protect you anyway."

"But this way you could be on the payroll, so to speak. We could cut you in."

"With the money you steal."

I sat up and crossed my arms. "*Really? You're going to give me a moral lecture?*"

"No," he said at last, conceding the point.

"Besides, we only keep one percent of the money when we empty these bastards' bank accounts. The rest goes to charities that help trafficked women." Our hacks were getting more and more effective, too. Arianna had helped—she'd made some calls to the CIA, who in turn had made some calls to the FBI, and we now had a dedicated contact we could feed evidence to, when we uncovered it. There were always more trafficking rings popping up, though, and the mysterious Carl was still out there somewhere.

"It's a good idea," Alexei muttered after a while. "But we will have to change the name."

I blinked at him, unsure if he was serious. "Really?"

He shook his head firmly. "I am not being a *Sister of Invidia*." He playfully spanked my ass. "You should try to sleep for a little while. You have college."

With the Dread held at bay—seemingly for good, although I wasn't taking anything for granted—I'd been able to enroll in college. Only part time, for now, but it was a step towards a normal life. And at some point, I was going to meet up with Lily—maybe Yolanda, too.

"There's not enough time," I said, looking at the clock. "I have to be up in an hour." I bit my lip as if thinking. "What could we *do,* to pass an hour?"

He grinned and started to whisper in my ear.

"No," I said, squirming. "Say it in Russian."

<<<>>>

Thank you for reading! If you enjoyed this book, please leave a review :)

Get my newsletter and I'll let you know when a new book comes out, so you can grab the ebook at the launch price of 99c instead of paying full price. I'll also send you *Losing My Balance,* an ebook novella that's exclusive to my newsletter readers.

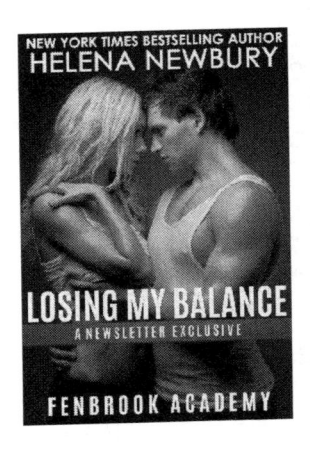

http://list.helenanewbury.com

CONTACT ME

If you have a question or just want to chat, you can find me at:

Blog: http://helenanewbury.com

Twitter: http://twitter.com/HelenaAuthor

Facebook:
http://www.facebook.com/HelenaNewburyAuthor

Goodreads:
http://www.goodreads.com/helenanewburyauthor

Pinterest: http://pinterest.com/helenanewbury/

Amazon Author Page
http://www.amazon.com/author/helenanewbury

Helena Newbury

Made in the USA
Lexington, KY
02 November 2016